SHIRLEY F'N LYLE

VIVA THE REVOLUTION!

CLAYTON LINDEMUTH

SHIRLEY F'N LYLE

VIVA THE REVOLUTION

Clayton Lindemuth
Hardgrave Enterprises LLC
SAINT CHARLES, MISSOURI

SHIRLEY F'N LYLE: VIVA the REVOLUTION/Clayton Lindemuth

ISBN-13 : 978-1686889608

FOR: DOROTHY PAVAO CALHOUN

So many women in the 50's were abused that no one even commented on black eyes. And I remember the conversations on how we were done taking it and then going right back home. We were totally dependent . No jobs, money or cars.

— Dorothy Pavao Calhoun

CHAPTER 1

S hirley Lyle sat in her car. Behind her, blackness. Ahead, bathed in bold Ford Festiva headlamp yellow, a pine. Every April, sap oozed from pores in the bark like hot glue pressed from a nozzle, until the sticky orbs dropped, becoming shiny pixels on her sunburned baby blue paint.

Hands on the steering wheel, Shirley noticed a dark smear on her arm. Blood.

Should have checked yourself before leaving the warehouse.

Did it come from the meth zombies? Or from where she cut open her chin on the cement? She tilted back her head, adjusted the rearview, saw her cheese-grated flesh oozing blood down her neck.

Shoulders bunched tight, she twisted the keys. The engine shuddered and died. Headlights dimmed, then went black. Sitting in the secondary glow of purple street lights, shaded by the pine, Shirley closed her eyes.

Coming home was unintelligent. Not the kind of mistake the woman responsible for VIVA the REVOLUTION could get away with. Although VIVA, brand new, consisted of her and Ulyana.

You don't come home after killing a drug lord and two meth zombies. You grab your cash, burn the rest of your life, and run.

Ahead, the pine. To her right, walking away exactly the way Shirley imagined a stripper who'd assisted a triple homicide ought to walk, Ulyana.

Be precise! It was not a triple homicide. More like a homicide with double-side of manslaughter.

Should have left Ulyana dead too. She didn't even really know her. How could she trust her? They were staging the crime scene to look like a drug deal gone bad, like on television, when the meth zombies snuck up from the back of the warehouse. Ulyana could have turned on Shirley, if that was her plan. Instead, the stripper had saved her. That bought a little trust. A little. She'd roll with things the way they left them. They'd get some sleep, join for breakfast in the morning and figure out their next move.

They should have a few hours head start.

Ukrainian.

Ulyana wasn't Russian. She was particular about that.

Details! Every detail matters!

"Shut up! I know!" Shirley smashed her hands into the steering wheel.

Collect yourself. You are not Shirley Lyle. You are Shirley Fuc—You are Shirley F'N Lyle, and Shirley F'N Lyle keeps cool. Shirley F'N Lyle walks between raindrops.

Shirley sat with the engine off. What were the odds of a drop of sap landing on her windshield while she debated burning everything she owned?

Ahead, the pine with the pitch. To her right, walking toward her own trailer, Ulyana the perfect blonde. . . except Shirley had noticed when they were killing El Jay that one of her breasts was heavier than the other. And a little to the left, close enough there was nowhere to park but under the pine, her trailer.

Burn it.

She reached for the cigarette lighter. Remembered she'd bought her Festiva used, without one. Not that igniting a trailer with a cigarette lighter—from the outside—was a workable plan.

She had matches inside the house, but it would be difficult to see her things—the photo of her son Brass, displayed above the television—maybe her blender and some of the rum in the cupboard—without losing her nerve. Thirty plus years of accrued knickknacks and baggage. All tying her to a life of subjugation. Lying on her back, head over the edge, throat open. . . On all fours, chest dragging. . . Or nose buried in a nest of crooked hair. She'd accumulated a lot of junk in (fifty-two minus seventeen) thirty-five years servicing men. All that rubbish tethered her like high tensile threads knotted to iron anchors.

Almost like those animal balloons at the big city parades.

"Yeah Shirley, go the easy route. Make a fat joke."

Shirley closed her eyes. Tried to allow the chatter in her head to still. Expanded her chest, listened to the wind rush through her nose, back the nasal passage, and deep into her lungs. Exhaled, allowing all the tension to escape into the cool Flagstaff night.

It didn't work.

Shirley pulled the latch and used the door as a support as she shifted her left butt cheek farther left, half off the seat. It was a miracle she could get into and out of the Festiva—and if it hadn't been for the john who was handy with a welder, it wouldn't be possible. She twisted out her left leg and, hanging on the door, followed out and up with the rest of her.

She stood. Looked at the trailer and gathered her resolve.

The street lamp buzzed.

Thirty yards away, Ulyana turned and waved.

No need to yell. Ulyana would soon enough see Shirley's trailer aflame. She'd figure it out.

Shirley squared herself. Set her jaw and lumbered toward the six-inch high deck.

At the door, she paused before inserting her key. VIVA the REVOLU-TION meant never going back. Never whoring again. Never taking abuse, from man or woman. Never beating up on herself for all the stupid things she did that landed her in Flagstaff, still hooking at the age of fifty-two, weighing four hundred pounds, *(to be totally transparent, you're only three-fifty-three)*, with an active client base close to a hundred. VIVA the REVO-LUTION meant rejecting the day-to-day, self-imposed and self-reinforced idiocy that kept her hewing to other people's lines.

VIVA meant she was fed up, pissed off, and fired up about staying fed up, pissed off, and fired up.

Momentum is important.

"Yeah, but it's eleven, and this particular fired up fed up gal is tired."

Don't go inside. . .

She inserted the key. Opened the door and entered. Flipped on the light switch.

Across the room, her couch sloped on the left side, where she always sat because it was closest to the television screen. To her left, on the wall behind the TV, a photo of her son, Brass. The only thing in her life she hadn't screwed up. He was married. Couple kids. Someday he'd be president of the United States.

It wouldn't do to burn the place down and leave his photo.

In fact, burning *everything* didn't make sense. The car had a trunk. VIVA the REVOLUTION didn't have to be so extreme as leaving behind the good stuff. . . She didn't have that much good stuff. You don't throw out the baby with the bath water, unless it's really bad.

She leaned against the television and removed her son's photo from its nail. Placed it on the counter top and grabbed an unwashed Mickey Mouse glass.

Mickey waved his white-gloved hand at her. Pointer finger out. *Don't do that. . . idiot.*

"I need a little pick me up. . . Before I set fire to my world."

Mickey held her stare.

"Stay in your lane, mouse."

Shirley fetched rum from the lower cabinet and poured three inches. Filled the rest with flat Coke.

Bed was going to feel good.

No. VIVA!

"But where will I sleep?"

You'll figure it out.

Shirley put part of her inner cheek between her incisors and chewed until it hurt. "Yeah. VIVA. This place needs to burn."

But not the rum. Shirley placed the liter next to the photo of Brass.

What else?

Clothes. She had a duffel in the second bedroom closet, packed tight with junk. But she wouldn't take many clothes. Only a few favorite items that fit. Certainly not the leather bustier, G-string and garter combo. No tools of the trade. She'd starve before she ever pleased another ounce of man meat.

Shirley gulped from the glass. Flat Coke and rum. She shook her head.

No men meant no income. She only had thirteen thousand dollars saved. No IRAs. No pension. She probably didn't even qualify for Social

Security. VIVA the REVOLUTION required commitment, because if she wasn't going to work her trade, she'd have to find another.

She read a book a long time ago. . . the good guy suffered misfortune after misfortune, but wherever life took him, he always found work washing dishes.

She grabbed Mickey. Silenced him with a stare.

Drank.

Washing dishes. If only. She couldn't remain on her feet more than twenty minutes. That was one of the benefits of prostitution. Not much foot time.

Could she hook a little? Help stretch the savings. . .

No!

Shirley finished her drink. With her head tilted back, her brain floated. It took a lot of liquor to buoy a brain as big as hers. She smiled. She'd killed a man and got the assist on two more. Considering all things, life was pretty damn splendid. She'd crossed a line and planted her heels on the other side. Revolutionary. Imagine that. Shirley Lyle, leading the charge! Head way back, waiting on the last drop of rum and flat Coke, she snorted. Dribbled elixir over her chin. It burned where she'd grated the skin on concrete. War wounds!

This burning-down-the-trailer thing was an opportunity. New horizons. Like how they used to burn bodies at funerals. Celebrate the past, or not. Burning meant it was done.

She'd pack her clothes, grab her computer, her life savings.

Cool! She'd forgotten about the money bag Ulyana took from the drug lord's car. Even better!

I can do this. I'm Shirley F'N Lyle.

Things were looking up! She'd live on savings. Find a desk job. Set up one of those 800 lines, and use her vast understanding of human sexuality to please callers from a distance, at eight bucks a minute.

No!

Screw servitude. Servility. Serfdom. Pretending, sucking up, smiling all the F'N time.

She'd go hungry, *(that never worked before,)* shed a few pounds, and with luck, the weight-loss line would intersect the standing-on-her-feet line in time for her to find a job that didn't attack her self-worth. Because if she understood anything at all with certainty—VIVA the REVOLUTION meant no feeding the kitty unless Shirley said the kitty got fed. And that wasn't likely for a long time.

You know what, sweetheart? You can buy new clothes. You're leaving now, with Brass, rum, and cash.

Shirley nodded. "Damn straight." She pulled a candle and matches from a cabinet, and a can of Pam from another.

VIVA the REV—

Pounding at the door.

Ulyana?

Or Lester?

Why did she and Ulyana leave the gun in the car with the body?

"If that's you Lester I'm about to go full nuts! I'm warning—"

She pulled the door; filled the opening. Halted.

"Maddix."

"Well hello, Shirley."

She swayed; steadied herself. Fought the chill climbing her back. He wore denim on the bottom and flannel on top. Sunburned face and hands. She'd seen the rest of him. Hands and forearms perma-tan, the rest pale as soaked feet. His fingers felt like sand paper when he slid them on her—or like a hammer when he balled them.

Maddix Heregger mostly liked it rough. Slapping. Choking. Demeaning words. But he owned a construction company and paid like a champ, so she'd always given him free reign. She'd worn Brass's motorcycle helmet one time, but Maddix didn't get the point. Serving Heregger meant a few bruises, but most of the time she couldn't make the bills work for the month without him. She let him have her his way.

You're not fast food.

She stared at him and held firm in the doorway while a random thought skittered across the back of her mind.

You have cash. Savings, plus what we stole. You don't have to wash dishes. Just kill bad guys and take their cash. . .

"I'm closed for business, Maddix. Out of business. I quit. So go along back to wherever you came from. Go see your ex-wife."

She swung the door. It bounced from his foot.

"Now Shirley—"

"Don't you—"

"Let's not have a shouting match on the stoop."

She glared. He reached to the door and filled the space between them. She stepped backward.

Don't let him in!

"Let's talk a minute."

He pressed close. She smelled alcohol. He placed his hand on her shoulder. Dragged it across her front, to the top of her breast.

She twisted away.

Maddix stepped forward and closed the door behind him. Shoved his thumbs through his belt loops and cocked his head like a dog pondering the mysteries of a television screen.

"I don't want you inside my home. I'm not in the business anymore."

"Yeah, see. That don't work."

"Why the hell don't that work? It's my business. I quit. I'm asking you to please leave my home." She placed her hands on her hips. "Before I do something stupid."

"I came all this way. Let me try to understand."

His brow lifted. His gaze drifted toward the ceiling. His mouth hung flat. She'd been with him sober and drunk. Sober he was smart and mean. Quick witted, usually with one form of deprecation or another. But intoxicated, she'd seen his brain stall. Like an old Zenith. She wanted to rap his head, help him find clarity.

"Yeah, Shirley. That don't work. I planned on seeing you tonight. Planned it all night long. And it's late enough I'm not going anywhere else. So you're the one."

"No, I'm not. You have to leave."

"For old time's sake?"

"Leave."

She squinted. It worked for Clint.

A smile pulled Heregger's lips. He reached, placed his hand on her shirt at the collar. She batted away his arm. He slammed the heel of his other hand into her mouth. She felt consciousness squirt out her ears, saw herself as if from the ceiling, staggering back and falling to the sofa.

Heregger stood above her. She blinked until he became one person. He pulled his belt flap from the loop. Drew it in, released the hook. Snapped the button free and dragged down the zipper.

"You'll always be what you are, Shirley. You're not going to change. And sure as hell not tonight."

"Don't you dare pull that out."

"Shirley. I'm going to give some advice. Look at yourself." He turned, scanned the trailer. Stomped down the hallway to the bathroom and returned with her makeup mirror. He held it in front of her face.

"Look deep. You're a whore. You're fat. If you didn't have sixty pound knockers and three holes, you'd have no value at all. But what you do have, you know how to work. That's why we have a business relationship. You're my supplier. If I want two by fours, I go to the lumber yard. I want a woman's tender care, I come to you. And you do what it takes to preserve the relationship. That's what business owners do."

Shirley stared into the mirror. Her eyes were bloodshot and how the hell would she know if they were puffy or not? Because he was right. She was monster fat. Radical fat. She didn't need him to remind her. She knew. That's also what VIVA the REVOLUTION meant. She wasn't merely over-throwing all the men who wanted to humiliate her, because you can't stand for something you don't respect. VIVA the REVOLUTION meant standing proud for herself first—but to do that, she had to be something worth standing up for. Not some giant hooker.

Maddix was right. There was no use pretending she wasn't what she was. Not until she was something different.

"Yeah, that's right, Shirley. I can see the wisdom taking hold."

She'd always put on a front like she was happy with herself. She'd throw back her shoulders and strut. Make the flesh jiggle. Put on a show. But in truth she was a buck fifty past what she personally thought was sexy. She only shook it because the men paid her to. Her health sucked. Her knees hurt all the time. Rolling over in bed was a pain. She snored like a man, farted like one, and for fifteen years she'd been plucking jagged black hairs that grew thick as pubes from her eyebrows. She hurt inside when she ate a tub of ice cream. It hurt to walk. To sit.

Fat, fat, fat.

Her weight crushed her spirit long ago, and day by day destroyed her health.

She was who she was. Nothing more.

But, VIVA the REV—

"Shirley, I'm not gonna ask again."

"Just because you got a tiny pecker doesn't give you the right to be an asshole all the time. I said *no*. I meant it."

She closed her eyes and cool tears trickled over. She lowered her face, and the blood on her first chin stuck to her second.

Then she felt his fist.

CHAPTER 2

FBI Special Agent Joe Smith parked at the entrance to the Mountain View Mobile Home and RV Resort.

He trembled.

She killed him. The man. The drug dealer. Stone cold murder by sex—and within hours she was back to work, servicing men. The woman was a fanatic. Banshee. Siren—but not crazy. Her stare held a freaky intelligence. She behaved like a woman who understood a much larger picture than anyone around her. Including Joe.

Shirley Lyle called mid-day. He was in Phoenix, staring at his computer screen. She had intel. Good stuff, she said. Get up here now.

He should have stayed in Phoenix.

Joe glanced at his glow-in-the-dark watch. Eleven p.m.

He joined the FBI straight out of college because he loved America and wanted to defend her good people. Until being posted in Arizona to work on the Baer Creighton case last November, life was good. Though his face was deformed, he built a network of friends and acquaintances who learned to value his wit and charm, his rock solid rural values. He had a home. Routines. To Joe Smith, home didn't denote four walls and a bed. It meant connections. The social element. The security of relationships.

The move to Flagstaff, and then Phoenix, changed everything.

Every move, from high school to college, and from there to the FBI in

New York, felt like ripping a band-aid off his soul. Upheaval. Self-consciousness. Indigestion. Fitful sleep. Acne.

Joe Smith was birth 1 and narrow, with a wedgy face. When he hit puberty, his nose ascended above his cheeks like a mountain range forming out of a jutting tectonic plate. His father once said he could use Joe's face to split a log.

He never in his life experienced a true kiss. First, because he was profoundly unattractive, knew it, and only attempted when convinced his charm might surmount his appearance. That is, he only tried to kiss girls when horribly intoxicated. Second, because the one chance he got, he turned his face so far to the side, her mouth didn't align. His only fulfilling kiss—lipwise—had been upside down, Spiderman style, with a girl whose tiny chin allowed ample room for his nose. Lips aligned and pressed, but the rest of his body was left unfulfilled. What to do with his hands? Reach for her breasts? He didn't dare. Thus the subtle touches and pressures that might ordinarily obtain... didn't.

Agent Joe Smith relocated to Flagstaff, and rapidly afterward, to Phoenix, a frustrated man at his biological peak. The move sealed his fate. Joe accepted he was built for solitude. A man designed to be a paladin. Nothing left but to fight for justice, and leave the tender ministrations and pleasures of the body for those who might more easily procure them.

Until someone mentioned a woman who might—for a fee—provide what he otherwise could not.

Shirley Lyle.

Months ago, he knocked on her door. Negotiated with wit and derring-do. An FBI man, haggling rates with a hooker, not as a sting, but for the same reason as any other man. He was physically lonely.

He bedded her. And returned, again and again.

When the FBI tired of chasing Baer Creighton in Flagstaff, and sent most of the task force home, they assigned Joe to Phoenix. Two hour drive, each way. Two hundred dollars, each toss under the covers. Four hours of windshield time for five minutes of sex and a half hour of cuddling...

It turned out, he wasn't physically lonesome so much as soul lonesome.

He stopped calling Shirley Lyle. Considered getting a dog.

Then Shirley called him.

Come here! Now! I have a drug lord chained to my bed and I'm extracting information by sexual torture!

She didn't say those words, but that's what he saw on arrival.

He raced up Interstate 17 because he'd paid her for sex and now he was at her beck and call. Because morally, he was a failed human being. Compromised. But also, he scrambled because Shirley had a drug lord's son tied up, was torturing him for information, taking video, and needed his help to bring down the entire Flagstaff drug trade in one swell foop.

Oh, what a tangled web. His father had said when you put your dicky in a woman, you're not just putting it in her, but everyone else she's ever been with. Beyond that, you're inserting yourself into her life. Tangling yours with hers. Be careful. There's some whacked-out women out there.

Head down, eyes closed, tearful, Joe Smith rued the day he knocked on Shirley Lyle's trailer door.

Earlier that night, upon seeing the scene, Joe told her to let the man go. She couldn't keep a naked man handcuffed to her bed, with electric stimulation pads all over, like leeches... Crap! He should have put a stop to the nonsense. Should have.

But she threatened to expose him, and Special Agent Joe Smith left the man cuffed hand and foot, to endure her cruel tortures.

Duty to respond! Duty to respond!

Joe lingered outside. While inside, he had been unable to confront Shirley. If she followed through on her threat to tell the FBI he bought sex from her—and showed them the videos—she'd rip open his soul. Everyone would know what they already guessed—he couldn't get sex unless he paid for it. And his penis was smallish, for a man of his height.

His career, right when his skills were blossoming, would be over.

He couldn't face her.

But standing outside Shirley Lyle's trailer, he couldn't give up his values. Right meant doing what was good and just, no matter the personal cost: time, energy, position, or wealth. Joe Smith would sacrifice any of them to be on the right side of the right.

Abject humiliation?

Yes.

Standing beside her trailer, knowing a man, inside, might soon be a murder victim... and Agent Joe would be an accessory... He couldn't abide. He drew his weapon and configured his mind to deal with the situation.

Consequences be damned.

Joe returned to Shirley Lyle's door and heard footsteps of the other girl, the stripper. He hurried back to the shadows. Within seconds Shirley Lyle emerged, the naked man draped over her shoulder. She pitched him in the trunk of an Impala.

Joe had parked farther up the road, so his car would never be associated with a prostitute's residence. After Shirley slammed the trunk, she and the pretty girl left in separate cars. Joe darted to his, then followed the procession from a distance.

Miles later, he parked outside an abandoned grocery warehouse, and after the girls drove both cars inside, hustled on foot to the entrance. They fought the homeless druggies who lived there, and shot two of them. They moved the sex-murder corpse from the trunk to the back seat, and set fire to the car.

Now, hours later, Shirley Lyle was back at work like nothing happened, and Joe Smith imagined one hundred and one scenarios that would doom him to a life in prison.

Shirley Lyle.

Joe shook his head.

What if?

He realized something. Turned the ignition and drove away.

What if Shirley Lyle didn't have to be his problem?

CHAPTER 3

Alone, Shirley sat against the wall with her legs straight out, arms at her side. Tears burned her concrete-grated chin.

Maddix Heregger had been his usual self, except a little rougher.

"Correct you," he said. "For the sake of every man burdened enough to seek your company."

She bawled.

Her knees ached like they always did, but worse, for hitting the warehouse cement before her chin. Her heart—not the emotional center of her soul, but the meat made to pump blood—ached. All her insides ached. She couldn't get enough air, even when her lungs were full.

She was going to die.

She hiccupped.

Rum.

After Maddix left, she slid down the wall. She'd been weeping so long her rump had fallen asleep. She never sat against a wall before. Maybe there was a reason.

She pushed with her left arm, but with the angle, didn't have the strength to rock her weight to the side. She leaned forward, until her belly prevented going farther. She twisted, but that hurt.

I am going to die. Right here. Pinned into a corner where I can't breathe. Held down by my own...

Her pulse quickened.

I don't want to be found like this!

Blood rushed to her forehead. The skin tingled.

"FOUNDER OF VIVA THE REVOLUTION DEAD—PINNED UNDER OWN BELLY"

Internet news would eat the story up, even if VIVA didn't exist yet. Always some asshat ready to laugh at another person in trouble. Or dead by Darwin.

She needed separation from the wall. With her butt pressed into the corner, she didn't have the strength to push away.

Shirley shifted her left leg directly in front of her. Her ribs ached from Maddix's punches. She pushed her right leg as far as it would travel. Twisted her right arm across her front, leaning, pulling, as if to straighten her body and drop parallel to the wall. She shoved her left breast off her thigh to make room, but—

Deep in her back, a muscle twanged like a plucked bass string. Nerves fired along its path, neck to rump. Down the leg. All she needed. Last time she had back trouble, she couldn't climb out of bed for a week, even with all the opioids her son could buy on the streets.

If I survive this, I'm going to change. Lord I'm going to change. I'll—

Inspiration!

She leaned left until her forearm was on the floor. She gritted her teeth through the rib pain. Reached across with her right hand and clasped left. She pushed her left knee to the right, straightening her body, then grunted and cussed herself onto all fours.

After ten minutes of effort, she stood erect.

"I need to sit down."

Sweat beaded on her brow. She swiped with her arm. Her ribs hurt, bad. Blood was still stuck to her arm. She gathered her breath. Closed her eyes and willed herself to take action.

In the bathroom she turned on the light. Prepared to study the ripped skin below her chin, her gaze lingered instead on the yellow-purple forming around her left eye socket.

VIVA the REVOLUTION was dead.

She leaned close to the mirror. Observed blood shot eyes rimmed in salt water, with traces down her cheeks. Flushed skin across her forehead. Man hairs growing out her lip. Shirley sighed. Looked downward.

No! We were going to change all this!

Slow, taking in everything, she lifted her gaze. Her belly swelled round, but saggy. Boobs like a double mudslide. Neck, chin, chin, chin.

"My face is still pretty. Mostly."

Except it looks stretched over a soccer ball. You're going to die.

"Not this second. I'm getting some rum."

Take responsibility!

"I need a drink."

At least go to Urgent Care. Look at those rocks in your skin. You want cysts in your chin?

"A little rum, first."

Shirley turned off the light. At the kitchen she poured an inch and a half of rum into Mickey Mouse. Gulped.

She grabbed her keys, locked the place she was going to burn only a couple hours before. Shirley looked at the a.m. sky. The cool air roused her alertness, and the alcohol gave her clarity.

Burn it now. Run!

"I am a stupid woman. But I am not that stupid."

Urgent Care was up the road, not a mile away. She fought into her car seat. Engine sounded like humping jackrabbits. She waited for the tiny pistons to smooth out.

On the drive she thought about Lester Toungate, the old man who, with his son El Jay, trashed her trailer. Not twelve hours ago, Shirley and Ulyana used naked female flesh to lure El Jay to his destruction. They tortured him with assorted stimulations until Shirley realized she couldn't let him live. So she held a plastic bag over his head while he thrashed against the handcuffs and nearly ripped her headboard from the wall.

That was the birth of VIVA the REVOLUTION. No more taking guff. Not just from men. From anyone. Including herself.

And here, not half a day later, she let a man beat her down.

Well, she could forgive herself for her part. He beat her.

But she beat herself down too. Called herself names. Let the stink-think take over. That's what VIVA was supposed to end.

Cresting a hill, a bright Burger King sign beckoned behind tree cover on the right. If the light was still on, the restaurant was still open. That was a rule. Maybe a burger and fries? Some nutrition to beef up her mental fortitude? Because if she didn't set her mind right, this was rock bottom. She'd been depressed before, like anybody. But her trailer had been tossed. She was a stone cold murderer by asphyxiation. Trailer trash harlot got the snot knocked out of her and if she didn't find a way to seize control of her life...

If you don't find a way to reassert VIVA the REVOLUTION, you'll be dead in three days or less.

"What are you talking about, three days?"

I pulled it out my ass.

"You shouldn't be driving."

I'm not. You are.

Nearing Burger King, red and blue lights broke through the tree cover. A full day after the dog murdered the boy taking out the trash, and police were still flashing their lights. Of course, she told them the dog belonged to the serial killer from North Carolina the FBI was so riled up about.

She slowed as she passed. There! Drug dealer Lester Toungate's truck —the one he'd parked at her place—when he and El Jay ransacked it.

Shirley drove by slow. The restaurant was dim inside.

Ahead, another quarter mile, Urgent Care. She put on her signal though the road was empty. Swung into the parking lot and waited, head-lights weak under the glare of the parking lot lamps.

She struggled out of the car.

Inside she stood at the counter. The television was on, but silent. No one in the waiting area. No one behind the counter at the computer. A toilet flushed. A man emerged, hands tucking his pants. He finished as he spoke.

"Can I help you?"

"This is Urgent Care."

"Uh? Yes?"

"So yes you can help me."

"How... can I help you?"

"Urgently. I fell on concrete and banged up my chin."

Shirley angled her head.

"That doesn't look good. So here's the forms. Fill these out. Here, here, and here. Initial here." He flipped the page on the clipboard. "Fill this section out here, best you can. And sign here, here, and here. This page is our HIPAA info. You know. Sign here. And this page is for your insurance. I'll need your ID and insurance card."

"I don't have insurance."

"Oh."

"I'll pay cash. How much?"

"Depends. I'll add it up. Fill this out, okay? You can sit over there."

Shirley wrote her name, address. Six feet, even. Three-fifty-three (?). Blue. Brown. Regular. Everything. She hoped blood would drip on the form. Alas, she clotted quickly.

She waved the clipboard. Take a hint? No? She resumed her feet and delivered the patient info forms.

"How long?"

"Should be less than a half hour."

"There's no one here. There's no one outside for a mile. You growing a doctor in the back lot? Why a half hour?"

"I'll see you."

A woman's voice. Shirley leaned. A mousy Asian entered from the hallway. Took the forms from the man and smiled. Her face remained unchanged as her gaze moved over Shirley's bruised eye.

"We'll be in the first room on your right. You can go in. I will be right behind."

Shirley entered but the woman lied. She wasn't right behind.

Shirley looked at a plastic chair with chrome legs. Years ago she broke a chair like that.

You should have sued.

"Damn right. Half the world is big people. Make some big chairs."

The examining table was too tall. She found and withdrew a step stool from below. Wiggled to get her thighs supported. Wished the table had a backrest.

Waiting...

Shirley thought of the man she killed only ten or so hours ago.

The act was nothing special. All her life she thought killing someone would be a big deal. In the movies, first time killers always freaked out. But she was stone cold clinical in her judgement and delivery of the sentence.

What had changed?

The door opened and the woman from before entered. Nonstop eye contact.

"I'm Doctor Kristanna Rong. How are you doing?"

"Okay."

It wasn't right, looking in someone's eyes like that. Shirley stared back until Rong looked at her clipboard.

"You fell? Let me look."

Doctor Rong stood beside Shirley.

"You want me to tilt my head back or something?"

"No. I can see."

"Does it hurt?"

"Only when I cry."

"Oh, sweetie. I'll get you patched up. You fell?"

"Yeah. Me and this stripper friend—well. A man swung a log at my head. I fell."

Shirley traced her fingers along the back of her skull for the first time in hours. Goose egg still there.

Dr. Rong observed. Shirley searched her face, but none of the muscles drew. No smile. No frown. No squint. Her stare pierced, but without wounding.

"He knocked me out cold. I landed on my knees, then my chin."

"I'll need to clean out the dirt. Looks like tiny pebbles, ground into your skin. Want me to numb it before I scrub?"

"What are you using? That?" Shirley nodded at a Brillo-looking pad in Dr. Rong's hand.

"Yes. But wait. Have you been drinking?"

"Of course."

"I can't give you a pain killer. It won't hurt too much. I'll be quick."

Isopropyl fumes lifted to Shirley's nostrils. Rong closed in. Shirley jerked. She'd felt a lot of pain before but debriding her cheese grated flesh with rubbing alcohol had to top the list of the worst torment ever.

The fiery misery passed. Shirley numbed. Rong pushed, dragged the scouring pad, rubbed.

"I'm almost done. You're handling this like a woman accustomed to pain."

Shirley closed her eyes and relaxed into Rong's touch. Strange—a connection with a human being that wasn't a transaction. Well, it was. Rong was treating her and would take money. But it wasn't some guy paying her to satisfy himself with her flesh. Dr. Rong caused more pain than most who touched her, that was the truth. But her concern made it gentle. The way she kept glancing into Shirley's eyes, trying to read her.

Caring enough to read her. Motherly.

Real motherly—not like Shirley's mother was motherly.

"A little ointment and I'll apply a bandage."

"So nothing needs sewn up?"

"No. None of the lacerations are more than a half centimeter, at most. It looks worse than it is."

Shirley smelled Rong. Some kind of spice. Like those Ramen packets—the imported ones that cost two bucks.

"When we're done, I also want to examine that bump on your head. You may have a concussion."

"I'm pretty sure I do. And pretty sure I don't give a damn. I've had worse."

"How did it happen? Most men don't pick up logs and club women with them."

"You're not hanging with the same men I do."

Shirley opened her eyes.

Rong stepped to the counter and used a stool to reach the top of a cabinet.

"What men do you hang with?"

"Oh, you know. Assholes."

Rong smiled, tight. Released, and her face resumed neutral. "I sense you don't take very good care of yourself."

"That's a little personal."

"True. How did you hit your chin on pavement?"

"I fell."

Rong nodded. Partial frown. Gaze steady on her. A damn inquisition perpetrated by eyeballs.

"You said a man clubbed you. You fell after getting hit on the head."

"So?"

"There are a couple kinds of abuse going on here."

"How about you patch up the one on my chin."

Rong gathered items from cabinets and placed them on the counter abutting the wall. Moved some to a wheeled stainless steel tray.

"You know, the thing about injuries like this—"

"Shit happens."

"To some people. But did you ever notice bad things don't happen to everyone equally?"

Rong squirted antibacterial ointment on a pad.

"Look, I don't know if you double as a shrink or something, but I came in for some stitches."

"No, of course not. I have a PhD in psychology, but I don't practice."

Shirley rolled her eyes. Deliberate, in your face. Then smiled to make light. Like calling Dr. Rong an imbecile, then saying, "bless your heart."

"Taking care of yourself is hard work when you don't like yourself, isn't it?"

Ouch.

"Look, I didn't come here—"

"Shirley, I don't criticize. Only observe. You are not healthy, and your lifestyle choices are likely to kill you."

Rong cut four pieces of white tape.

"What do you know about my lifestyle?"

"It puts you in the presence of men who club you. And being beaten is ordinary enough you don't expect better. Your choices also have led to morbid obesity, and since you drink alcohol to mask your troubles, you likely have an addiction problem as well—not to mention what the poison is doing to your organs. These choices are hallmarks of a personality—"

"Hold your damn horses."

"Let me finish. All of this is very clear to anyone who bothers to look. It is uncomfortable to hear, but I only tell you because you have the power to take back your life. If you don't, you will lose it."

"Take it back?"

VIVA the REVOLUTION?

"Yes, of course. Take it back. The beliefs you hold about yourself, that animate you, are negative. They bring you to act out great harm upon yourself."

"I didn't club myself in the head."

"No. You put yourself somewhere a man could."

"Hello? A man can club you anywhere."

"And yet—a majority of women don't get clubbed."

"Maybe not the ones you run with."

"Yes, because I make deliberate choices about the people I go near. Shirley. Listen to me. Your choices lead to results. If you disavow the choice, you are a victim of the result. You are powerless... because your decisions are the only power you hold. In all the universe the only power you have rests in your ability to make decisions."

"None of this was my fault."

"You are not hearing me. You are not responsible for what other people do—but you are responsible for making yourself vulnerable."

"Look. Finish my chin. I'll pay, and we'll be done with it."

Rong closed her mouth. Pursed her lips. Relaxed and said nothing. She placed the pad with ointment on Shirley's chin and applied tape.

"Like yourself more," Rong said. "Give yourself a little grace. Everyone has a past. Forgive yourself and move on. Doctor's orders. Otherwise you aren't going to live much longer."

Three days?

"We're all done," Rong said, and smiled faintly.

Shirley looked to the cabinets.

But—

Shirley tried to think. Not feel, and act, but *think*. Dr. Rong peered inside her. Stupid to think it, because no one looked inside anyone. Her gaze communicated a desire to *understand*. Her look said she was processing what she saw, not with animal responses, but concern.

Dr. Rong was with her on an uncharted level. She cared.

Rong opened the door. Waited.

"Me and this other girl, we were getting rid of a—something bad," Shirley said. "I had to take care of myself and that made some evidence... to get rid of. So—hey, this is all confidential. That's what that form said."

"Well, medical privacy. Not, um, criminal?"

"Okay. I'll leave out the good stuff. So I was getting rid of, uh, this thing. I took it someplace no one would find, except I didn't see some people sneaking up. One clubbed me. That's how I fell on my chin."

"How did you get away?"

"My friend, she had a gun—" Shirley shut her mouth.

"Never mind. Why are you telling me this?"

"You said I can take back my life. I'm trying. I'm *really* trying."

"What I mean is—"

"Shush. That was only the start. See, I know I'm a disaster. When the, uh, man who became the criminal stuff I can't talk about came and upended my whole trailer, I decided no more. Never again. VIVA the

REVOLUTION, baby, you know? I wasn't gonna take no bunkum from nobody. I wanted all that stuff you're talking about. Good decisions. Self respect. I'm worth something. You know that old saying, if you take all the chemicals in the human body, somebody's only worth thirty four cents? Well, look at me. Double! I'm worth at least sixty eight! You find little things to tell yourself, to keep up the fight. But I know I'm not healthy. I know it. So right when I was ready to change the whole world, kick some ass, this happens."

Shirley grabbed her shirt at the bottom, tucked her chin, and pulled her top over her head.

Rong peered at her bruises.

"Look at that. I sat and took all that. I said *No! I don't do that no more.* And this is what he did."

"Did you call the police?"

"So I can get arrested for hooking?"

"You said 'no.'"

"I took money."

Rong walked around the table, studying the damage.

"All this is from him? Nothing from the, uh, criminal stuff?"

"All this is from him. I took it. Sat and let him beat on me."

"Why?"

"Good question, right? You're the shrink."

"Why did you meet him?"

"He came to my place."

"Why did you let him in?"

"He put his foot in the door."

"Did you resist?"

"Some. But he pushed in. Pressed my buttons, so I pressed his."

"Meaning..."

"I told him he had a teeny pecker."

"Shirley."

"I did."

"And he started punching you?"

"No. I blew him."

"I don't understand. He pushed his way in, you insulted him, and then you submitted? Something else happened. What did he do? What did he say?"

24

"He said I'm fat. I'll always be fat. Worthless, and I'll never be anything but."

"Now we're getting somewhere. So let me ask you. If he said he doesn't like salmon, would that have made you allow him to beat you and use you?"

Shirley wrinkled her brow.

"Of course not. You don't care what he likes to eat."

"No. Salmon is delicious. And he's an asshole."

"And a criminal, and all sorts of other things. Regardless. His opinion about food doesn't matter. So why does his opinion about *you* matter? Why is he a better judge of you than he is of fish?"

Shirley stared at Rong and parsed revelation.

"Because I think it's true?"

"He said what you believe about yourself. At that point, why keep up the charade?"

"So I gave in."

"Think of it this way. You ever see a movie where someone is accused of a crime they didn't commit, and they never confess? They take all the punishment, all the abuse. They refuse to cut a deal? Why do they do it?"

"Because it isn't true."

"Right. Some people don't care about what is true. They'll say anything they need to say. Others can't deal with untruth, at all. They see clearly. That's a great advantage. You're like that."

"So you're saying I am fat and worthless."

"No, I'm saying you're fat—and you are honest about that. You don't lie to yourself about that. But here's your mistake: your size and your worth have nothing to do with each other. When the man who beat you equated your size with your worth—that was an opinion that was as valuable as whether he likes salmon. Who cares?"

"I fell for it."

"Only because inside, you equate the two the same way. You tell yourself the same lie. That's what you need to change."

Shirley felt a tickle in her heart. Not a leap. A tickle.

"I don't know if I can do that."

"Grace," Rong said. "Nothing is harder. We think our past defines who we are and determines our worth. When we make mistakes, we believe we are less valuable and we lose self respect. We need to give ourselves grace." Rong closed the door and leaned on it. "I know about a group. You could—"

"I'm not going to a battered women's group. I'd beat them even more."

"Shush." Rong smiled.

Shirley smiled.

"They have meetings. Private, like alcoholics anonymous. The women who attend rely on one another to help them process their worlds, and learn how to steer themselves to better situations."

"I don't like to talk about myself."

"You don't have to. The first time I went, I listened. I found that seeing other people share their experiences helped me understand my own. I heard a woman say what she was going through and I saw her problem. I realized I was doing the exact same thing. You might go and listen. You could make a connection or two. There are counselors who can—"

"I don't want a counselor. I get sick of the high and mighty crowd. Tell me what's wrong with me."

"You can think about it." Dr. Rong nodded. Appointment over. She stepped forward, took Shirley's hand. "Give yourself grace. That's first."

CHAPTER 4

Hours ago, Lester Toungate fell forward. A bullet nicked his skull and knocked him unconscious. Even asleep, he knew he lived.

Lester Toungate would never die. Couldn't. Because that would mean two things Lester couldn't fathom were true.

First, God existed.

Second, He was just.

Lester awoke crumpled against a boulder. Earlier, he took cover when the fugitive from North Carolina went in the cave after his dog. Lester's head throbbed and pressing it, his finger slipped. Blood—not yet dry. Maybe he was only unconscious a moment. But his whole body ached with the discomfort that follows being crumpled, unmoving, for hours. His neck flashed pain. Awkward angle.

Lester opened his eyes.

Darkness.

He rolled to his back, twisted his neck opposite the knot until muscles twanged and the joints crinkled.

Pinch in his ribs. Maybe he'd broken one, falling.

Lester felt along the ground for his hat, and finding it, kept it in his hand. He rested. Allowed his awareness to seat. Somewhere during his eighty-three years he'd learned not to take heady action until it wasn't heady. A man who didn't understand his whereabouts was a man at risk. Lester looked. Waited. Listened.

From the chill in the breeze and the shiver giving birth in his back, the hour had to be close to dawn.

He took in the black sky, stars punching through the tree canopy. Looked East, but the forest was too dense to betray the gray glow of predawn. Air poured deep in his lungs, and out, while he listened for footsteps or other signals.

None came.

Lucky was dead.

He remembered, now. The white pit bull in the cave killed him. And the man from North Carolina took the dog from the cave—or that was the plan. The man had nicked his head with a bullet before leaving, so maybe the pit was still in there.

Unlikely, but possible.

Lester blinked.

Why assume the man had left?

If only a few seconds had passed, and not half a night, the spree-killer could still be in the cave. Waiting to see what Lester did.

For the moment, Lester had cover behind the boulder. He patted along his body, not expecting to find additional wounds, but needing to be certain before attempting to stand. He found none. Only the bullet creasing his head.

He braced. Stooped forward, hands propping his weight at his knees, he peered over the boulder.

Nausea. Stabbing pain. Felt like a broken rib. Muscles and joints didn't work the way he expected—his left side hardly followed orders. Weak and numb—but that was because he'd been crumpled on that side half the night.

Standing, Lester sensed the predawn gray in the east. The whole hemisphere lighter than the west.

He leaned on the boulder, collected his thoughts.

Lucky was dead.

Lester nodded, slow, as the right perspective took hold. The German shepherd was old. At least ten. And with the grit in his lungs from being a 9-11 search dog for the police, hacking up blood and more unsteady on his feet every hour, his days were numbered anyway. The pit bull killing him meant Lester didn't have to.

His cheeks tightened with a smile and coolness rimmed his eyes. All the men he'd killed without emotion... but putting down that dog would have been rough.

After a couple minutes upright, lucidity returned. His brain felt like a six cylinder firing on eight.

He'd leave Lucky where he lay. Rites were ridiculous. The same treatment he'd want—if he was capable of death.

Time to put on the CEO hat. That's what the last few days had been about. Why his first son, Paul, was dead. Lester had to reevaluate the mission. The goal wasn't to capture the pit bull with the incriminating thumb drive in a barrel on his neck—a story which required more credulity than he could muster, in the cool clear night. The goal was to restore the business his sons drove into the ground.

Step number one was to get to his truck. Fill his belly with sausage, eggs and cakes.

Work to do.

Lester pressed his hat to his head, his left arm against his maybe-broken rib, and stepped forward. He was only a mile or so from his RAM. Probably be light by the time he reached the Burger King parking lot.

If he remembered right, there was an Urgent Care right down the street.

Lester probed with his right foot, stepped out. Listened to the noise from his feet on dry leaves. It wasn't a soft echo, but a thickening of sound, that confirmed the rock wall was close. He put out his arms and lowered his head. If he struck stone, it would be his crown, not his face. Easy does it. One slow step at a time. Didn't matter if it took three hours to walk one mile. The end would be the same.

Trudging along, his heart waxed stronger. He was on top again.

Paul was dead.

Hard to believe the man carried Lester's genes. Maybe he didn't.

Either way, he was gone.

Other son El Jay—Lester Junior—would expect to ascend to Paul's position.

Lester'd nip that in the bud.

He didn't off one idiot son to hand the reins to another. No, it was him alone. El Jay would keep running the paving company. He'd tell him he wanted a straight life for him. Didn't want him to be hiding from the law all his life.

His right toe caught a root. He stumbled. No problem. That's why you walk slow in the dark. Step after step.

The gray in the east became yellow. After a bit, long shadows formed. He wondered what it would be like to stand atop a dune at the Sahara, at dawn, and see his shadow touch eternity.

Same, most likely.

The terrain rolled slow and coming down the final hill, he angled for the Burger King light. Different muscles, walking downhill. His broken rib seemed less broken. He let his arms hang free, swinging with a normal gait.

He arrived at his truck. Up the road, Lester swung into Urgent Care. Empty lot. He completed the forms. Waited. No one else inside.

A sleepy Asian woman in a white coat led him down the hall, pointed to room. "You can sit on the table or the chair."

"I was involved in that fracas last night, with the dog and the serial killer you heard about on the news. Need to get patched up."

"I didn't hear. Please remove your hat."

Lester sat in the corner and placed the fedora on his lap.

"You are a lucky man."

"If you call it that."

She got close. He smelled her. Not bad. Spicy.

"That cut appears to be from a bullet. It's to the skull. Were you unconscious?"

"About six hours, my guess."

"You were concussed. That goes without saying. It wouldn't be unusual to have a hematoma. Or a brain hemorrhage."

"Those the same thing?"

"No. Subdural or epidural hematomas are bleeding between the skull and brain lining. A brain hemorrhage—a brain bleed—is inside the brain. You should be at a hospital, not an urgent care."

"Not gonna happen."

"Do you have any problems with balance?"

"No."

"Your speech isn't slurred. Any numbness or weakness on one side of your body?"

"Uh—no."

"You sure? Because either of these conditions can kill you quickly."

"I'll take my chances. Just patch me up. And I might have broken my rib. Though maybe not."

"Can you remove your jacket? Your range of motion doesn't indicate a broken rib."

"I took a walk this morning and it loosened up."

He took off his jacket. Winced.

"You're bleeding. Did you know?"

Lester looked.

"Shirt off."

He complied. Feisty little snipper.

"You've been shot here as well. Lift your arm. High. Above your head."

"Okay.

It looks like another crease, like the one in your head. Never fully penetrated, so the likelihood of any internal damage—other than bruising—is small. The primary risk is infection. You should go to the emergency room."

"Again—"

"I'll clean both wounds and dress them."

"Attagirl."

Her lips tightened. "You are a lucky man."

"Yeah. That's what you call it."

CHAPTER 5

R apping at the door. Shirley's chest drew tight around her bouncing heart.

Another client? Another Maddix Heregger?

Or Lester Toungate, ready to exact a pound of hell for the snipe chase she sent him on?

Frozen, Shirley remembered holding Ulyana's pistol in her hand before the meth zombies attacked. She'd never felt similar power. Certainly not from wielding her mini baseball bat.

Speaking of which, she tiptoed down the hallway until her feet gave out and she had to walk. She grabbed the stick.

You need a gun.

Nothing like the power. Knowing she could send a little piece of metal out the barrel, going a million miles an hour, so fast that a wee chunk of metal could remove half a man's head. Capability like that erased fear.

You need a gun. A giant one.

Rapping, louder!

She imagined Lester Toungate's face, snarled back in rage, saying he learned her story about hiding the thumb drive on the dog was total nonsense...

Well, Lester wouldn't have El Jay with him this time.

She'd beat his octogenarian ass to pudding. He couldn't weigh a buck fifty.

Unless he has a gun. You need a gun.

Pounding on the door...

Shirley arrived in the living room walking on the sides of her feet, gently resting heel to floor, rolling the foot forward. A walk she learned as a promiscuous teen, sneaking about the house for exit. Can't let the heels land hard.

She neared the door.

No one gets in unless I say so. This is my domain!

Hand to the wall, she leaned, bent a single strip of metal blind back from the window, admitting a shaft of light from the bright morning sun.

Ulyana.

Shirley released a breath she hadn't realized she'd been holding. Maybe Lester was still looking for the dog. They needed a plan to deal with him. Shirley unlocked the deadbolt. Opened the door.

"Ve need plan for Lester," Ulyana said. "What happen to you?"

"What?"

"Your eye. What happen?" Ulyana strode inside. "Is zat from last night? At varehouse?"

Shirley gave her a look. Peeked outside. Closed the door.

"El Jay did not do zat. What happen?"

I need an accent.

"I don't want to say."

Ulyana raised her hand. "Fine. Did Lester do zis? Bekause ve need to talk about him. And El Jay. He still out zere, in kar."

"Yeah, *dead*. And that was the plan. Burn him and leave him with the car. Nothing connects us to that."

"Did you vakuum hair and throw it in dumpster tvo miles avay?"

"What?"

"Hello? You shave him all over your bed."

"I knew there was a reason I wanted to light this place on fire. Well, a bunch of hair will only matter if police come here and search for his pubes. They won't, because we burned his body—and they won't see he doesn't have any. Nobody suspects us. No one even found him yet. Most likely maybe. He's not the problem. Lester is."

"I know, da? Zat why I kome. Ve need plan.

Shirley sat. Shook her head. Yawned, and raised her arms back to stretch.

Ulyana came to her, peered at the purple and yellow under her arms, where Maddix beat her, while holding her down. "If not Lester, who?"

"Maddix Heregger."

Ulyana smiled with the left side of her mouth. Frowned with the right. "Who?"

"A john."

"What hell?"

"What?"

"VIVA? You said you vere done vith zat. Zat's REVOLUTION, da?"

"Well you're part of VIVA and you went out flashing titties at half of Flagstaff last night."

"Zat different. Zat is job."

Shirley shook her head. "You're only nineteen, but try to think, just a little, before spouting nonsense."

"I zirty-four."

"Oh."

"And difference is my job is job. I'm good at it."

Shirley looked her up and down. Ulyana wore that flesh-tight running outfit that showed every perfect ounce of her. "Yeah. That's fair."

How come every five minutes I want to bawl?

Ulyana stood beside her. Touched her shoulder. "Zis okay? You're not bruised here, too?"

"No."

Ulyana caressed with her thumb—one second. Sat on the edge of the chair opposite the sofa. Leaned forward, elbows on knees, legs wide to accommodate the forward lean.

"So who's Maddix Heregger? Bekause I, how you say. Got konnected."

"He's a builder. Has a small company. When he finishes a project he's flush and comes every day 'til he's broke. Well, I haven't seen him for a few weeks. He just showed up last night."

"Why you let him in?"

"I didn't. I tried to close the door."

"You're tough girl. What are you, six feet five?"

"Six. Even."

"You kould have stood up to him. Like vith El Jay."

"That was different. I had you there."

"You're one vith attitude, going crazy on assholes. You vere super hero last night. You kill drug lord."

"El Jay? He was just a drug lord's moron son. He drove an Impala."

"Vell, he trash your place and you torture him, and suffokated him."

"You wearing a wire?"

Ulyana's jaw fell. "I shot druggies."

"I'm kidding. I couldn't fight back with Maddix. He—"

"What?"

"I guess he knows how to make a girl submit."

"What that mean?"

"He said I was fat."

"You are."

"I understand that. Honest. I'm aware. But he didn't say it that way. He said that's all I am. All I ever will be. I don't want to go through all this. I already talked to a head shrink, okay? I have a plan."

"Yeah. VIVA, Shirley. VIVA. We need to kill zis Madd—"

"No. I don't want to murder people. Unless it's really important. Or I really want to. Maddix is all right. He's just an asshole."

"Niet, you kan't zink like zat. You kan't make exkuses. You have problems, but you don't go around terorizing people."

Shirley leered.

"Zat's different. He vas drug lord."

"Idiot son."

"Whatever. I don't take crap. I show people body of me. Tease zem. Put it right up in their faces. The only way you can work in my business—or yours—is to nip that nonsense in the bud. The moment they turn wild —Bam!"

"You sure speak good English, allasudden."

Ulyana smiled.

"Yeah, busted. What's your story?"

"I do not understand. Busted? My English is not too good—"

"Bull."

"Okay, seriously," Ulyana said. "I'm not from Ukraine. I'm from Philadelphia. I studied Russian in college, and when I moved here, I had to choose a stage name. A persona."

"So you're not Ulyana?"

"I am Ulyana. But I'm not 'Ulyana the Ukrainian.' I never said that. I just sang Russian songs to drunk men, and whispered Russian nonsense in their ears."

"Really?"

"They love it when you say Putin. They think you're saying something else."

"Wonder what that could be." Shirley looked away, gazed at the wall, for relief. Sometimes the trickery, everywhere around her, was too much. Maddix Heregger—at least he was who he was. "That kinda pisses me off. You lying like that."

"I didn't lie."

"You spoke with a fake accent, knowing good and damn well what I'd think."

"I told you the truth, now. I only met you... was it only yesterday?"

"So you meet the whole world with a lie?"

"I have to. I know people. Russian people. I—pretended to be Russian to earn their trust. Now I'm in. *Really in.*"

"That's exactly what VIVA the REVOLUTION is all about. We don't have to lie to nobody. We don't have to take a role, or fit into somebody else's box so they have terrific self-esteem and we think we're worthless. We don't have to keep all that crap in our heads, shouting ourselves down, making us think we're garbage, unless our heels are in the air or our mouths are sucking. You dig?"

"Exactly. So why don't you want me to have my friends whack this guy Maddix?"

"Because he's mean, but he's honest. He's being what he is."

"Oh, the scorpion being the scorpion. You like him."

"No. But... One time, when he was really messed up, he couldn't finish. He kept trying, but he just wore himself out. He rolled off, but didn't get up. I almost fell asleep. And he started talking, distant, like his brain didn't have enough air. He said his parents beat him. Sick stuff. 'That's the way everybody grows up, right?' Those were his words."

"Nah. That's crap," Ulyana said.

"I know he's an asshat. But it's not his fault. Not really. When you think about it."

"What did he say when he beat you last night?" Ulyana bounced from her chair and lifted Shirley's arm. "What did he say when he did

37

that? Because those black circles are his knuckles. He punched you in the underside of your arm. That's sick. His parents didn't do that. He did."

"I cried."

"Yeah?"

"When he did that, I cried. And he said, 'How the hell you feel anything, through all that fat?'"

"And that's all it took to throw VIVA the REVOLUTION out the window?"

"All it took?"

"People use names. They're like a gun that shoots out of the mouth. I can't believe you don't know this. You've been heavy a long time. You've been insulted before, right? You understand words don't matter. They don't even mean the same thing to everybody. I studied language, remember? When some drunk boner tells me my tits are lopsided, he thinks he's insulting me. Truth is, boobs are supposed to be lopsided, and he's oblivious because the only ones he's ever seen were photoshopped by some other asshole. You arrive in heaven, every woman's gonna have one heavy tit."

"That isn't the same," Shirley said. "You're perfect."

"Well, yeah, the body. But I got issues."

Shirley smirked.

"Sometimes I throw up after I eat. Out of fear. If I get an ounce of fat on my ass, I lose money, so I run six miles every single day. And I only allow myself one slice of pizza per month."

"Damn. You got a nazi in your head."

"Yeah. And instead of being a captain in the Army as an interpreter, I'm a stripper. Instead of being a spook for the CIA or something, I'm taking my clothes off for a living. I'm not ashamed of who I am, but I'm not what I wanted to be."

"You?"

"I got issues, right? So don't give me this, *I'm perfect* nonsense. Or I'm different. You're bat-mad and I'm bat-mad. It's all rouge and lipstick. In the end, if you're not convinced you're worth something, and somebody says you're not, you believe him. So I guess you're right. Your fault, not his."

Ulyana spoke truth. Shirley was in the right place to see it. Sometimes low self-esteem is a fair assessment. Shirley imagined a clock ticking. The second-hand clicking one notch after another. Around.

Around.

Ulyana returned to her chair and sat.

Ulyana stood. "If you're an overweight prostitute and you don't want to be, what are you going to do about it? Lose weight, or stop being a prostitute. A skinny virgin can't call herself a fat whore, and have it mean anything. That's just how language works."

"Simple," Shirley said. "I'll just be skinny, and forget I screwed half of Arizona. When every *single* diet I ever tried just left me fatter, and I got men showing up at my door three times a day."

"No, not simple. But possible—because other people have done it. If someone else did something, you can do it. You're not inventing losing weight. You're not discovering it. Other people been there done that. So you go there and do that. And the other part—the hooker thing. I don't have a problem with it. But you do. You can end it with a decision. You say you won't ever sell sex again, and from that moment you don't. You are what you are, not what you were. Remember that. Say it."

"I am what I am, not what I was."

"As long as you believe it, you get the benefit of making the change when you make the decision. You believe, and it is."

"So how's a girl with issues got it all figured out?"

"Yeah? Well you had it all figured out last night, too."

"Yeah."

"Yeah?"

"Dammit! Yeah!"

"So VIVA's back on, right? VIVA the REVOLUTION. We hunt down Lester Toungate and make sure he never comes after us. And Maddix Heregger—"

"No. I'm going to handle Maddix. I don't want some mafia guy to kill him. I want to punish him, so he can learn from his mistakes. Be a better man."

Ulyana shook her head. "Fine. But we're killing Lester. These people don't mess around. If we don't take him out, he comes for us. You started that when you killed his son."

"Okay. Whatever. Later."

"I need sleep."

"Oh. You worked last night?"

"I got called in."

"At midnight? Right after we split up."

"It happens. Girl got sick. And I need to be back by noon."

"Thank you," Shirley said. "Ulyana. Is that your real name? Truly?"

"Da. My grandparents on both sides are all Ukrainian. Tight kommunity. Accent kame easy."

"Well, thank you, Ulyana. VIVA the REVOLUTION."

"VIVA, baby."

CHAPTER 6

R oddy Memmelsdorf lifted his Budweiser, plugged the hole with his tongue, and tilted. No beer made it through. He placed the bottle on the table and fake-swallowed. Smacked his lips. Wiped his mouth with his sleeve. Looked around.

People ignored him. Good. That's how you keep them from noticing. You act it out. Even the little stuff.

Stupid people.

The Ukrainian tormented him.

Three months had passed since the big prick leaning on the wall—bald, white guy with Cyrillic tats—threw Roddy to the sidewalk.

He'd looked up at Mike from his back, seeing PINK PANTHER in neon behind him.

A black man originally owned and named The Pink Panther, *Panther* signaling the place was cool. Down with the struggle. Hep to the jive. But there weren't very many other black men in Flagstaff, and they were all family guys. Eventually the founder sold—at gunpoint—to Vanko Demyan.

So said Foster—the old guy who was always there, at the corner, not even scoping the girls. The bouncer they called Mike was actually Mykhaltso Babyak, from Volgograd, the city formerly known as Stalingrad. He'd been in the States three years, had no life outside the club, except whatever tough-guy tasks the owner demanded of him.

Roddy Memmelsdorf was a genius. Not, "oh wow you solved the crossword" genius. More like Einstein. Hawking. Those guys. That's what pissed him off. All his life, he was better. Faster. Smarter. He understood things no one else understood. Cosmic. Metaphysical. But more than that: he was like Jesus and never had a broken bone. He remembered faces. His peripheral vision was wider. His olfactory system—he could distinguish thyme from rosemary at a hundred yards. His problem solving. His accent. Every damn thing about him was better than other people.

And life never gave him what he deserved.

Like that Ukrainian girl. All he wanted was a quick toss under the covers. Nothing exotic. Missionary, even.

Nothing in his life had been more frustrating than seeing her, and not taking her. Owning her, the way a man owns a woman when she weeps for more.

Not to take his world view from a comic strip, but long ago he'd seen a sketch of a cave man dragging a club in one hand and a woman, by the hair, in the other.

The clarity of a bygone era.

Roddy's history with Ulyana the Ukrainian stripper spanned 129 days.

Smart people aren't spontaneous. They lurk. Roddy observed her for a month, and then, three months ago, made his move. He'd already seen her a dozen times before he paid thirty dollars for the all-included private dance— "all included" being the term that allowed him to touch anything above or below her leather underwear. He followed her to the cubby at the back of the joint.

Not being a lifelong romantic, and having no language to announce his hopes, he recycled the line he'd used on his wife.

"I'm a man. You're a woman. I want a woman that'll do as I say."

"Of kourse, Baby. *Putin vedet Rossiyu.*"

But the funny thing—Ulyana quit working for the Russian, which no one was supposed to be able to do.

After a couple weeks spending ten to two a.m. shivering next to the January snow banks at the edge of the parking lot, and not finding her car, or seeing her leave, Roddy checked the other four clubs in town.

He found her at a joint owned by the Toungates. The business license was in the old man's name, but the son, Paul, managed. Roddy knew because he sold property and casualty insurance. He didn't own the account. He'd overheard the colleague who did.

Paul Toungate had money. Ulyana sat on his lap while he searched for places to tuck singles.

Then—two nights ago—Ulyana disappeared again.

Roddy checked the other clubs. He hadn't been thrown out of them, so he walked in, did a circle, asked a couple girls about the Ukrainian, and left. His desperation grew by the strip club. At last he defied illogic, and returned to where she'd quit: the Pink Panther.

Roddy found her car in the lot.

He smacked his steering wheel. Continued driving, turned around after a half mile, and drove by the Pink Panther again.

There was no place nearby where he could park in anonymity. The club sat by itself on a road that led to a small brick warehouse, and nothing else. He turned to the Pink Panther lot and backed into a rear spot. Slouched until his line of sight passed between the upper curve of the steering wheel and the dash.

Mykhaltso had already bounced him once. A colleague from work he sometimes ate lunch with had asked him about his photo being up, behind the bar, on the "do not serve" cork board.

Must have grabbed it from a security video.

He had to see her.

Had to.

He spent the next day thinking about her, even more than usual. He didn't go out that night, but drank beer and watched the idiot box.

His wife asked about his wistful look.

"You're up to something. Don't you have to make your rounds tonight?"

"Everything's taken care of."

"You have the strangest clients."

"Well, they put food on the table, so I meet them when they want to meet me."

"But always at night. It's just strange."

He'd looked at her the way he'd taught her not to want him to look at her.

Sitting with beer in hand and the television burping noise, he slipped into his plan. He'd create a disguise. Practice a couple moves, like changing his walk. And instead of buying Heineken, he'd go lowbrow. Bud. No—Bud Light.

Fit in.

First thing in the morning, he went to Party City and grabbed a wig and a pack of mustaches.

He was near the club... may as well drive by...

Ulyana the Ukrainian's car was parked on the side, by the building.

A little brazen for his taste, he parked at the club in broad daylight. Kind of surprised by the afternoon crowd. He donned his disguise. Mykhaltso wasn't the brightest bulb and three months had passed since he bounced Roddy. Things would be fine. His hair was blond now, and he had a brown mustache. New eyeglasses and salesman's wrinkled suit. He'd always worn slacks, before.

Roddy stepped out of his car. Walked cool as blue Jello to the double doors.

As he entered, he remembered the last time...

She'd tormented him. He'd seen her almost every day for a month. Ever since the first he saw her, he fevered for her. It was maddening. He'd paid her thirty bucks to possess her. To grab her like he owned her, and dominate her. Just sex. That's all he wanted. Nothing deep. No soul searching. Just a good animal romp, some sweat, and glory.

But she pushed him off and shouted. And three seconds later the big dumb vodka farmer Mykhaltso lifted him by his belt and jacket collar and threw him off Ulyana. Then chased him down, grabbing him just short of the door, to chuck him outside.

Roddy was already leaving with haste. The last throw was pure insult.

And evidence Mykhaltso was predator-fast.

Well, you can get away with insulting dumb people, Mike.

But not Roddy Memmelsdorf.

ULYANA TOOK THE STAGE. Roddy snapped back to present. She wore a leather top and bottom—but the leather looked fashioned from the narrow strips used for whip making. Milky skin everywhere else. Curves all around. And red welts where she smacked herself, for effect, with the music.

Ulyana stomped her heels. Threw her pelvis high. Rolled. Pursed her lips. Smiled wide. Stuck out her tongue. Rubbed her backside on the chrome pole.

Roddy shifted in his seat. Placed his fingers in his pocket and adjusted the pinch.

Mykhaltso hadn't looked his direction at all. It was three p.m., and Roddy fit in with the afternoon crowd. Business guys.

It was unfair, almost, how smart he was. She was just a stripper. Months had passed since he'd been thrown out. He didn't look anything like his usual self.

She'd never guess it was him.

Roddy fanned a twenty and a ten. Wished he had some singles, to widen the spread.

The green caught her eye.

Now she was topless.

She finished her set, slunk down the steps from the stage. She sauntered to him. Beaming smile. Eyes.

Nipples.

Every ounce of her as perfect as he remembered.

She sat on the chair beside him. Placed her hand on his thigh. Stroked with her thumb.

Like he was too stupid to know what she was doing. Shameful, almost, matching wits with her.

She leaned to him and whispered, *"U menya skuchnyy den'. S Putin-ym."*

Ah, the equalizer. Women didn't have minds. But they had everything necessary to short-circuit a man's. Biology didn't play fair.

He grabbed her breast, tugged.

She squeezed the hand still resting on his thigh. Shifted it closer to his center.

"I'm just a man," Roddy said. "And all I want—"

"YOU!" She ejected from the seat. Bounced the little round table. Launched his beer.

Roddy froze.

"Mykhaltso!"

Roddy jumped up. Tripped on his left foot and pitched into Ulyana. Swinging his arm for balance, he struck her shoulder.

She shoved him off. "He hit me!"

Roddy fell. Climbed to his knees.

Mykhaltso arrived with balled fists in motion. One to Roddy's left temple, the other glancing his upper arm as he collapsed, vaguely aware of Ulyana's perfectly toned runner's calves... how they came low to her ankles, not like his wife's skinny-girl bony ankles.

Roddy's head bounced. Mykhaltso grabbed his neck. Hand slipped. He shoved his fingers under his shirt collar, locked tight by Roddy's tie. Lifted. Roddy hung, still conscious. He choked. Tried to get his fingers between his neck and Mykhaltso's fingers. Swiped behind him, blind.

Ulyana yanked his hair. The wig pulled from his head. She thrashed him with it. While Mykhaltso held him, she yanked off his mustache. Then chick-punched him.

Pretty good, for a chick.

"It's him," she said. "From a couple months ago."

"*Kto?*"

"You threw him out. Remember?"

"*Akh ...*"

Mykhaltso jerked Roddy's collar. Roddy, leaning backward and perpetually unable to gain his balance, stutter skipped along while Mykhaltso dragged him to the door. Behind him, he heard the bouncer's foot slam into the horizontal release latch.

Air beneath him, askilter, offidaddle, ajumbo. Heat flashed to his face. Fear? His skull already ached. Roddy's head smacked blacktop. He expected to hear something. Mykhaltso's voice. A taunt or threat.

The door closed.

That was it. The final insult was... no insult.

Intolerable.

Laughter arrived from the parking lot. Male voices.

Roddy relaxed into the April-cold but afternoon-warm blacktop. He shut his eyes. Maybe they'd pass without a word.

He choked. Coughed. Rolled his head and the spit smelled nosebleed fresh, good like blood straight from the vein. Warm. Nauseating.

"Whooey," said one of the approaching men.

His head sideways, the man leaned on his buddy. There were five of them. In overalls and flannel. Big hair. Silver on the tips of their boots. All five.

Got spiffed up to see some strippers.

One punched another. They staggered together. Swayed and laughed together.

A man pulled his buddy's sleeve with one hand and pointed at Roddy with the other.

"Yeah, they just tossed his ass."

"Dude—what you do?"

They arrived. Circled.

"Really, Dude. What'd you do? 'Cause you can get away with damn near *anything* here."

"Leave him alone."

"No! I don't wanna do what he did."

"He probably grabbed something. They tossed this feller I knew—"

"Dude. Don't be slipping fingers—"

Roddy swung his right leg, caught Dude in the shin. Felt ankle connect with bone. The man lurched back.

The other four closed in, planted heels, lobbed feet. Hoots. Silver toed sparkles. Howls. Line dancing. Kicking.

Roddy bruised. Bled. Curled in a ball and shook.

HIS SUIT WAS RUINED. Both eyes swollen, one closed—right after a heel came down. He'd somehow provoked a nosebleed when Mykhaltso threw him out. It only worsened. Roddy swallowed blood while they kicked him.

The men soon tired of his whimpers. One rubbed his boot clean on Roddy's shirt. The five entered the Panther.

Stooped with hands braced on his knees, Roddy staggered back to the double-door entrance and spewed the blood he'd swallowed. He spat the proceeds a little higher, on the handle.

Unable to stand upright for the pain in his chest and abdomen, he scampered sideways from under the extra-wide eaves. Each time he got too erect, his stomach cramped and ribs flashed white hot torture. He rounded a Ford Taurus. Spat a new mouthful of blood on the windshield.

Onward, across the lot.

He arrived at his car. Leaned on the door while watching the Pink Panther entrance.

He inserted his key, and though it hurt to remain upright, he let his hand fall. Turned, and rested his back on the window.

Roddy tried to open his left eye, but couldn't control the muscles. He slipped his finger into the slit. Felt his finger—and his eyeball. That was heartening. But he couldn't part the eyelid enough to see light.

He shut his good eye and thought hard about what he'd say if he went to the emergency room. He'd been jumped by some thugs at the mall. Transients. Migrants.

Leaning against the car door, spitting blood with lessening frequency, his fear of further assault morphed into glee at surviving. As he analyzed the plausibility of each made up explanation for the attack, his emotions evolved.

It was unjust. Life always piles more adversity on the most advantaged. And Roddy, with his intellect, looks and charm, was among the very most advantaged.

Walking across the lot, he'd felt devoid of energy. Weak to his core. But now, umbrage animated his cells. Against the pain, he forced himself to stand erect.

Face pointed at the Pink Panther, he discerned details he'd never before seen.

The building had a smoke stack. Odd, on a bar.

The powerlines coming in from the back hung with a lot of slack.

From the shape of the roof, there was an attic. Just below the apex, he spotted a square door, secured by...

Nothing.

Roddy Memmelsdorf nodded. His gaze bounced. Powerlines. Attic. Smoke stack.

Much to work with.

He opened his car door and lowered himself through a forcefield of pain. Roddy dropped to the seat, thankful he'd kept his hand on the door, and pulled. He hit the locks. Slapped his palms to the steering wheel. Then the dashboard, in case he somehow triggered the horn or airbag. Aware of his rage while in its midst, he nurtured it. Fed himself insults from other life situations. Thieves were everywhere. They snuck in some extra taxes on his phone bill. Potholes. The boss was incompetent but kissed the right ass. Keep it coming. You want sustainability, not fireworks.

You want cold fusion.

All his life when things were unfair and people didn't show him the respect due, he let it slide. Let the slag sit there, burning. That's where the ambition came from.

But someday, at some point, you have to break free. You have to stand up for how good you are.

The door opened. Mykhaltso stepped out, covered his brow with his hand, and surveyed the lot. He walked to the corner and peered around the side. Back at the door, he waved someone forward.

Ulyana emerged from the Pink Panther.

She entered her car.

Roddy waited until she pulled out and drove a hundred yards, then turned his ignition.

He thought about finding those cowpokes and kicking their asses. Or returning with a gun. He could stay hidden at the back and see which vehicles were theirs.

Visit them alone, in the order they stood while kicking him. The order of their deaths would be the only clue...

But the truth came to him. They were drunk. He was on the ground, an obvious target. It wasn't their fault.

Ahead, Ulyana braked. Turned right.

Roddy slowed. Arrived at the turn.

Fault didn't rest with the men who beat him. Or even, so much, with Mykhaltso.

Roddy turned right.

Fault sat square with Ulyana the Ukrainian stripper.

Except the bitch was really from Philly.

CHAPTER 7

S hirley Lyle stood next to a red brick church. Where she came from, churches were white.

Her stomach churned with disquiet. What was worse? Going where God was supposed to be, or going there to listen to abused women?

She turned from the door as it opened.

"We're about to begin."

"No. My mistake. I shouldn't have come."

"Miss?"

"What?"

"Come in. You'll be glad you did."

Shirley studied the woman who spoke to her, a sixty-something hippy with straight gray hair, parted at the middle like the Ted Bundy girl who got away.

"I just—I can't listen to sap, you know? I got my own life to deal with."

"Why did you come this far?"

"A doctor sent me."

"Rong?"

"Right."

"Yeah, she's great."

"Does she actually come here?"

The woman shrugged. "We don't talk about fight club." She grinned. Held Shirley's eye.

Shirley smiled. "Sure. But if the situation gets real bad, I gotta protect myself. I cried enough. I'm looking to kick ass."

"You'll be fine. Come in. Make yourself comfortable."

"You don't go around the room, 'Hi, my name is Bob'..."

"No. You can lurk. If you want to share, you can. If not, you can listen. We're a pretty forgiving group."

"That's what I'm afraid of."

"Come again?"

"I don't want to be copacetic with everything. I spent my whole life giving in. Taking whatever people dish."

"Uh-huh."

"Yeah, well. Like I said, I don't know if this place is right for me."

"Maybe not. You can decide. I'm going to hold the door another minute or two. You can go in. Or not."

Bundy girl smiled. Forgivingly. Couldn't be all bad. A little grace in the right places, maybe. Forgive the little things, at least.

Shirley stepped inside. Her knees hurt again. And where her jacket was tight on her arms, her brand new Maddix Heregger bruises throbbed. And the bruises on her ribs. The knot on her head. Plus the bandage on her chin. She wanted to yank the corner, but number one, the tape was made of the adhesive 3M invented to hold the tiles to the Shuttle, and number two, nobody wanted to see blood and lymph forming bulbs on her chin.

She scanned the room, at ease, but feeling a little weird about being in a church. She could take God or leave Him—that had nothing to do with church. *Church* was where the happy hypocrites went. The guys she took money from.

Metaphysicalities aside, the basement didn't smell mildewy and stagnant. They had air fresheners, and good circulation. Maroon carpet, like rich folks put on their patios. Fold up tables, unfolded along the wall, with a thin, white box, no one had yet opened. A coffee thermos with a handwritten sign she could read across the room:

DECAF

Women sat on metal chairs arranged in half moons. She expected a podium, but the stage was bare. People had to stand there exposed. Unzip their souls with nothing to hide behind.

Yeah. No.

Dr. Rong said some attendees would tell stories so silly, Shirley would spot her own mistakes.

The metal doors closed and the room quieted. Bundy girl squeezed Shirley's fingers as she passed, before taking the stage.

Shirley sat in the back, on the left side, far away from the others. With luck, people would interpret that as a signal.

She looked to the donut box.

What kind of people put out donuts, and don't open the box?

Bundy girl took the platform.

"Thank you for coming tonight. If you're visiting, know that you are welcome. You'll find our arms are open to embrace you, and give you warmth. And to listen. We're here to listen."

A woman sitting in front leaned to the woman beside her. They touched foreheads. One lifted her arm to the other's shoulder. They adjusted their postures after sharing a sniffle.

Shirley grimaced.

"Since I'm on stage," Bundy girl said, "I'll go first. I'm Rosalind. Rose. I've been coming for three years. I first came after I tried to, um, solve my problems with a razor blade. No success. I freaked out when I saw the blood. My husband... well he isn't my husband now but at the time he was. Anyway I'm Rosalind, and I love you all so much. Because this is hard, right?"

Mutters. Yesses.

"Stay strong, Rosey."

"So after my ex took me to the hospital, I found out later he went out with his lawyer to some strip club that night and they figured out how to take my 401k. Since I was the breadwinner. So now I take life day by day. Powerless over some things, but not what matters. Thank you."

Almost in unison the room repeated, "Powerless over some things. But not what matters."

Clapping. Hugs.

I'm not going to last through two hours of this.

BREAK. Other women wandered to the donut box. Thank God. Because without nutrition, she wouldn't survive the next hour.

Each woman who took the stage repeated the mantra. The audience echoed. *I'm powerless over some things, but not what matters.*

Shirley ignored it the first couple times. But she found herself looking for where the next speaker would insert the phrase. She rolled the words around in her mind until they resonated.

The sun would rise, or not. Shirley was powerless. If the world ended, she'd breathe deep and watch the ultimate show.

But she had the power to control other stuff with her decisions. Like Dr. Rong and Ulyana said. Being a hooker wasn't coded in her DNA. Prostitution wasn't destiny. She traded sex for money, or she didn't. She got to decide.

There were only three ways for sex to happen: consensual with money, consensual without money, or rape. Nothing else.

Last night, she could have taken the first two options off the table. She could have said, Maddix, No. If you continue, I'll call the police. And if they don't throw your ass in jail for rape, I'll burn your body and leave you at a warehouse where meth zombies will think you're overcooked pork.

She had power, so long as her mind remained resourceful.

So the mantra wasn't bad, just quickly losing its freshness. For everybody. All the women repeated the words in unison, but no voice stood out. No one seemed to resonate. No one was jazzed up, rejuvenated, assertive.

Maybe I'll slip on outta here...

The group was supposed to last two hours — maybe more — until every woman who wanted to speak had an opportunity. The night could go on for years...

One woman filling a Styrofoam cup with decaf said the longest meeting she ever attended lasted four hours. Then the woman looked at Shirley, as if her backside somehow was more protected against sitting on metal.

Or maybe that wasn't what she thought.

Shirley reminded herself of the Mickey Mouse glass. Her son Brass said he always thought Mickey waved his hand to say, *You can do it! C'mon!* Shirley always thought Mickey was saying, *Don't do that, dumbass.*

Perspective.

The woman who eyeballed her size—or didn't—approached.

Shirley inhaled like a bullfrog before a battle.

"Excuse me. I noticed your pants."

"Uh-huh."

"I love that pattern. You know, I have a pair like those, only in gold."

"Oh, yeah! And I love your necklace. Is that real vermouth?"

The woman blinked.

Time to sit.

The woman sat beside her. "I'm Lois."

"Hi. Shirley."

"First time?"

"I heard you say these meetings can last all night."

"You can leave when you have to. No one minds."

"It's not that. I have to—"

Lois sad-smiled. "You don't have to explain. Everyone takes it at their own speed. Come when you need support. Or need to give it."

"What are you here for? Get or give?"

"They're both the same, for me."

"Are you going to speak tonight?"

"Next time maybe. You?"

"Shit no."

"Oh, this is Ruth. She's such a dear. Much stronger than she looks. Heart of a lion."

A mouse on four-foot legs took the stage. She held her hands crumpled at her belly, and turned.

The crowd inhaled.

"Ruth! What happened?"

From the front row: "Roddy Memmelsdorf happened."

Memmelsdorf. Don't forget that.

"It's okay," Ruth said. "I'm stronger now than I was before. Everything happens for a reason."

"Did you call the police? Please tell me Roddy's behind bars this time."

"No, you see, I didn't need to. Because I learned how to—"

Shirley Lyle gritted her teeth. She looked at her legs. Her arms. Underneath the padding she had muscle like an ox. Not many men could pick up and carry four hundred pounds, like she did every day. Though in truth she was less, and only started saying four hundred when she raised prices two years ago.

And that Ruth girl on the stage, a skeleton with a little skin stretched over. Bony knees visible through her pants. Widest part of her arm was the elbow. Her back curved like the bookworm who spent her life curled up in another world. Body atrophied because she was seldom in it.

In short, a weak, weak woman. A natural born victim—like some men prefer.

Shirley looked again at her arm. Felt an urge to cloak it around Ruth the way a hen might spread its wing over its chicks.

No—this wasn't a mother hen feeling. It came from her inner hawk. Or eagle. Shirley's nostrils got wide. Her medulla fired kill signals.

Roddy did it. Roddy Memmelsdorf.

Ruth told the story. She asked too many stupid questions and Roddy got tired of it. He was the man of the family and that was always her deal. She wanted to surrender the decisions—and protection—to a man. And now she had to take the good with the bad.

"I am powerless over some things, but not what matters. You see, I've decided—"

Shirley stood. "You got it backwards, Ruth!"

Mutters.

"Excuse me?"

"I only come here the once, but that's not what the mantra means. You're powerless over the world, but you're not powerless over yourself. You got it backwards."

"What did I say? I'm powerless over some things. But not what matters."

"You meant it like, you can't influence whether your husband beats the hell out of you. But *what's really important* is that you have the power to submit, so he can keep beating you. See?"

"That's not what she said."

"I didn't hear that."

"You're putting words in her mouth. Maybe you should try to be more supportive."

"Who are you?"

"Who invited you?"

"Ruth is trying to share."

"What?" Shirley said. "Are you freaking kidding me?"

Bundy girl sad-smiled, again.

Shirley pointed at her. "YOU said this was Fight Club! But this is Shut Up and Take it Club."

Lois, beside Shirley, cringed like a dog beside the bathtub on the fourth of July.

"The first rule of Shut Up and Take it Club—all you do is talk about shutting up and taking it. I don't believe this. I thought you people came here to get encouragement to be strong."

"We are strong. As a group. To support one another."

"But you keep getting the daylights beat out of you?" Shirley read the faces turned to accuse her. "Bruises. Welts. *Scars*. That's being strong? Look at this." Shirley pointed to her bruised eye. "Check this out." She lifted her top, exposing more purple flesh. "I'd pull the bandage off my chin, if I thought it would matter."

Shirley noticed Dr. Rong didn't attend. Maybe that had been her point. Maybe she knew Shirley would recognize in the groups' hopeless submission, her own.

And see the bald stupidity of it.

Eight women had taken the stage to confess their misery. Each told a story worse than the one preceding her—as if the whole show was choreographed. Or each woman knew the pecking order.

Without fail, with every story, the audience women asked if the police did anything.

None of these girls ever hooked for a living, that was damn sure. You don't trust police to save you. All they do is book you. And you don't let people beat on you forever.

Except you kinda do.

You can't expect a man—who thinks in terms of power, and asserting his will on the whole damn world, and bloating his ego, and sticking his pecker in anything that wiggles—you can't expect him to become enlightened on his own. He didn't have brains to support both his organ and enlightenment.

Except, you sorta did.

Shirley shifted sideways into the aisle. Retreated a step.

Ruth oozed sadness and misery. Pointed it like an instrument of war at Shirley.

To hell with this.

These people didn't know what they didn't know. Too weak. But some looked athletic, spear-chucker types. What were they doing here? Only thing weak on them was their minds.

It was sick.

Well, that's where they were different. God gave Shirley points and sharp edges—probably so she could stab and slice a little. He gave her a broad back. A ferocious, mama-bear heart.

She stepped backward, keeping her face to the women still shocked by her gall. Glanced at the donuts.

That would undermine the moment.

Insight glowed within. Even if she wasn't exactly fond of herself in her present condition: knees aching, having to turn sideways to enter her trailer and likely to die tomorrow from any of sixteen ailments—according to Dr. Rong, she had to recognize her strengths. If she didn't stick up for herself, she had to do it for the others. Because some of them—the Ruth Memmelsdorfs of the world—were what they were. There was no reaching them.

No changing them.

Only saving them.

Shirley reached the door. She pointed at the women, her arm traversing the room, then straight up.

"You don't have to take this bull crap! No one has a right to be an asshole! VIVA THE REVOLUTION!"

They gawked.

"What's VIVA the REVOLUTION?"

"You ain't VIVA material. Yet."

She shoved. The door flew open. It looked good. She rolled with it. Pumped fists and stomped on the cement sidewalk all the way to her car. She threw open the door and rocked inside.

She needed to change. At least so everything stopped hurting all the time. She didn't want to be muscle bound and sickly-looking. But it would be nice to fit her clothes better. And the car.

And her door.

And bed.

Okay... maybe a couple of pounds. The ones getting in the way of life.

Locked on a vision of the future-to-be, Shirley saw herself in a kung fu place, with a six foot tall chick in a white robe bowing, presenting her a black sash.

She was at the gun range, pointing out the problem that caused a fellow badass's weapon to misfire. She lowered her shooting glasses. "Son, that pin don't go there. You need the hydraulic one, from the shop. Radium tipped works best. And fetch me a lemonade from the cooler."

Maybe after kicking all that ass she'd slip into a black dress, mount a chip on her shoulder, and holster a pistol on the inside of her thigh— because there was room—and disappear for a night on the town.

Some guy grabs a girls ass and she don't want it?

Shirley punched the air.

"P-kow!"

She stomped.

"Splat!"

Criss-crossed her arms to defend against attack. Ducked. Glared. Grimaced. Pummeled the air, each fist a piston.

She held her hand like a gun.

"Pook-Chow!"

Suddenly self aware, Shirley dropped her arm. Lowered her head and looked around the church parking lot.

Shirley nodded, a little.

She could take it, herself. She could handle getting beat on every now and again, only because she'd endured so much. Sometimes the way you win is to avoid losing even more. Life demanded humility, sometimes. She'd taught herself to tolerate the rules, and always think about long term consequences.

But seeing a mouse like Ruth Memmelsdorf get pounded on, and make up lies about how it was right. How she was smart to keep taking abuse...

Shirley Lyle wanted blood.

"Nobody has a right to be an asshole."

CHAPTER 8

As Lester moved, he became comfortable. Life starts out and the body is fresh and awkward. Growing pains. But after a few decades it gets agreeable, and after eight, feels like a paper sack that's been used to carry a hundred lunches. No stiffness at all, just fuzz everywhere. Rips at the edges; corners getting weak.

A worn paper bag accommodates a couple bullet creases pretty easy.

Lester made coffee and sat at the kitchen table, vapors lifting the smell. He drank. Waited. Thought of his cell phone. Damned thing was a nuisance. He pressed the power button and sipped coffee while the gizmo went through a startup routine. Big red Verizon check mark. Buzzing. Signal located.

A text message arrived. Lester thought a moment, then pressed the notification. Held the icon too long and got a menu. Remembered to press the button on the bottom. Held it too long; it wiggled. Damned idiotic devices made by adrenaline junkies for kids with ADHD. You barely had to touch something. He sat the phone on the table, drank more coffee. The screen went black. He tried again. Just a quick tap to the speech box icon.

A message from El Jay popped up.

. . .

HOOKER CALLED. Going there for the thumb drive. Need to talk about the motorcycle thing.

"THE HOOKER CALLED?"

Lester ran the message through his head. More coffee.

She'd cried and cussed. Put on a show. Against his better judgment, he believed her.

Lester dialed El Jay's number. Frowned.

"Hey. Call me."

He brought up the text message again. Finished his coffee.

A punk named Clyde Munsinger—the new owner of the trailer court where Shirley Lyle lived—had threatened Lester. Upon buying the mobile home and RV resort, he'd discovered a decade's worth of old books. He studied them and deduced a money laundering operation.

Clyde didn't die of natural causes so much as a natural force: Lester Toungate's ire.

Before his death, Clyde swore he'd made copies of the evidence on multiple computer thumb drives, which would be sent to the FBI and other law enforcement agencies, if Lester did anything to him.

Always one step ahead, Lester knew Clyde made no copies, and gave his original to Shirley Lyle, before driving out to threaten Lester, and die.

Next day, Lester and El Jay tore Shirley Lyle's trailer apart. No memory stick. She insisted she'd placed the device on the neck of a pit bull... which happened to belong to a serial killer from North Carolina. Hence the law enforcement interest at Burger King, where the dog killed a man before bolting to the woods. Lester tracked down the animal, only to trade conversation and gunfire with the very fugitive they hunted.

A bullet creased his head and Lester was out. The North Carolina man got away, and with him, the dog. If Shirley Lyle planted the drive on the dog, the killer from North Carolina was in possession.

Hell of a fuss they were making about him—not that Lester felt a competitive tingle. Stack up Lester's bodies against the other man's, from what he'd learned on the news, their piles were even-steven. Lester couldn't die, and the other man could. He'd take the lead someday.

As was Lester's wont, he pondered. You don't live to be eighty-three in the drug business without learning to make well-considered decisions.

He'd discovered long ago, most folks do such hair-brained impulsive fool-ishness, a person of mediocre intelligence who bothered to think could easily outwit the person with a 190 IQ, but never fired it up.

If the man from North Carolina—on the news they said his name was Creighton—actually had the thumb drive, what benefit could he derive?

He wouldn't be able to dicker with law enforcement.

Being from back East, he wouldn't know anyone local who might be interested in acquiring such information.

Probably fair to assume this Creighton fellow, if he had the drive, didn't fathom what evidence he held and had no way to find out. The news said he was a moonshiner hillbilly who lived under a tarp. No, if he had the thumb drive, it wasn't worth losing any sleep.

The real question provoked by El Jay's text: Why did Shirley Lyle call El Jay?

They warned her if the dog returned, she damn sure better tell them. And they said they'd be back if they didn't find the dog, or if they did, but no thumb drive.

Could the dog have returned to her?

No. Creighton couldn't exactly talk to the white pit bull and find out he wanted to head back to Shirley Lyle's place. That dog, as the saying went, didn't hunt.

More likely, Shirley never put the drive on the dog. Lester and El Jay scared the bejeezus out of her, she got her mind right, and called El Jay to offload the device and keep her life.

El Jay, if he had any sense, put her down. Maybe that's why he mentioned the motorcycle...

Lester looked at his coffee mug. After the first couple sips, he'd forgotten to drink.

Bah. Barely warm.

He gulped it anyway.

LESTER OPENED HIS GARAGE DOOR, filled a 1977 Hodaka 250 dirt bike's gas tank from a red five-gallon plastic gas container. Cussed the jackwad who created the twist flow-stop mechanism, made a million bucks, and turned a clean and simple refueling process into a messy pain in the ass.

Lester wiped off the splashed gasoline with a rag he kept handy, because the overflow happened every damn time.

He restored the can to its place in the corner. Looked at the garage wall... unfinished two by fours, plywood. What the hell was he doing? Nonstop bitching. That wasn't him. Never was. He saw the woods, hunted, killed. No room for complaining. Things were what they were; he made decisions to ease his crossing. Simple.

Must have been the bump on his head had riled him up inside, so he didn't even know.

Good to be aware if he was prone to anger and rash thinking. That's how mistakes happened.

He pulled on an open face helmet. Backed out the bike. Closed the bay door. Kick started the Hodaka and followed a trail through the woods behind his house until it caught a dirt forest road. Nearing the lake, he cut a random path between trees. Allowed instinct to guide him toward the truck he'd left hidden in undergrowth, the night he dispatched Clyde Munsinger to the black unknown.

That night, Lester had Clyde's body to deal with, and then coincidentally—almost—his son Paul's body. He'd used Clyde's truck to dump the corpses over the cliff at Sycamore Rim, and assigned cleaning the truck, driving to the desert, and burning it, to El Jay.

Lester thought on that. If El Jay went to see the hooker, how'd he have time to drive the truck halfway to Yuma, then two hours past the last desert road?

His stomach churned.

Was Clyde's blood-filled truck, with Lester's DNA all over the cab, and his fingerprints, in El Jay's garage? With Lester's Harley-Davidson in the bed?

Lester pinched his lips together. Gassed the Hodaka. He had business to attend. Shipments to arrange. Needed to touch bases with his suppliers and mules. Rebuild at least three distribution channels. With Paul dead and the execution-style hit a half week back on a couple carriers, the operation might appear to be in disarray. Though he had an arrangement with the Russian, *détente* was just another word for dogs sniffing assholes while they growl and jostle for advantage.

Lester jammed the Hodaka brake, slid the rear tire sideways, and launched a dust cloud on his Dodge RAM. He sat on the vibrating machine and looked things over. Truck appeared unmolested. Most likely, the ten or fifteen vehicles that had driven by hadn't noticed it tucked back in the growth.

He held his gaze on the door where Lucky last jumped. Old dog.

Dead dog.

Lester bowed his head. Maybe he'd see about getting a pup, since people weren't worth a damn.

He drove a little farther into the woods. Over the years, he buried a lot of bodies in the soft ground adjacent the lake. Sometimes that required disposing of vehicles in distant locations—which meant returning on the Hodaka to retrieve his RAM. He had a routine. Long ago, on a hunting excursion, he'd discovered a boulder abutting a hill, sloped on the back side, and next to a logger's double track on the front. It was only a couple hundred yards into the woods beyond the lake. He drove the Hodaka up the back and onto the top of the boulder.

Dismounted, stood the bike on its kick stand.

Most modern dirt bikes didn't have stands anymore. Lester couldn't noodle the nonsense. They must have let the guy who designed the gas can work on the motorcycles.

After a few minutes' walk, Lester got in his truck, drove, and parked the Ram with its open tailgate next to the boulder. He loaded the bike, tied it down.

In the bed of his truck, he withdrew his cell phone.

No coverage.

He entered the cab. A half hour later he parked at El Jay's. His wayward son's Impala wasn't in the driveway. El Jay was likely at the pavement company. Lester walked to the side window of the four-bay. Cupped his hand over his eyes and pressed to the glass.

The F-150—rife with blood and fingerprints—sat inside.

With the extra-tall doors, El Jay hadn't needed to remove the Harley from the bed to drive the truck inside. So Lester's Sportster sat there, tires resting in the mingled blood of Clyde, Paul, and four college kids who should've stayed in their tents.

Lester stepped back from the window and studied the grass underfoot. An ant crawled on the cement block garage wall, below the siding.

Lester thought on that.

Before murdering Paul, Lester had already concluded any lasting Toungate imprint on humanity, any significance, would derive from his own actions.

He'd contemplate the implications of being done with El Jay, too.

The ant followed a grooved seam of cement between blocks, cut a hard left, and disappeared under siding.

Meantime, that truck behind the glass was evidence.

Lester stepped a few feet, twisted the knob. The side door opened, unlocked.

Lester closed his eyes. The door was unlocked. He clamped his teeth. El Jay's fate sealed—

But hold on, maybe... Just maybe hold on.

Lester tingled. Hair stood on his neck. He released the door knob. Eased back. Shut the door.

Listened.

He turned. Looked across the street for a misplaced shadow. A guy in a suit walking a dog, or some other law enforcement anomaly.

Leaving the door open, Lester returned to his truck and pressed El Jay's phone number again.

No answer.

He looked up the street, down the other direction. Again he scanned the neighbor houses for shadows, motion. Across the street, down a ways, to the high school parking lot. Sometimes cops sat there, at the corner by the trees, in a speed trap.

Nobody, nowhere.

Do it now? Or come back at night?

His disposal plan—that he'd tasked his derelict soon-to-die-son El Jay —would take at least ten hours to complete.

With his other plans waiting, Lester had no time to delay. He strode to the garage, opened the bay door from the button on the inside wall. Entered the F-150 and found keys in the ignition.

Naturally.

Clyde Munsinger sat behind the wheel when Lester shot him. He hit the gas and Lester let him bleed out twenty minutes before approaching the truck, stuck in a ditch a half mile down the road. A man with a couple holes in him can bleed a lot in twenty minutes. To avoid sitting in blood when he moved the vehicle, Lester placed floor mats on the seat bottom and back. They were still there.

Imagine explaining that to an officer of the law. Naw. Get pulled over, it's a gun fight.

Lester placed his .357 on the passenger seat and backed out the truck. Swerved to miss his Ram, with the dirt bike on top.

He again searched the adjacent houses, driveways, parking lots. Something about this whole setup was dead wrong. But the truck had to go, and there was no way to be one hundred percent sure the evidence was gone, except when you turn the whole thing into cinders and scrap.

Spotting no police, Lester backed onto the road.

From Flagstaff he drove Interstate 17 to the north side of Phoenix. 101 West, around the smoggy metropolis. 10 West, toward Los Angeles. After three and a half hours, he exited to a road that offered a gas station on the left, and nothing at all on the right.

Lester turned right, followed a dirt road that just kind of got tired, turned into a double track, then a single, then a turnaround.

Straight through, over baked rocks that tinkled like glass. Beyond where some good old boys came out to shoot a hundred boxes of ammo at a rusted refrigerator.

Even in April, the desert heat was more than Lester preferred. He drove until hemmed at both sides by arroyos. Got out, studied the terrain, and finding a suitable location, eased the truck over a bank. Dropped the tailgate and offloaded his Sportster.

Doused the truck in gasoline, inside the cab, all over the bed. Over the hood. He removed the cap from the gas tank, so the fumes could mingle.

He stood back so far he could barely see the truck in the gulch, and tossed a lit flare.

On the Sportster, he wondered which problem to solve first.

El Jay?

Or Shirley Lyle?

CHAPTER 9

S hirley Lyle squeezed into her Ford Festiva. A client sold it to her, after modifying the seat, console, everything, to allow her to fit inside. He was one of the nice guys. Could turn a wrench.

Handy with a tool.

One of the rare johns she'd close the door saying, "It's a pleasure doing business."

Still, driving a Festiva was like climbing into a sardine can and rolling the lid back on. She didn't have to step on scales. The car informed on each additional pound. Today the door closed like she'd scarfed a bowling ball for breakfast.

Which didn't make sense—she hadn't eaten all morning. Probably stress-bloat.

Her stomach wouldn't stop yelling at her. To escape the commotion, she'd grabbed her mini baseball bat, a map, locked the trailer, and got in her car.

She'd woken ready to kick ass, and the last thing she needed was to succumb to brain garbage. Shirley F'N Lyle didn't suffer fools. Even if the fool was the voice in her head. Too many Ruth Memmelsdorfs in the world to rescue.

But she couldn't go full-swing into saving other people without saving herself, first. What was the saying? Put the oxygen mask on yourself, not the ugly baby.

Hence the plan. She'd skip breakfast, shed a few pounds, pair up with Ulyana to kill Lester Toungate and visit some proportional justice on Roddy Memmelsdorf—both standing patiently in line behind Maddix Heregger.

Because the rest of them didn't carry around a bushel bag of kryptonite, like Maddix.

Why take on Maddix first? He'll kill you.

"Because."

You can't do this.

"Bull. Yes I can."

You're too fat.

"Piss off."

He'll beat you up again.

"So be it."

He knows what to say to turn you into a quivering spineless slob.

"Yes he does. But Superman couldn't float. Look at me."

Shirley caught her reflection in the rearview. Stared the bitch down.

She slammed the door against her flesh and it latched on the first try. Fired the engine. Jammed her elbow against the door, as if to make it move and give her some room.

"I'm sick of this car."

You need new wheels. Use El Jay's money.

Hmmm. Ulyana had found a pouch of cash in El Jay's car.

"No. That's burn-the-trailer money."

You're no fun. And you're stupid for taking on Maddix.

"You're psychotic! Leave me alone. I'm not gonna face him right now. This is called doing a little homework, so you know everything about your enemy there is to know! Besides. I'm undercover."

At a stop sign, she looked at her map. Twisted it. Searched for the sun. West is always on the left because West and East spell WE. Except if you're driving south.

She turned the map again. Cut the wheel right. Another right... getting close.

His truck! In a parking lot.

Shirley swerved. A small grocery, a laundromat, an out-of-business bank, and one of those new e-cigarette shops. She drove to the far end, parked beside a minivan where her car was mostly hidden from the businesses, but she had a line of sight to the laundromat.

The A/C was on. And her headlights. Being surreptitious demanded a whole new set of skills. She rolled down both windows and killed the engine. Put down the sun visor and donned the sunglasses that fell on her bust. Big with pink flower frames.

Shirley sat motionless. In the excitement of seeing Maddix Heregger's truck, she'd forgotten her appetite. But now...

She glanced at the grocery store entrance.

Back to the laundromat.

Back to the grocery.

They have ice cream bars in the back, kind of on the left side.

"Shut up, Old Shirley. Eyeballs, this is a direct order from your commander. Don't listen to her. Look at the damn laundromat."

Maddix crossed in front of the wall of windows and stood behind a table. He dumped a bin of clothes.

Look at that.

She squinted. To do surveillance right, she ought to have binoculars. Shirley leaned closer to the wheel.

Was he.... folding laundry?

Trying... to fold laundry?

Maddix lifted a button down shirt, upside down. He held the back seams together, the middle folded like an accordion, with the front flaps hanging.

"He doesn't know what the hell he's doing."

You should go in there and help him. He'd appreciate you more.

Shirley blinked. Considered.

"Shut up, Old Shirley. Shirley F'N Lyle does no man's laundry. Ever."

She waited. Maddix swiped the pile of clothes from the table into a basket and charged out the door.

Great. You're following a man who gets pissed folding socks.

Maddix entered his truck and drove. Squealed a tire at the turn.

Shirley waited. His house was only a block away. It was dumb luck she'd spotted his truck in the parking lot. Fortunate... because now when she parked down a ways from his house, she knew he was home.

What would she look for? A weakness in his plan, she could exploit? Vulnerabilities in his security?

Maddix Heregger didn't have a plan. Or security. He was just a guy designated to be the bully in any room he entered.

Wouldn't that be something? You reach heaven and find out, some people don't have a choice... Like, at birth, we're all actors, and some people are assigned the bad roles. Good, talented people. They could have been anybody. Gandhi. The Dali Buddha. But they draw the card that says, Hitler, so they have to spend their lives providing the disasters that give everybody else the chance to grow.

"You're just full of ideas, aren't you, Old Shirley? Well riddle me this. What about all the people they kill along the way? They don't get to grow, do they? Your cosmic good-will crap is just crap. Maddix Heregger—and everyone like him—is an asshole. And nobody has the right to be an asshole."

No mercy.

"That's right."

So what, exactly, are you looking for?

I'll know it when I see it.

You could grab a box of ice cream Snickers bars... They're easy to spot.

Shirley closed her eyes. Bit her tongue. When she tasted blood she opened her eyes.

She needed momentum. Confrontation, before the anger faded and her confidence crashed out the bottom.

"I need a gun."

CHAPTER 10

R oddy Memmelsdorf did the only thing befitting a man of superior
emotional intelligence, after being bounced from the strip club and
beaten in the parking lot.

He killed his wife's cat.

The scrawny feline had death coming. Always hissing, clawing. Roddy
worked all day to bring home the cat food, and what appreciation?

Cats.

Seven years back he'd said to Ruth, I'm a man and I want a woman
that'll do as I say.

"Yes."

"So you'll marry me."

"If that's what you say."

"That's clever. Well, first rule, the cat stays with your mother."

They married in winter. Ruth had been true. She'd left the cat, and
then pouted nonstop. He hadn't yet bought furniture, so she spent her
days on a blanket on the hardwood floor. He came home from work, and
instead of having his favorite budget-sensitive dinner ready—mac and
cheese with sautéed spam—she'd look up, legs crossed, head propped on
wall like a prisoner in the White Tower, waiting Death's tender mercy.

Pitiful. How the hell were they going to look back on these as the salad
days?

He'd inspired her. The sex was good, especially when she seemed least willing. Getting her there... even if he had to be a little rough... kind of made him feel stronger. Like he was stepping into a more atavistic vision of manhood. He did things to surprise her, keep her nervous. Pinch, instead of squeeze. Bite, instead of kiss. From her response, she loved the technique.

"I want to find a job. Help out with the bills. All I do is sit all day."

"Start a garden."

"The plants would freeze. Besides, how would I buy plants with no money? Why can't I work?"

"You'll be pregnant soon."

"I'm worried about that."

"Why?"

"I'm not pregnant yet."

"That's your fault. And no, you can't have a job. That's not your place."

"Can we at least go to Goodwill and buy chairs?"

"I don't want junk."

"You have a chair at the office to sit on."

"We don't buy anything until we can pay cash. Period."

"Then you should make more money."

Roddy ended the conversation with a movie-move he'd always wanted to try. Almost without premeditation, he crossed his arms, shoved the V against Ruth's throat, pinning her to the wall. He grabbed her shirt collar with each hand, and rolled his wrists.

Choked out in seconds—on his first try. No marks. Just peace.

Ruth Memmelsdorf learned. She was quiet, most of the time, and rarely needed reminders of her place. She never got pregnant, but developed mean skills with tomatoes, bell peppers, and especially zucchini. Roddy hated zucchini. Ruth knew.

He permitted her rebellion—but watched.

Over the years, Roddy's brutal work ethic brought home plenty of cash. He siphoned some dollars away from a savings plan calculated to make him a millionaire in fifteen years, and the furniture situation improved.

Then one day, three years into their shared bliss, Ruth's mother had a stroke walking the mall. She died with spittle pooling on brown tile.

Roddy would have avoided the funeral, but his mother-in-law had referred some business to him and those clients would attend. In sales, appearances mattered more than anything.

The good thing about being in insurance: he could work anywhere people gathered. After the funeral he shook hands, passed out some cards, made some new contacts to call for auto and home owner's quotes.

Driving home from the service, Ruth asked to stop by her mother's place for a couple items. Roddy said he'd spare a few minutes, so long as he returned to work quickly. You call fresh leads fast, or not at all.

Ruth entered the house and emerged three minutes later holding the cat. Roddy jumped out of the car.

"We're not taking Mister Shonky!"

"I know. We can't leave him in the house. It's been four days already. There's no one to feed him. He'll shred the furniture and everything else before we can sell it. *We'll lose a lot of money.* And since no one's going to want an old cat, you need to put him down."

"Take the stupid thing to the shelter or something."

"And *pay them money* when you could just do the job yourself?"

Roddy nodded. Squinted. Was she playing him? Couldn't be. She wasn't smart enough.

"Yeah. I'll put him down. But later. I need to call some leads while they're hot."

Four years later, Roddy still hadn't found time to kill the cat.

Clumps of fuzzy hair lay all over the house, regardless of how often Roddy reminded Ruth to clean. To listen to her, owning a cat was a never ending losing battle.

But when Roddy thought of ending the insanity, Mister Shonky hissed and ran.

Roddy felt like Jesus at the wedding, saying Mother, it's not yet my time. But he thought with tremendous frequency about killing animals. Who didn't, with neighborhood dogs barking, cats running loose? But thinking and doing were different. Crossing the line and taking life... wow, the metaphysics. Life only happens once. At least to each individual life.

If his damned emotional intelligence wasn't so high...

Still...

Roddy sensed himself growing. Someday he would shed the constraints of the lesser intelligent. What were morals anyway? Nothing but primitive rules designed to limit the behavior of the least informed, least capable, leftmost on the bell curve of society. Roddy was like Nietzsche's Overman. So highly evolved, he must create a new morality.

Roddy waited. His time would come.

It arrived the day after five cowpokes kicked his face into a swollen ball.

He woke tickled and near-sneezing on cat fluff.

His left eye remained swollen shut. His brain pounded.

He opened his right eye.

Mister Shonky lay on the pillow beside him, haunch to face, tail on Roddy's forehead—giving him the evil eye.

Roddy sneezed. Shonky jumped and hissed. Arched back, tail high.

The sneeze triggered incendiary brain pain, which awakened Roddy's other torments. He grabbed Mister Shonky's neck. The old cat's raspy screech failed. Using both hands, Roddy squeezed until Shonky went limp.

Cat urine deflected from Roddy's trembling arm. Some flowed to his elbow and dripped. The rage inside him flashed from his pores. His pain went away. He threw the cat against the wall. The outside door made a racket. Ruth's footsteps pattered. She stood at the bedroom door taking in her dead cat and mangled husband. He saw her intellect sputter, trying to account for both his swollen, bruised face, and the cat crumpled on the floor.

She looked from the cat to his face.

Ruth ran to Mister Shonky.

"He loosed his bowels. Clean that up."

Roddy dismounted the bed.

"What happened? How did the cat do that to your face? You weren't like that when I got up this morning."

"Yes—"

"Yes what?"

He tried to lower his eyebrows, to warn her off questioning him. But with his one eye swollen, Ruth merely stared, all the more confused.

"Yes. I agree. The cat did this. He slept on my face."

"So you killed him? You killed him?"

"I panicked."

"No you didn't."

"Excuse me?"

"No I won't do that either. You killed Mister Shonky!"

She stood with the cat in her hand, dangling at the end of her lanky arm. She lifted her knee.

Swung her arm.

Roddy, seeing her windup, cat tail whipping, remembered she'd said in high school she would have been the girls' softball starting pitcher, if she could only control the pitch.

The cat zipped by Roddy's head. Smashed the bedroom window.

Ruth stomped to the closet. Pulled the lanyard and the yellow light came on. She spun, strode out of the bedroom. He heard her feet stomping the steps to the basement. Less than thirty seconds later, back up them.

Whatever.

Roddy stepped to the bathroom and relieved his bladder. Washed his arm, then hands and gingerly, his face. Meanwhile Ruth pounded back and forth between closet and bed, stacking clothes in a suitcase.

The cat was dead. He'd give Ruth a little room. She was more animated than he'd expected. He'd let her burn it off. If he gave her instruction now, with one side blind, she might actually land a punch.

Over the years, he'd slowly discovered, there was a lot more to Ruth Memmelsdorf than he saw on the surface. And with women—especially in their crazy moments—it was more efficient to defer a lesson until it would take.

But one thing was certain.

No way in hell Ruth Memmelsdorf was leaving.

CHAPTER 11

Having forgotten his jacket and gloves, Lester Toungate pulled his Sportster into a gas station before climbing the five thousand foot elevation plateau on Interstate 17, forty minutes north of Phoenix. Filled his tank and bought a Mexican parka made in India, and an Arizona Cardinals football team sweatshirt. He marveled the Indians were cheaper than the Mexicans. Learn something every day. As for football—the NFL, and instant replay—could go to hell.

He arrived in Flagstaff so cold his guts rattled. The temperature had fallen to the upper forties and Lester climbed off the Sportster shaking, but ready for what came next.

Big moves.

First, he needed to retrieve his truck and dirt bike from El Jay's. Then he'd deal with Shirley Lyle.

Ten o'clock at night. El Jay's place was four miles.

Lester made coffee and drank it while soaking in a steaming bathtub. When his skin stopped burning and warmth radiated through him like sleepiness, he climbed out of the tub, toweled off, and called a cab. He dressed in long underwear and denim.

Big picture: he needed to tie loose ends. The last few days sported a greater density of killing than any since, damn, you had to go back to 1992. Police were better at finding evidence and connecting dots nowadays, and before making his move against the Russians, he had to ensure nothing regarding Clyde Munsinger, Shirley Lyle, or his son Paul, would come back and haunt him.

As a sub-strategy, Lester arrived at a fine plan to deal with Shirley Lyle. A stroke of elegance. He considered the angles and every conceivable outcome tested good.

A cab waited outside, on his driveway. Lester gave the woman an address for Walgreen's, a couple blocks from El Jay's.

She drove. Spoke. Lester said yes and no until she quit.

"Want me to wait?"

"No."

He exited and walked toward the drugstore until the cab disappeared. Lester pivoted. In minutes he knocked on El Jay's door. Peered through the kitchen window, then the living room. The garage remained empty.

El Jay had typical young man habits. Night clubs. He liked entertaining women. Usually, several.

Not finding El Jay at home, and Lester's inability to raise him on the phone, didn't necessarily mean ill. El Jay probably worked the morning at the paving company office, then went out on the town. He maybe lost or damaged his cell. Any number of scenarios could assemble into a good reason to believe El Jay was out somewhere being El Jay.

But Lester knew different. You don't live forever seeing patterns indecipherable to others, and not develop a nose for smelling the earliest, faintest stink of shit hitting the fan.

Someone had done Lester a solid.

He stood on the cement patio. Watched his breath cloud the air.

How'd it play out?

El Jay likely visited the hooker, like his message said. Shirley Lyle. Big girl. Maybe-probly, somewhere between there and home, one of the Russians caught up with him. Or maybe they planned a meet. El Jay was cocky like that.

More likely scenario—he made inroads weeks before, when he and Paul started working against Lester Toungate Enterprises. Regardless. If the Russians snuffed him, that only confirmed Lester's estimation of El Jay.

The complication: if El Jay visited Shirley Lyle, he might have been carrying the thumb drive when whoever done him, did him.

Lester's chief rival, Vanko Demyan, might now possess all the information about Lester he'd need to eliminate him. For Vanko, giving the thumb drive to law enforcement would be a good move. A better play, if he had the balls, would be to extort Lester. Fold him into his enterprise. Secure his labor and organization for the price of his freedom.

If that was the case, Shirley Lyle still saw the contents of the thumb drive... and still needed eliminated.

An equally plausible history of El Jay: he visited the hooker to steal a piece of ass. A man like El Jay might find a woman like Shirley Lyle irresistible. Something to conquer. Then driving home, El Jay met the Russians. In that case, Shirley still had the thumb drive, and Lester's plan would still provide an elegant conclusion.

He unlocked his truck, looked to the side where Lucky used to sit. Maybe after the show he'd go to the rescue and find a new old dog that would lay around all day and offer him a sullen eye and a short wag of the tail, once in a while.

He sighted The Mountain View Mobile Home and RV Resort. A minute later, Lester turned on the gravel entrance. He looked right. Shirley Lyle walked a dead-end road with a dozen trailers on each side. Elbows wide and thrusting, she looked like a sprinting turtle. Good for her.

Last day of her life, exercising.

Shirley being out and about gave him some time. He parked at Clyde Munsinger's office.

Thought better—since he'd recently killed the man—and tooled to a trailer without a vehicle in front. From here he could see the homes of both Shirley, and the stripper from Ukraine.

Headlights—from the back entrance.

Lester was motionless. No need to shift around. Nobody looked where the light went, let alone where it didn't. The car rattle-zipped by. One of those foreign jobs with the muffler removed. Throaty roar of a four-banger.

Ah!

The car stopped at Shirley's place. Blonde popped out like her ass was on a spring and her legs were made of rubber. Woman like that could have a mind like Einstein but she'd better serve humanity by taking off her clothes.

She bounced to Shirley's door. Rapped. Looked through the window.

Walked the length of the trailer, studying the ground, everything. Knocked the door again. Put her ear to the surface.

Vibration?

Made sense.

After a few seconds, Ulyana strode to Shirley's car, then turned a circle.

Why was Ulyana in such a frenzy to see Shirley?

Lester relaxed his mind and allowed the associations to reveal themselves. His son, Paul, had been availing himself of Ulyana's charms. Lester suspected El Jay and Paul had joined forces to unseat him from his business. And El Jay had texted that he was meeting Shirley last night.

Was it possible Ulyana and Shirley played roles in El Jay's conspiracy with Paul?

The stripper returned to Shirley's door and this time, tried the handle. Locked. She walked to her car and drove to her own trailer, farther up the gravel road. She popped out, and without glancing at her surroundings, unlocked and entered her place. Lights on. Flicker of a television. Bedroom light on. Bedroom light off.

Lester nodded, slow.

Talk to her a bit, before getting reacquainted with Shirley?

Lester leaned, looked off to where motion caught his eye. Shirley walking between trailers, a hundred yards off.

He didn't dislike her. She'd made him coffee when he asked, while El Jay emptied everything she owned on the carpet. Fact was, his mother was a big boned woman and Shirley's pissed off face put him in the mind of her. In a pleasant way.

He'd give her a few minutes. Say hello to Ulyana.

Lester keyed the ignition; drove. Parked at Ulyana's.

What tied Ulyana and Shirley? How did that connection happen?

Well, since he and El Jay ransacked Shirley's place, and Paul was sleeping with Ulyana, and spied on Shirley, was it possible that Ulyana had somehow tipped off Shirley?

Lester raised his fist to the door. Hesitated.

What would motivate Ulyana to risk her situation with Paul? That wasn't a dumb stripper move... it was a conniving stripper move. Action taken by a person with access to different puzzle pieces.

Maybe.

Girls form packs. Evolution taught them that. A stripper befriending a woman of the night wasn't exactly a stretch. And if Ulyana was worried about Shirley for some reason, and El Jay was going to see Shirley for the thumb drive, it seemed pretty possible, likely, that Ulyana knew something about it.

Lester rapped on the door. Added a short kick for emphasis. With women, it often made sense to rattle their nerves before asking a question.

"Who is it?"

"Lester. Open the door."

No answer.

"I said open the door. I won't hurt you. I'm looking for my son."

No answer.

"Three seconds 'til I come through this door."

"I got a gun. I know how to use it."

"Mine's bigger, I'm sure. And like I said, I'm not here to harm you. Where's El Jay? I need him."

"I don't know."

"I believe you and that—Shirley—are in cahoots."

"Think what you want. I'm calling the police."

"Yeah, you do that. I'm going to keep poking around. And when I find you know something about El Jay, I'm going to come back. You understand me?"

"Go away!"

Lester drove his boot to the bottom of the door. Maybe he should have left the woman unrattled. Little difference. El Jay was gone and by the time Lester completed each step of his plan, he'd own Flagstaff.

He drove to the burger joint down the road, but before pulling into the drive-through, turned around. Cameras everywhere. He retook the street, motored to Cinder Lake, turned around, and figured in the forty five minutes he'd been gone from the trailer court, Shirley Lyle had time to exhaust herself. Good chance by now she was back at her trailer, turning in for the night.

Lester stopped at a gas station and bought a pair of thirty-two ounce Gatorade bottles. He dumped them on shrubs. About to move his truck to the gas pumps and fill them with gasoline, he thought of the cameras. They were everywhere in the modern world.

Filling the Gatorade bottles could haunt him.

Without looking up, or around, Lester drove back to his house. He pulled a six of Budweiser from the refrigerator. Twisted the caps, sipped from one and dumped the rest in the sink. He loaded the bottles back in the cardboard holder and carried them to the garage. Grabbed a funnel and poured gasoline from a red plastic can.

Splashed.

Cussed.

Cut rag strips for each, and packed the openings. He rolled down his window, cranked the heat, and drove to the Mountain View Mobile Home and RV Resort.

CHAPTER 12

Shirley entered her living room. Closed the door behind her and leaned against it. She shut her eyes and savored the steady thunk of her heart. The chill between her shoulders, where sweat cooled. She was stronger than she thought. In the last forty five-minutes, by her quick calculation, she'd walked approximately sixty-three miles around the trailer court.

She dragged a chair from the kitchen to the living room, placed a pillow from the sofa on top of the seat, and stretched her legs. She kicked off her shoes and wiggled her toes.

With more ambition, she might remove her socks. But getting there…

This is what success felt like. Painful—because achievement was out of the ordinary. Change always meant turning aside from comfort. Heroism demanded hurt.

She'd quit surveilling Maddix Heregger after determining she had absolutely no idea how to come at him. She needed to know her mind at a higher level. More than strategy or tactics.

What should be her goal?

Did proportionality make sense?

She knew what her son would say. Brass used to talk about Franklin Delano Roosevelt nonstop. Someday when Brass ruled the United States, he'd model his reign on FDR's. Anyway, you don't respond proportionally,

Brass said. There's no such thing as proportional victory. Or being friends with enemies.

What did Heregger deserve? What was justice?

Shirley considered. Her response didn't need to be just, if that meant legal or through legal channels. Police. Courtrooms and stuff. Maddix didn't assault her through the court system. Why the hell should she respond through it?

She'd bedded too many cops, lawyers, and judges to think they were anything but ordinary fellows, with itches like anyone else. Their views weren't special.

Opinions are like elbows. They stink.

But you took money. That's the same as saying yes.

"Because! If I'm gonna work I'm gonna get paid."

You just said it was work.

"The electric company doesn't run juice out here for free. Besides. I *always* have to think of the economics. Should I go behind on my bills so I can look like I didn't want to be raped? Talk about stupid, Old Shirley."

Maybe rape was the wrong word. She'd serviced plenty of men she hadn't desired, but always by choice. The pleasantness of the intercourse didn't determine its name. It was whether she submitted herself, or not. Top or bottom, on her knees, whatever. Penetration meant yielding, submitting, and rape boiled down to one or two. Yes or no. Gift, or theft.

Life or death.

Maddix used mental and physical force to gain her acquiescence. He gave her a choice between experiencing more violence, or giving him what he wanted. And he berated and belittled her to ensure she made the decision he wanted.

"Old Shirley, that's rape. And that demands payback. VIVA the REVOLUTION!"

You'll get yourself beat up again.

Shirley ignored herself and enjoyed a moment of total clarity.

She pressed her toes against chair spindles, back and forth, hitting the pressure points.

"Was it? 'Cause I don't feel raped. More like..."

She rested her head on the sofa. After a life in the sex business, intercourse didn't require enthusiasm. Sex didn't create emotion, by itself. She'd performed so many acts in so many combinations, her Maddix-wound wasn't from shock, shame, or physical pain. For an adolescent, rape was a violation of sex. But for Shirley—and maybe other extraordinarily well-fornicated women—rape had little to do with sex.

What stoked her growing rage was the power play. The use of force toward reducing her existence to the tiny relevance of making a man's helmet pop. There was no interaction. No back and forth, the way lovers engaged for mutual excitement. Even when working for pay, she enjoyed faking the back and forth.

Maddix made intercourse one-sided, where he was the only player, and her supporting role, coerced.

The act? Really… who cared?

Shirley could handle the emotional side of the whole sordid nonsense. She wasn't some dainty flower just had her petals plucked. But being demeaned, tricked and coerced with violence… and all at the hands of a man who could have known her spirit, but chose to plunder her sex…

"I don't feel raped. I feel a little soul-murdered."

The window next to the television shattered inward.

Shirley looked. Hardly moved.

She retracted her right knee. Realized the object that had exploded into her living room, and bounced off the bottom of the sofa, was a brick-sized rock with white paint, from the corner where she parked her car.

Shirley blinked.

Again.

"Wait a damn minute! I'm having a revelation! What the—"

She dropped her leg. Pushed off from the sofa and grabbed the chair for leverage.

Accident? Kids being evil?

Grab the mini baseball bat—

She stood square to the window.

You need a gun.

She stepped to the chair and grabbed a shoe. Sat. Looked out the shattered window.

Flames, swinging in an arc. She shrank inside as fire flashed into her home, bounced from the faux walnut paneling, splashing an orange glare over her wall.

The object bounced and rolled on her carpet.

A beer bottle?

87

She shoved her foot into her sneaker.

Another firebomb flashed into the trailer. This one hit a picture frame.

Shirley rammed her other foot in the other shoe.

She looked to the hallway leading to her bedroom. If she ran outside now, whoever was there might kill her. She needed her mini baseball bat.

You need a gun!

Shirley navigated the kitchen. Entering the hallway she heard another window shatter—in her bedroom. She hurried. Fire flashed ahead. She spun, noticed the dish with the thumb drive she used to lure El Jay to his death. On her way to the front door, she grabbed the thumb drive and a chrome metal kitchen chair.

El Jay's money!

She left the chair at the door and hurried down the other short hallway. She'd hidden the money bag in the bathroom under some folded towels.

Another window shattered.

I'm gonna die.

She grabbed the money bag. Hurried back and swung open the front door.

Lester Toungate, holding a gun.

See? If you had a gun...

"Ah—you have the thumb drive. Throw it to me, and you'll live."

Shirley gawked.

"If you lay on the floor, you'll breathe easier. But I imagine you'll die there. You have about twenty seconds to make up your mind. Throw me the thumb drive."

Shirley gritted her teeth. She stepped backward into howling orange and black smoke curling around the inner walls and ceiling. After a moment she stood in the doorway. Pushed back the screen and locked the arm.

Lester snarled.

Door open.

Screen open.

"VIVA THE REVOLUTION!"

CHAPTER 13

L ester rolled from his back to his side. His ears roared. His skin tingled with heat.

He opened his eyes. Flinched, remembering the chair Shirley Lyle launched at him. His brain throbbed, and somewhere in that orb of pain, his back felt pretty damn rotten too. But the pressing situation, as full awareness arrived, was the inferno beside him. He needed distance from the roaring flames. He sat and the elevation increased the heat. Lester pressed his hand to his head where the serial killer's bullet furrowed his scalp. That's where the pain was. Lester ground both hands to his head.

No relief.

Hemorrhage? Hematoma?

No reason to fear death—at the moment, the pain of living was enough.

Lester got to his knees, then feet, stooped and braced, afraid of the last bit of elevation.

He stood, the motion increasing the torment in his brain. His ribs hurt too—where the bullet creased and bruised.

Lester turned a circle, remembering.

Ah.

Shirley Lyle was out cold, her head next to an evergreen. Lester placed his hand at his holster. Empty. He looked at the ground. Stepped farther from the flames and tried to recollect.

Standing at the door, she had the thumb drive in her hand. She locked the screen open. Stepped into the blaze and next thing, metal flew at his head. He fired. She charged out and clocked him.

He looked at her, then the gravel. His .357 had to be nearby. And the thumb drive that was in her hand. Maybe she threw it in the fire before grabbing the chair, but what sense did that make? She would have no proof—so he'd keep coming. She would know that. Besides. She only disappeared a fraction of a second—otherwise she couldn't have caught him off guard.

He saw her again in his mind's eye. Moved pretty damn fast, when she wanted. He'd remember that.

Lester stooped, and that hurt his brain too. Anydamnthing he did. He closed his eyes, hard. Pressed his temples again.

Had to find his gun.

The .357 wasn't nearby. Couldn't have gone more than a few feet. The area was so bright with flames, no way he'd miss it.

His revolver was under Shirley Lyle.

Lester shook his head. Swung his arms back and forth, and breathed in hard. No adrenaline; just fatigue.

He knelt beside Shirley, mid-frame. She lay face down. He pressed her side, at the hip.

Shirley wobbled.

Leverage. He needed a two-by-six. Something.

Why not use Shirley's body against her?

Lester shifted to her right foot. Grabbed her shoe and pulled the leg back and leftward, hoping the additional travel would decrease the load.

Shirley's sneaker popped free. Lester's arm swung. The shoe flew. He landed on his backside, too close to the heat.

Lester smelled bacon. Must be his head acting up.

Next plan?

Lester remained sitting. Drew up his legs. He didn't have another firearm in the truck. Stupid on him. Police and Fire would likely arrive soon. Revolving lights—and a pillar of fire—would attract witnesses. Plus he'd already fired his pistol.

See if any people watched, then brain Shirley with a rock?

Nah. Situation was already too risky. He shouldn't be anywhere near the scene. Surprising, no crowd gathered yet.

The smart move: leave and reassess from safety. Lester twisted. All fours. Resumed his feet.

A limestone chip bounced from his head. Stung, hard. He lifted his forearm as a shield and turned.

Ulyana, winding up for another. She girl-grunted and swung her arm.

Lester scooted.

A rock hit his belly. "Stop!"

"Leave her alone!"

Ulyana bent to the ground, reloading.

Lester gritted his teeth. Balled his fists. "I'll be damned if—"

She wound up. Jiggled and whirled. Another stone zipped by his ear.

"Go away, you monster!"

No accent. Hmm. He'd liked that about her. Lester backed from Ulyana, away from Shirley's parked car. Ulyana advanced behind a hail of zinging gravel. Lester dropped his arm. Bent forward, he scooted around the other side of Shirley's inferno trailer.

Lester stopped.

Ulyana hadn't followed. Maybe she'd have more luck moving Shirley.

If he could somehow find his gun...

Lester rounded the burning trailer and sought a view from the same side Ulyana surprised him from.

Illuminated in fire, Ulyana bent to the ground beside Shirley and picked up a rock. Put it in her pocket.

What would she want with a rock?

Ulyana prodded Shirley's shoulder. Shouted at her.

Lester placed his hand at his head and pulled it back with blood.

Why would Ulyana put a rock in her pocket?

CHAPTER 14

Shirley's lungs burned and her skin felt about to melt. She whirled the metal framed chair. Released.

Lester fired his pistol.

The hurtling chair jerked, reversed spin, crashed into Lester's legs.

Shirley rushed out the door, stumbled on her steps, and fell forward. She swung her right arm and toppled the old bone sack Lester.

His pistol flew.

Her legs gave out.

Shirley splatted on her driveway gravel. She clonked her head on the pitchy pine tree and zonked into blackness.

"SHIRLEY! Wake up! Shirley! Are you awake?"

Something jabbed her shoulder. Pebbles pressed into the flesh above her eye socket. Her neck was sticky. A sharp edge pinched her belly. Her knee was warm and wet.

Shirley opened her eyes. Groaned from deep in the throat. Flames poured from each window in her trailer. Smoke clouded black against the half-mooned sky.

"Brass!"

"Is Brass inside?"

Wha—? Ulyana

"No. His picture."

Ulyana prodded her shoulder. "We have to go! Before Lester comes back!"

Shirley remembered. She saw his pistol flying in the air, almost within her grasp, as she tumbled upon it.

She started to lift herself.

"Where's my shoe?"

Ulyana bounced from her squatting position and retrieved the shoe. "Lester tried to drag you off his gun... probably so he could shoot you."

Ulyana undid the laces. She lifted Shirley's foot and shod her. Retied.

Shirley grabbed the pistol and struggled to her feet. She faced her burning home. Gawked, to make sense of it.

"Lester wanted the thumb drive. He wouldn't let me come out of the trailer without giving it to him."

Ulyana darted fifteen feet to the road. "He was parked beside that trailer. The empty blue one. He's gone. Come on! We have to go!"

"Where?" Shirley strode toward Ulyana, giant steps that hurt her feet and told her of pulled muscles in her back and shoulder. She stopped. Patted her pockets.

"What?"

"The thumb drive! And El Jay's money—I dropped them when I fell!"

Ulyana bounded back. Heads down, they searched.

"Damn that's hot," Ulyana said, turning to the fire. "Oh—wow—the wall's caving in!"

"We need that money!" Shirley pointed.

"Wow. You must have chucked it with the chair." Ulyana hurried twenty feet, grabbed the money bag. "We'll never find the thumb drive. We need to go!"

"That memory stick is the only insurance I have. When Lester gets it, he'll kill me. Us."

"Does he already have it?"

Shirley closed her eyes. Grimaced. "Damn! Just damn!"

"We have to go! Shirley?"

"Where? We can't go to your place."

"We can't go anywhere as long as he's alive. He'll keep coming for us."

Ulyana stared at the pistol in Shirley's hand. "Unless we come for him."

"You drive."

Ulyana walked. Shirley limped. They arrived at her car. Ulyana opened the passenger door. Shirley mentally rehearsed the process of riding shotgun. Just reverse everything she ordinarily did. Grab the door. Left leg into the car first, followed by left butt. Rotate. Scoot. Kick. Lift right leg and pull door.

Cake.

Shirley put the gun on her lap.

"Would you uh—? That thing is aimed at my guts."

"My bad."

Shirley placed the firearm on the dash.

"How about the floor? Or where you had it, only pointing the other way."

"I can't reach the floor. I need a smaller gun. This one's legit, don't misunderstand. But the *fung shway*, right? The ergonomicals—"

Ulyana revved the zippy engine. "Could you—I'm sorry. Please move your leg out of the way. I can't budge the shifter. Reverse is all the way right and back.

Shirley pressed her body hard to the right. Her thigh didn't displace, just expanded. She grabbed her leg.

"Dammit." Shirley opened the door. Moved out her right leg and squirmed away from the center.

Ulyana found reverse.

"Can I get back in?"

"We can try."

"I'm buying a big automatic tomorrow. This is ridiculous."

Shirley returned her leg to the footwell. The door remained ajar.

Ulyana eased the clutch. They reversed. Ulyana turned the wheel.

Shirley's flaming trailer filled the windshield.

"Wow that's horrible," Ulyana said. She braked. Put the car in first.

"I don't know. Might be horrible. Might not."

Shirley shifted her left cheek more leftward. Then the right. Closed the door.

Ulyana nodded. The car lurched. The engine died. Ulyana turned the ignition. Eased the clutch. They crept forward.

Shirley rolled down her window and felt the heat as they passed. Between other trailers she saw flashing red lights. The firetrucks arrived before they reached the exit. Ulyana swung into another trailer's parking space and killed the headlights.

"I wish you hadn't done that."

"What?"

"Reverse?"

"Damn."

The firetrucks passed. A police car arrived.

"You're clear."

Shirley repeated the shifting drill.

They reversed, reseated Shirley, and stopped at the exit.

"So how do we find out where Lester lives?"

Ulyana revved the engine and the car surged forward. She turned right.

"Where are you going?"

"Lester's."

"Oh. Have you been to Lester's place before?"

"I worked for Paul. And Lester."

"WHAT?"

"A few months ago. You knew I was with Paul."

"That was paying rent, like the rest of us. But you work for Russians."

"Now. And before. But in between, they sent me to the Toungates."

"Like, top secret, super spy?"

Ulyana smiled. "Sorta. They wanted me to strip at their club for a while. See if Paul slipped up and said something useful."

"And that involved Lester? Like, at Lester's house?"

"A couple times."

"You let Lester screw you?"

"Not really. With Lester, you mostly screw him. He puts a saddle—like for horse—on this futon—"

"Oh, that's too rich. Don't tell me any more. I want to keep the image the way I'm seeing it." Shirley looked out the window. Let her open hand glide in the air. "I used to do this as a kid."

She closed her eyes and let the seat absorb her. They needed a strategy for Lester. On whom Ulyana had slept. *Whom...* another word for her

Pretentious Folder. Let's see. *Ergo* was in there. What else? Couldn't think of it.

"That's terrible, your trailer burning down."

"Not terrible... *per se*." Shirley grinned wide. "Not terrible *per se*. When we came back from leaving El Jay at the warehouse, I sat in the car and tried to find the gumption to burn it myself."

"Why didn't you?"

"I wanted to keep some stuff. And I got raped."

Ulyana was silent. Then: "You want to swing by Maddix Heidegger's and kill him next?"

"Let's finish this job before we start another. But yeah, then Maddix. And there's this other guy, likes to pound his wife. He's next."

Ulyana turned. "Up here a little ways. What are we going to do?"

"You being naked worked with El Jay."

"You think a little nipple's going to take Lester's mind off killing us? Even for one second?"

"Yours? Yeah."

Ulyana pulled to the side of the road under trees. "We need a strategy. Using that gun."

"We go up and shoot him."

"Which one of us?"

"I get to!"

"Okay," Ulyana said. "What do I do?"

"Like I was saying. A little distraction..."

"He came to my place before burning yours. Asking about El Jay."

"What?"

"I told him I was calling the cops. So I can go up to his door and knock. When he sees me, he'll think I'm there because of how he threatened me, earlier. You'll be standing behind me. Off a little.. That'll give you a second to shoot him."

"Past you?"

"I'll jump away. Then you shoot. Don't look at me like that. I can jump."

"Be a whole lot cooler if you was naked. His eyes would stay right where we want. Then I step around the side and—P-Kow!"

"You can do that without me being naked."

"Why is it suddenly a deal breaker?"

"Because it's fifty degrees out."

"Even better for the nipples. But fine. Whatever. Your way."

"Shirley?"

"What?"

"Do you want to see me naked?"

"No! Jeez. Tramp. Get your mind out of the gutter. I just wanted Lester distracted by sex. I'm not an old hand at killing people. Yet."

"Just checking."

"Let's go."

Ulyana drove ten feet. Stopped. "So, I can't just drive up there to his house. He might see you get out of the car. Can you—"

"Walk? How far?"

"I don't know. A mile? A half mile?"

"Do you know what a mile is? Point to a mile."

"Down there. That house."

"That isn't even fifty yards."

"Can you walk that far?"

"Once. If my pants was on fire. Or they were giving out Snickers ice cream bars up there. Get closer."

Ulyana engaged first gear. Pulled on the road. A few moments later, she swung into a driveway. Trees on both sides. The driveway sloped.

"Keep going farther. You didn't say it was uphill."

Ulyana crept along.

"Okay."

The car stopped. Shirley exited, jazzed by adrenaline, .357 swinging in her hand.

Ulyana eased ahead. Shirley crossed to the other side of the driveway and walked close to the trees on the side.

The porch light came on.

Did he know they were there? Or were the lights motion sensing?

Ulyana parked. Headlights went out.

Shirley hurried, best she could. Her feet still throbbed and the skin where her thighs rubbed was getting hot. She swung her gun hand level, for practice. The pistol rocked. Really sweet. But it was heavy and shooting someone shouldn't feel like exercise.

It's like lifting weights. If you shoot enough people, you'll be healthier.

Ulyana leaned against her car, facing away from Shirley. She looked back, super casual. Shirley nodded toward the front door.

They approached in parallel, separated by twenty feet. Nearing the house, Shirley vectored for the door. She stopped next to the outside wall and Ulyana entered the recessed stoop.

Both hands on the gun grips, barrel level, Shirley flicked the pistol.

Ulyana knocked.

CHAPTER 15

Left hand on the wheel, Lester steered onto his driveway. His head rested against the seat back, until the juddering truck bounced him. All his life, never brain pain like this.

Never.

What did that nurse say? Hema... Hemorrhage. Stroke. Said he should have gone to the ER.

Lester said, God hates me. I'm safe.

He killed the engine and sat under the yellow light. After a long while, he pressed the button on his visor and the garage door shut. He closed his eyes.

Ulyana bent over and picked up a rock. Not very damn likely.

He needed to make a pot of coffee, grab a gun and go get her.

Lester pulled the truck's door latch. Lifting his arm increased the pressure in his brain. Throbbing moved behind his right eyeball, and waited, as if the glowing pain prepared to scorch open his head from the socket.

Whiskey. Not coffee.

One arm forward, his right eye squeezed shut, Lester entered the kitchen from the garage. He swiped a snifter from a cupboard and a bottle of Evan Williams from the liquor hutch. Slammed his hip into the counter top. Steadied himself and poured the snifter full. He drank.

Keeping his right eye closed, he followed the wall with his hand.

Entered his bedroom and opened the unlocked gun cabinet. From the bottom, between rifle stocks, he lifted a pistol. Replaced it. Grabbed the next, a .38 Special. He spun the cylinder and put the grip in his right hand. With his left, he closed his fingers.

Lester grunted and followed the hallway back to the kitchen. He filled the glass again, steadied himself on the kitchen island, and pitched to his favorite chair. With his drink on the lamp table, he drove his hip into the armrest. The chair faced the door.

Lester sat with his right arm on the rest, .38 pointing at the knob.

CHAPTER 16

Ulyana knocked on Lester Toungate's door. She turned to Shirley. Shrugged.

Shirley whispered. "Maybe he didn't come back."

"Can you look inside the garage? I'm not tall enough."

Keeping the pistol pointed at the door, Shirley stepped from behind the corner.

"Point the gun at the ground! Don't you watch TV?"

Shirley aimed at the sky.

She followed the log wall toward the garage doors, but stopped at a window. Pain in the patootie—six foot woman bending and half-crawling to avoid being seen. Maybe she didn't have to. She eased her head around the frame. A lamp, over toward the front door, cast a dim yellow glow throughout an otherwise dark chamber.

Over in the chair... Lester?

The angle presented a distorted view. She moved farther into the open. Cupped her hands between eyes and glass.

He wasn't moving. His arm hung over the armrest.

That doesn't look natural.

A small whiskey glass lay on its side on the floor.

Shirley backed away. "Knock again. Call his name and tell him yours."

Shirley resumed her place at the window. Ulyana knocked and called out. Lester didn't move.

Couldn't be...

Shirley returned to Ulyana.

"He's passed out or dead. Sitting right behind the door."

"I hit him in a head with a rock. After he tried to drag you."

"A big one?"

"No. From the driveway."

"A pebble? Really? Besides. He made it home."

"What should we do?"

"He looks dead. His booze glass is on the floor. But we should kill him again, in case. See if the door's unlocked. Quiet. He might be sleeping."

Ulyana reached for the handle and twisted. Her eyes popped.

Ulyana stepped back. "You have the gun. You go."

Shirley lifted the .357 and pushed open the door with the barrel. Even with the lamp, the interior seemed dark. She spotted Lester. His eyes were closed. His left arm had fallen over the side of the chair—she'd seen that from the window. But his right arm—and a new gun—lay on the armrest, pointed at the door.

Shirley held the .357 on him and pushed the door all the way open with her shoulder. If he twitched, she'd fire.

Wait a minute. Would his eyes be closed if he was dead? He's sleeping!

Shirley eased nearer. With the .357 aimed at Lester's chest, standing so close she could smell his whiskey, She said, "My name is Shirley F'N Lyle. You burned my trailer. Prepare to die."

Lester did not move.

"If he—"

Shirley jumped. Ulyana was right behind her.

"Crap!"

"Sorry."

"What?"

"If he moves at all, you should shoot him."

"Ya think? Move over there. Get off to the side so we're apart. A tactical consideration."

Ulyana slunk to Lester's side, opposite his gun.

Shirley came closer.

Closer.

She aligned the barrel with Lester's head.

He can move his head fast. Aim at his chest.

"Good thinking."

"What?"

Shirley pushed the tip of her barrel into Lester's sternum. "I want you to open your eyes, so you can see what's coming."

She glanced at Ulyana, then kept her gaze fixed on Lester's pistol.

"You so much as twitch, I'll blast a hole through you. You threatened my life and I made coffee. Well—no more. Lester Toungate, I sentence you to die."

"Wait. Don't shoot him."

"What?"

"He's already dead."

"Can't be. His eyes are closed."

"Some people die with their eyes closed."

"No they don't."

"Look it up."

"Yeah. Help me yank this dictionary out my ass."

"Uh. No, really. If he's already dead, you don't want to shoot him."

Shirley shoved the gun barrel, hard. Lester didn't rouse. "You see a mirror?"

Ulyana approached Lester from the side and placed her ear to his nose. Put his wrist in her hand and pressed the vein.

"He's dead."

"I don't believe it."

"Check for yourself."

Shirley rested the pistol on the table beside Lester. Ulyana frowned. Picked it up.

"If you think he's dead why are you worrying about him grabbing the gun?"

"He scares me. Even dead."

Shirley grabbed the chair back. Leaned into Lester, half expecting him to jump up and scare her. All a big prank. But he was deader'n—

"Check his pulse too."

Shirley pressed his wrist. Nothing there but bone and sinew.

"What do we do now?"

"What do you mean?"

"I'd kind of like to burn his house down, you know?"

"No, don't. When he's found, they'll think he died of natural causes."

"He did."

"But if you burn the house, they'll wonder why he sat in a chair while the house burned on top of him. We should leave. Don't even keep the gun. Clean it off and put it in his holster. No one saw us come here."

"Like I said. I'm kinda fixed on revenge."

"Save it for the guy who beat your face."

"I want revenge, now."

"We'll go there next."

Shirley looked around the cabin. It was damn nice. Plank floors. Fireplace. Dead animals on the walls. A nifty lamp made of copper and cowhide. Horsehair pottery.

"You know what I'd really like to do is move in. Bury Lester in the back yard and plant a garden on top. Get rid of the stuffed animals. And maybe the dark curtains. Imagine this place with sunlight coming through those top windows. Yoga mat on the floor over there."

"Hold on. Don't light anything on fire. Don't shoot anybody."

Ulyana jogged back the hallway. A drawer slammed. Door thudded.

"You aren't leaving fingerprints, are you?"

"I'm wearing his socks on my hands."

Ulyana's noise moved from room to room.

Shirley shifted her weight from her left foot to her right. Could she sit a minute? Why not? She eased onto the sofa facing the fireplace. Dead Lester to her right.

"You know, old man, you gave me a scare back there. And if you wasn't already burning in hell, I had it in my mind to kill you with your own gun. To add the insult."

She looked, still expecting him to rouse, and answer.

Ulyana returned with a small duffel bag. "Check this out!"

"More cash?"

"Uh huh. A lot more than we got from El Jay."

"I love drug lords. You think there's any more? You check all the rooms?"

"I looked everywhere I could think. Let's go."

Shirley grabbed the cushioned arm rest and found her feet. She followed Ulyana to the door; looked back at Lester. "I saw his chest move!"

"He's dead! Put the gun back in his holster and let's go!"

"I want the gun."

"Think! Why would you want a gun that's probably connected to a bunch of murders? Go buy your own. We got money now."

"I'm going to regret this." Shirley moved to Lester's side and tried to figure out how to push the pistol past the cushion, into his holster. "This is stupid."

She wiped the barrel and grips with her shirt. Dropped the .357 on Lester's lap.

Shirley followed Ulyana out the door.

CHAPTER 17

U lyana turned the car around before Shirley entered.
"That wasn't nearly as satisfying as I wanted, and now I don't have a gun."

"What do you want to do?"

"I should get my car. So I can find someplace to stay."

"Did you grab your keys?"

Shirley patted her pants. "They were in the trailer."

"You can stay with me until you find a place."

"Thanks, but I'm flush. We're splitting that cash, right?"

"Fifty-fifty."

"I'll get a hotel."

"Just a waste of money. You can stay a few days in my spare room. Get your head right. Get situated."

The dashboard clock read a quarter of eleven. Plenty of time to find a hotel. They were flush with cash, but needed to divvy it up. From the size of the duffel—if it had the same size bills as El Jay's money bag—the score could be a few hundred grand. A few hundred large.

"There could be a hundred *large* in the there."

"*Laaaj.*"

"*Laj.*"

Counting that much money would take time. After that, she'd wake a hotel clerk, because Ulyana was fun by the minute but intolerable by the hour. Always popping and bouncing around. Smiling like a centerfold—and doing it well. Plus the accent was fake. That was just wrong. A million reasons not to stay at Miss Perky's trailer.

"What about renter's insurance?" Ulyana said.

"What's that?"

"Like car insurance on your stuff. You know. So if something happens—"

"Like everything burning to the ground?"

"Exactly. So if a drug dealer sets your place on fire, the insurance company pays you for what you lost."

"Isn't that the responsibility of the landlord? I mean, damn. Right?"

"No."

"Oh."

"So you lost everything."

Shirley sighed. Wiggled in the seat, even more uncomfortable. "Well, I don't plan on getting nothing from nobody. Never did. So this is just par for the game."

"For the course."

"It's an Americanism. They don't have those in Ukraine. Oh, wait—"

"Listen. You should take the money from Lester's place. He burned your home to the ground. The money's yours."

"No. That's not how we roll at VIVA the REVOLUTION, Incorporated."

"Now we're incorporated?"

"I just said that. Sounds justified, right?"

"You really should take the money," Ulyana said.

"Let's count it before I hold you to that. The bag's heavy."

"I was hoping you'd say that. I like money too."

"Vunderbar!" Shirley said. "So while we're out on the town, let's go beat Maddix Heregger until his eyes bleed."

"You don't want to kill him?"

"No. He didn't kill me. I want to shove a broomstick up his ass."

Ulyana gulped. Drove. Turned on the radio.

Shirley turned it off.

Ulyana said, "We should just get some rest and think about things, before we do anything else. Now that Lester's dead. Be careful, you know?"

Ulyana turned the wheel. Shirley rolled down her window and put her arm in the wind. Ulyana twisted the heater knob. Shirley closed the vent on her side.

"Okay," Shirley said. "I thought about it. I want Maddix Heregger tonight. Look at it this way. The world isn't right until justice is served. One by one. El Jay tossed my house. We killed him, and I felt pretty damn good. Things were looking up. VIVA the REVOLUTION. Then I got beat up and raped, and I don't think I'm going to be quite my new self until Maddix Heregger suffers some medieval consequences. Besides. We got momentum."

"That's when people make mistakes."

"So we make them."

"And go to jail."

"It's better than going back to the jail I was in."

"For you. But Shirley—how you say in Americka? I got life."

"Yeah, that accent thing still pisses me off."

"Well, you're not making sense. What's the harm in thinking about things?"

"The other night I decided to think about things. I sat in my car and stared at the trailer, thinking, I should go away right now. Burn it to the ground. Leave everything behind. Soon as I decided to play it safe, Maddix Heregger showed up. I don't want to go to your place and relax. Lester's dead. His son's dead. All those kids out there are safe from drugs. Well, I want to keep kicking ass. Tonight, tomorrow, every day. Shirley Lyle—Ass Kicker. I don't want to ever go back to being Shirley Lyle—Punching Bag."

Silence.

Burger King.

The car approached the turn at the Mountain View Mobile Home and RV Resort. Ulyana slowed.

Shirley regarded her. Then looked out the window.

Ulyana braked. The turn was to their left. The car stopped on the road.

"What are you doing?" Shirley glanced at the side mirror. Twisted around because she couldn't see.

"There's no one coming," Ulyana said.

"What are you doing?"

"If we do Maddix, we need a better plan than we had with Lester. Maddix sounds like he can handle himself. We don't have a gun. All we have is... us."

Headlights behind them. Shirley twisted.

Ulyana said, "And no more after Maddix. Not tonight. Deal?"

"Deal!"

Ulyana gunned the engine. Burped the front wheel. The engine died. "Sorry. I'm used to driving alone." She started the car. Revved and released the clutch slow and easy. They surged forward into the yellow glow.

"Turn up here," Shirley said. "Right. Yeah, that one."

THEY PARKED a block from Maddix Heregger's house. He lived on a street where every home had two maples in the front lawn, a single line of trees spanning the block. In the sixties it probably seemed groovy and wholesome. But knowing the sort of man who lived in Heregger's house, Shirley easily imagined the secrets held by his neighbors.

"That's his place, with the big truck in the driveway," Shirley said.

"Lights are on. So what's the plan?"

"Easy. All you do is get naked and ring the doorbell."

"Here we go again."

"Once you tie him up, I come in. I'll do everything else if you're too skittish. This is my justice, anyhow."

"No. That last part. VIVA isn't about justice for *one*. Maybe one at a time, but not one."

"You don't get to—say, that's a good point. VIVA the REVOLUTION is for all of us. Woke or not."

"And no to the first part, too. We need a way to solve problems that doesn't involve me getting naked every five minutes."

"Why? You're good at it."

"So are you."

"What?"

"He came to your place, not mine. He wants you."

Shirley's face clouded with deep, nonsensical delight.

"Sooner or later you're going to have to face it, Shirley. You're one sexy, sexy mama."

Shirley giggled. "Buck naked? Right there on his doorstep?"

"Hell yeah. It's dark out anyway."

"So where do we get the rope and broomstick?"

"You were serious about the broomstick."

"Well, in lieu of having a penis…"

"I'll sneak in after you go in. I'll find something."

"What about the rope?"

"Even better. There's a bag in my trunk. Accessories. I'm doing a new routine on stage. I handcuff myself to the bar and try to escape. You know. Contortionist stuff. Guys love it."

"You keep handcuffs in the trunk?"

"Yep."

"Where's my morals? I can't complain about what he did if I turn around and use sex to get him back."

Ulyana glanced out the window. "Don't fall for it. Justice first, then morality. Otherwise it's just the other guy's trap. You don't have a gun. You don't have a knife. You have his desire and your ability to fulfill it. Get justice. Then live the good clean life."

Shirley popped open the door. "I need a gun."

Shirley stood at Maddix Heregger's front door. She climbed eight steps to get there, and triggered a motion sensor light. She turned around.

So this is what it feels like to strip on stage.

"VIVA the REVOLUTION," Ulyana whispered. "You sexy, sexy mama."

Shirley placed Ulyana's two pairs of handcuffs between her thighs. She removed her top. Her bra. Held the cuffs in her hand. Kicked off her shoes. Wrestled out of her pants and underwear.

She tingled in the cold air.

Ulyana peeked around the corner and whispered, "Be sure to leave the door unlocked."

Shirley waved her away. Tried to think of an erotic way to display the handcuffs, but vertical, nothing came to mind.

She inhaled deep. Held her breath. It was only a man. He'd look like Maddix Heregger, but for now it was only a man who wanted what she had.

Shirley rang the doorbell.

Nothing.

She turned around. A man walking a dog stood on the sidewalk on the other side of the road.

"What are you looking at?"

He kept walking.

Noise inside. The door opened.

Maddix frowned. "What the hell do you want?"

Shirley took in his sunburned, stubbled face. The width of his shoulders. Tried to imagine how her plan might find success against Maddix, given his strength.

"I—I felt bad about the other night. I don't know what I got in my head. You've always been one of my best steadies, you know? I treated you so disrespectful."

"Damn right you did. Why I had to knock some sense in you."

"So this one's on me. I'm only what I am and I need this work. I need good men like you, or my business..."

Shirley sniffled.

Revolting. You should get an Oscar.

"...I don't know what I'll do if I can't rely on—"

"Get in here. Come on, before the neighbors know I'm with a whore."

Shirley stepped inside Maddix's house. She pulled the door. Maddix blocked.

"I'm going to gather your things from the step."

"Such a gentleman."

Maddix returned with her clothes in one arm. He locked the door with the other. Shooed her toward the stairs.

Shirley looked at the door handle.

Don't be obvious.

"Upstairs?"

"First bedroom on the left." He smacked her left cheek. "Get that bandage off your chin."

"Honest, you don't want me to."

He smacked her again. Same place.

Shirley lumbered up the stairs. Stopped before the top to allow her heart to steady out.

"Keep moving. The room on the left."

Shirley advanced the last step. Realized, if she happened to fall now, with Maddix beneath, she could easily shatter every bone in his body before they hit the floor. But it might kill both of them, and if not, would certainly hurt.

She advanced down the hall. Turned left.

"Wow. I wouldn't have expected a bedroom this big, for the size of the house."

"Get on the bed."

"Maddix, I must insist. I've been thinking about how to repay you and, you really need to let me handle it my way. I promise to rock your world. New senses and stimulations like you've never had. Guaranteed."

He was still. "Those cuffs better be for you."

"They are. They are. You ever had a woman in control? You know. Not really, but pretend."

"Never."

"So we're going to play a game. You know Simon Says, right? We're going to play Shirley says. Get on the bed, Maddix."

He tilted his head. Advanced his left foot.

"No. See? Shirley didn't say. Now Shirley says take of your shirt."

He stared. His left nostril twitched.

"Maddix, you're no fun. Shirley says take of your shirt so she can give you a back rub."

"Why didn't you say so?"

"I want your head this way. Your body along the bedframe at the foot, here. So I can stand beside you."

Maddix removed his shirt. He stretched along the foot of the bed.

Shirley stood beside him and pressed her palms into his shoulder and neck. Down his back. At the curve above his blue jeans, she kneaded down under the belt.

"We need rid of these pesky pants. Let me get your belt free."

He lifted his belly from the bed. Shirley expertly unfastened his buckle.

Keep that handy.

She lay the belt beside his legs and tugged his pants down over his rump. Down his thighs. Where the cloth bunched at his ankles, Shirley smoothed out a section.

"I got them all jumbled up. Hold on just—"

She slapped the handcuff over his ankle. Slammed the other side to the bed frame.

"Hey!" Maddix jerked.

Shirley dove to his back and pinned him to the mattress. She climbed slow across his body. Maddix pushed up, but Shirley crawled across his back. He collapsed, face down.

Careful to keep her arms and legs off the mattress, so her entire weight rested on Maddix, she grabbed his arm and with both hands, maneuvered it close to the frame. Maddix fought, but after a half minute, was limp.

She handcuffed his wrist to the bed.

He's not getting any air. You could kill him like this.

Shirley rolled off and lay on the bed beside him. She propped her arm under her head.

Maddix didn't move. She shoved his shoulder.

Nothing.

Shirley thought of Lester, dead so easy. Now Maddix. As if she was a black widow or something. Like a Midas touch, except a Black Widow touch.

"Hey, wake up."

She pushed Maddix.

His unchained forearm lashed out. Swung above her neck and dragged her down. His arm was like bent steel. He dragged her tight to the bed and squeezed her face to his chest, like he wanted to pop her head from her body. Her brain filled with air. She couldn't connect words into thought, except...

You're going to die...

Shirley opened her eyes. Jumped. "Waaaah!"

"Easy. It's over."

Ulyana stood at the side of the bed with a bloody crescent wrench in her hand.

"What's over?"

"He won't hurt you any more."

"I missed this one too? He's dead?"

"Not completely. He was strangling you. I had to."

"I have the worst damn luck."

Shirley flopped to her back. Her face was wet. She pressed her cheek with her hand.

"Sorry about that."

Shirley held up her red hand. She squirmed and pushed herself to a seated position. Leaned over Maddix. Welts, lashes and bruises covered his face. His arm hung over the side of the bed like he had a second elbow above the first.

"You broke his arm."

"And his head."

"Oh wow. This isn't what I thought we would do."

"No, you were going to shove a broomstick—"

"Still could."

"Well, yeah. He was trying to kill you. That ups the stakes. Now we have to kill him."

Shirley frowned. "Where's my clothes? I can't think naked."

Ulyana nodded at a pile on the floor. "If he wakes up, he isn't going to let things rest. Men aren't wired to get their asses kicked by women. It messes with their heads. We need to finish him."

Shirley pulled on her underwear. "We do that, we have to clean the place."

"What?"

"Hair. DNA. Fingerprints."

"We could burn it."

Shirley wrestled her breasts into her bra. Jumped and bounced until they seated.

Maddix groaned.

"No, we can't kill him for what he did to me. I want to, but that wouldn't be a revolution. It'd be more of the same crap that makes the world so miserable now." Shirley finished dressing. "You got a key for those handcuffs?"

"I pick them with a hair pin. Part of my act."

"No kidding. Let me see."

"You want me to take them off him?"

Shirley nodded.

"You're not going to use the broom handle on him, either?"

"You might have broken his skull. I almost suffocated him."

"Okay, if you say so. But he isn't going to be happy when he wakes, and my face is the last thing he saw."

Ulyana dropped the crescent wrench to the floor. She fished a bobby pin from her pocket and released Maddix's leg. She moved to his wrist. "You sure?"

Shirley nodded.

Ulyana released him.

Shirley braced hands on knees, her face next to Maddix's face. "You ever come for me again, or her, we'll kill you. Flat out, no mercy like this time. You better hear me."

CHAPTER 18

Lester Toungate opened his eyes. He tried to adjust his posture because his neck ached and his rear end tingled, but his body didn't respond. He remembered the white pain that had been in his brain, when he'd taken the chair. Lester turned his eyes and took in the room. His .357 rested on his lap.

That meant something. What?

Just who the hell am I?

Someone had been in the house. He sensed it. His heartbeat increased and his chest constricted. He tried to turn his head, but his body still slept.

I'm Lester.

He closed his eyes. Reopened them.

He used to have these waking dreams as a kid. Total clarity, inside a body that wouldn't obey. Fourteen years of age he woke like this for the first time. Total darkness, save a clock with hands glowing green. He rotated his eyes to the faint blur. His bed floated two feet above the floor —judging by his angle to the clock. Desire alone moved the bed, back and forth, a few inches maybe. Up and down the same. While his body ignored command. Lester focused on shouting, but he couldn't even change the pace of his respiration. Couldn't open his mouth, but moaned a little.

His brain rejoined his body in sleep, and he awoke unsure if the paralysis had been dream, or real.

Lester experienced the same imprisoned awareness several times through his youth. Never as an adult. He recognized what was happening. Now, when attack might spring from any direction, his body laid siege to his mind.

Birdsong from outside. Maybe close to dawn.

No footsteps. No voices.

Yet someone placed his .357 on his lap. The .38—he remembered—was in his other hand. Why would he have left his .357 on his lap, with the chair angled at the door? He couldn't remember, but he knew himself and this kind of nonsense—he didn't do stupid things. Had to be others involved.

Eyes closed, Lester thought about his right index finger. If he could contract the muscles, the .38 would fire. The noise might rouse his sleeping body. He'd asked a doctor years ago, and learned the phenomena was common. The conscious brain woke, but the motor control part slept. If he could pull the trigger, the noise might rouse the rest of him.

His finger wouldn't move.

Useless.

Eyes shut, Lester allowed a memory to float into view: that blond stripper who knew how to take a cowboy in the saddle. She threw rocks at him. He circled a burning trailer, and she lifted something from the ground.

LESTER JOLTED. Pulled back his elbows and shifted in his seat. A shaft of sunlight rested on his face. Late morning.

.357 on his lap.

.38 in hand.

He remembered. He'd moved the chair and sat expecting the stripper and the prostitute. He set about killing her and incinerating the memory stick, solve two problems at once. Wily.

She charged him from the door. Knocked him out. He came to. She lay unconscious on his gun and he couldn't move her.

Ulyana chased him off with rocks.

He'd returned home to grab his .38, planning to re-engage. End the whole nonsensical affair. His brain didn't agree. The pain laid him low. He drank whiskey.

Lester adjusted upright in his seat. Moved his .357 to the arm rest. Let his heart and lungs steady out before testing the brain. Because if he had to sit in that chair until he died to avoid more of that blinding pain from last night, he'd take his sentence. Not to be a puss, but a return visit to the misery of last night—he'd be compelled to end it.

Lester leaned. Braced with his arms. Scooted to the seat edge. Stood.

He'd live—of course he would.

Now how did his .357 arrive on his lap?

Lester opened the .38's cylinder. Full load. Clicked closed. He checked the .357 and holstered it. Turned about, taking in every detail. The lamp, still on. Sofa pillow moved. He never sat on the sofa. Someone had. Fireplace mantle, nothing different. Kitchen... Evan Williams bottle open. Volume a little lower than he expected.

Full circle, he stopped. The door was unlocked. Someone brought his gun back to him and sat on his sofa.

Ulyana.

She'd ridden him on the futon next the bookcase. Unfold, toss a saddle, mount and be mounted. More comfortable than flat on his back in bed—and Lester had always preferred the upright posture. Kept him wary. You're never caught flat footed when you screw standing up.

Ulyana knew the house. She knew what he was.

He'd seen the phenomena before, plenty of times. Women heard stories of his station in life. They'd see him pay cash, regardless of the ticket size. He didn't often reflect on it, but he carried himself with an unusual gravitas. He behaved as if he owned everything near him. Women noticed that. They were like moths. Afraid, yet drawn.

One time he hired a girl as a runner. A mistake he never repeated—though today's young women were snotty and ornery and he might benefit from testing the premise again. After she lost a kilo to robbery, instead of running, she came to him. Promised she would never make the same mistake.

Something in a woman's nature made her good at begging.

He killed her, but the insight mesmerized him. Women were hard wired to beg, and men, to make them.

Ulyana probably returned his .357, thinking she'd giddyup on his mess and all'd be forgiven. If she begged.

Maybe. It took something special to get his blood pumping, and she had it. Be a shame...

One last thing to check.

Lester kept a go-bag in his bedroom closet. Cash, in old, oily bills. Plus a change of socks and underwear. A fake passport.

Lester walked to his bedroom.

CHAPTER 19

E ngine almost inaudible, Special Agent Joe Smith crept by the charred remains of Shirley Lyle's trailer.

He looked to the far end, where her bedroom had been, and remembered the sweet pleasures she'd given him. How she moaned and wept with sensual delight at his stamina and size.

"Girth is what it's worth," she said.

No girl ever said that to him before. Because no girl ever slept with him before.

Her trailer was ashes and bent tin. Memories were all that remained.

The night Shirley Lyle handcuffed El Jay Toungate to the bed, she threatencd Joe that she would reveal video of their times together. The threat momentarily hit its mark. Joe Smith left her trailer, but outside he decided to do what was right.

So he hid, and then followed her and the blonde to where they disposed of the body.

Now, with her trailer gone, the likelihood of her having escaped with video evidence seemed small.

If by some crazy miracle Shirley Lyle suddenly disappeared, it would be like he never paid her for sex. The only evidence would be his memory.

Evil like that... he foresaw the need for penance. He'd have to be a super good guy. Serve ordinary Americans. Work really hard in the FBI. He could never atone, but perhaps his deeds might offset?

Joe drove past the burned trailer, turned at the end of the street.

CHAPTER 20

S hirley sat in the passenger seat. Ulyana drove to the back entry of the Mountain View Mobile Home and RV Resort. Ahead, the still-smoking remains of Shirley's home. Ulyana nodded. "You want to talk to anyone down there?"

"No."

"They might think you're inside. Burned up."

"CSI would never fall for that."

"Still, that was your home."

"That was *Old Shirley's* home. I'm done with her. I was renting from Clyde, anyway. He owned the trailer. My stuff is gone, but I'm not the one they need to talk to."

Ulyana parked.

"You got a couch for me?"

"I could also grab an air mattress—put it in the back bedroom."

"I'm going to be miserable either way. Let's go with easy. I'll take the couch."

"Don't forget we have to count the money."

"Oh yeah. Slipped my mind."

Ulyana entered the trailer.

Shirley closed the car door, grabbed the black duffel, and headed for the step. Inside, she dumped the bag on the table.

"Gross," Ulyana said. "Old man underwear—where I eat."

Shirley chucked them at her.

"Is that a sock? With a hole in the toe?"

"I heard of this book that says millionaires are plain old assholes like the rest of us."

"Get it off my table."

Shirley pitched the socks. Moved a passport to the chair. She lifted her arm, made a sword motion. "My side over here. Yours over here."

"Don't you think we should count it?"

"It's bigger if we don't know how much is there."

"That doesn't make sense."

"I'd rather let it look like ten million, instead of knowing it's two grand."

"That makes even less sense. It's easy. All we have to do is count one stack. Then all the stacks."

"I know how to count money. I'm just saying it's fun to dream a little. Before you mess things up by making them real."

"New Shirley, Old Shirley, I'm counting all of this. I won't tell you if you don't want to know. But we are not divvying up a pile of money without knowing exactly how many dollars are in it. That isn't respectful."

"By all means. Respect the money. I'm tired. This my couch?"

Ulyana nodded. Organized stacks. Removed a rubber band and slipped the first bill off the pile.

You know," Shirley said, "seeing all this money—how much it is—I should have shot Lester to be sure."

Ulyana froze, arm between two stacks. "Five hundred fifty two. Five hundred fifty three. I'M COUNTING. Five hundred and fifty four." She slammed the hundred to the stack.

Shirley turned on the television.

SHIRLEY'S EYES burned from the late hour and flickering gamma rays. She needed a splash of water on her face. But if she got up and farted, Ulyana would chew her ass. *Nine hundred ninety thousand I'M COUNTING blah blah yada.*

She was fine talking when she wanted, though. "Damn, Damn, Damn."

"What are you cussing for?"

"I'm counting!"

Two minutes later, Ulyana added the final wad of bills to the pile.

"It's one million."

"Dollars? BWAHHH!" Shirley hurried to the table. Ulyana had stacked the bills in a small cube.

"He coulda put that in a bowling bag," Shirley said.

"It looked so much bigger, all scattered."

"Wooo! That's crazy money. Woo. What's wrong? Isn't that a lot of money to you?"

"No, it's fine. I just thought the bag was deeper or something."

"Wait. Five hundred thousand each. That's still a lot of money."

"I know."

"What? It doesn't change anything for you? Quit work? Go back to college? Didn't you want to be a translator or something?"

Ulyana met her stare. Frowned. She walked to her bedroom and returned with a small gym bag. She split the pile and put her half in the bag. She carried the bag to her room and brought back a blanket. She gave it to Shirley.

"Goodnight."

Shirley placed her cash in Lester's duffel. She dropped it beside the sofa, where it would be close.

"I want to smell you all night long, baby."

Shirley turned off the kitchen light and the lamp. Snuggled into the sofa and threw the blanket over herself.

She drifted to sleep inhaling the sweet finger-oil scent of drug money.

"YOU DON'T HAVE BACON?"

"No."

"What you eat for breakfast?"

Ulyana wore a cotton robe. Bare feet.

Well check that out. A mole on her leg. Don't get excited. Its a beauty mark.

"Piss off, Old Shirley."

"What?"

"I said, what do you eat for breakfast?"

Ulyana held a plastic tub of spinach.

"I'm going to throw up."

Ulyana removed a giant blender from its base. Filled the bottom third with water, and dropped in two handfuls of spinach. She opened the refrigerator. Carrots, beets, asparagus, parsley, and—

"I don't even recognize that. What is that?"

"Just a little celery root."

"You're putting me on. I'm not kidding. Where's the bacon?"

Ulyana smiled. Cut vegetables into large chunks and dropped them in the blender. Last, she added a tablespoon of cocoa powder. Blender half full, she rested it on the motor base. Pressed on a heavy rubber lid and flipped the switch. She turned a dial. The motor increased pitch. Vegetables jumped and bounced and turned into mud.

Ulyana poured the disaster into a glass and lifted it to her lips.

Shirley leaned closer.

Ulyana tipped the glass.

Shirley's jaw parted.

Ulyana swallowed. Again and again. She lowered the glass, leaving a frothy, vomit-looking mustache on her lip.

Shirley closed her eyes. Dry-swallowed.

You gotta do it. You're Shirley F'N Lyle now! You take care of yourself!

"Old Shirley? You sound different."

No. Not Old Shirley.

"What?" Ulyana said.

"Do you... Uh. Have enough in the fridge for another?"

Ulyana poured another glass from the sludge remaining in the blender.

"Here you go. Enjoy."

Shirley lifted the elixir to her nose. Not horrible. Unlikely to cause instant death. Still, one hundred percent certifiable gross.

"I can't believe I'm going to do this."

"You better. You need to live a long time. For VIVA."

Shirley dumped the glass into her mouth and allowed the entire contents to pour down her throat. Mildly chocolaty. Mostly disgusting.

"I guarantee this'll clean me out."

Ulyana smiled big. "Let's make more!"

"This is how you stay so thin, right? You only eat gross stuff."

Ulyana prepared another batch. Shirley sat on the sofa. Ulyana poured.

Shirley's lower abdomen rolled. She felt pressure at the exit. Nausea crept from her belly, past her lungs, up to the back of her throat. Her intestines burped and danced. More pressure at the exit.

"Uhhhhhh! Which bathroom! I gotta—" Shirley held her breath while fighting free of the couch. Ulyana pointed back the hallway.

Shirley twisted, swung her right leg— "Oh crap! Oh crap! Oh crap!"

She pounded to the bathroom, yanked her drawers, dropped to the commode.

Shirley placed her head in her hands.

That's your body rejecting all the nasty food you've been eating.

"I don't like it."

It's a purge.

"Like Stalin? You don't sound like Old Shirley?"

No Baby. I'm Viva Shirley.

"I'm going nuts."

You're going to like me. I promise.

LATE MORNING. Ulyana came to the kitchen, dressed for work. She placed a hand bag on the kitchen table. "What are your plans for the day?"

"I'm going to buy a gun."

"Where? Do you know a dealer?"

"No. I thought I would search the Internet."

"Will you pass the background check?

"I don't know. I didn't think of that."

"What kind of gun?"

"What the hell? Twenty questions?"

Shirley's throat still felt hairy from exposure to raw vegetables. She filled a glass of water and lifted it to her lips. Through the sink window she saw the next trailer down from Ulyana's. Beyond that, unseen, a pile of bent metal and ashes.

Her car keys were in that mess. Her computer.

"Hey!"

Ulyana headed for the door. "Yeah?"

"Yeah. Let me go with you."

"You want to strip at the club?"

"No, a lift."

"I'm leaving right now. Jazalyn's been riding me nonstop. I can't be late. You ready?"

"Thirty seconds!"

Shirley grabbed a couple stack of hundreds. "I don't feel responsible, leaving this bag out in the open."

"Put it in the back room."

"Maybe I should put it in the bank."

Ulyana snorted. "If Vanko heard you say that, you'd get a lecture. No, the bank's the last place in the world to put your money."

"Who's Vanko?"

"My boss."

"Oh. Who's Jazalyn?"

"My other boss. Vanko's the big boss. Jazalyn's the club manager. You know. Used to be pretty. Used to do what I do. Now she bosses people around and tries to make sure no one stays long enough to threaten her job."

"Oh."

"Put the bag in the back room, or bathroom. I have to go."

Shirley stooped. Jerked the couch forward a foot. Tossed the bag behind and slammed it to the wall.

"Let's ride."

SHIRLEY POINTED AT A SIGN. GUNS AND GLORY. They were passing a strip mall a mile from the Pink Panther. Ulyana pulled into the lot.

"Don't go in there if... you know..."

"What?"

"Police are trying to arrest you, somewhere.

"An outstanding warrant for my arrest? I watch all the cop shows. I'm good. I'm clean."

"How are you getting home?"

"I got cash. I'm getting set up right."

"Oh."

"Not that I didn't sleep like a baby on your couch. But that ain't VIVA."

"Uh, okay. See you later?"

"Roger Wilco." Shirley saluted. Ulyana drove off.

Shirley entered Guns and Glory.

A man stood behind the counter, leaning on his forearms, pistol in his hands. Across from him, a woman geometrically similar to Ulyana. She stared into the man's eyes, while he kept his on the gun... Until he glanced at Shirley. He stood upright. "Be right with you, miss."

If you were in the market, he'd do...

"Viva Shirley?"

She's not his type. You are.

"Pardon?" he said.

"Thank you." Shirley smiled. Nodded. Turned to a glass counter-top displaying beautiful firearms and knives.

Ohh. Wow! All these pistols and only two hands to shoot them.

"Viva Shirley likes guns," Shirley said.

She remembered the small pink pistol Ulyana carried, that burned in the car with El Jay. Shirley wanted a larger one, but not like Lester's. Small enough for comfort and ease of use. Big enough to bag an elephant.

She glanced at the man and the woman he was helping. She leaned away, now. Something wasn't right, between her expression and her stance.

She's playing him.

The man shook his head. Placed the pistol back under the glass. She gave him a card. Walking past Shirley, she smirked.

Don't worry, that was fake too.

"I want a gun," Shirley said.

"I can help." The man paused. He shook his head as if to refocus; snapped his attention back to Shirley. "Do you know what you want?"

"A gun. What was her deal?"

"Oh, Miss ATF?"

"A-T what?"

"Alcohol, Tobacco, and Firearms. Government people."

"All the cool stuff."

"They come in every couple months and try to get me to sell without the background check. Anyway, this gun you want... What's it for? Targets? Home defense? Concealed carry?"

"Just a gun. Targets. Homicide. The regular."

He laughed. "Uh, yeah. So—uh, you're not supposed to say that."

"I meant, in a self-defense situation."

"Of course. In that case, perhaps you meant *noncriminal* homicide."

"Or manslaughter. That sounds cooler."

"Uh."

"I'm kidding. I just want a gun. The world's getting crazier by the minute."

"True—"

"And I got a Constitutional right. That's always been super-important to me."

"Of course. I didn't mean anything by it. I'm a retired homicide cop. My ears perk up, you know? So what caliber you have in mind?"

"A-1. Top notch."

Blank stare.

"The best," Shirley explained. "I got cash."

"I meant, what size cartridge do you want it to shoot?"

"Love, that's what I need you for."

"Okay. I see. Have you been to a gun range? Do you know what you like to shoot? What feels right in your hand?

"I want something that'll shoot like a cannon but fit comfortable between my boobs." She pointed at her sternum.

Again the man looked at the counter. He smiled.

At last.

"I can help. Can I ask your name?"

"I'm Shirley Lyle. What's yours?"

"Donal. O'Laughlin."

Donal stood eye-level with Shirley, making him six feet. He looked like a Kenyan marathon runner. Except Irish with gray hair and blue eyes. His face had been around the block a couple times. Maybe dragged from a truck. But now that he found his groove, his expression lit up and he shifted along the countertop toward the front of the store. He moved like his body always did what he wanted it to.

Sad envy flashed through Shirley.

You'll get there, honey.

"That one," she said, pointing. "Right there. That's the right size."

"This?"

Donal unlocked the case and removed the pistol. "Great choice. You ever shoot a forty?"

"Sugar, all that means to me is chugging Old English 800."

"Forty caliber?"

"I doubt it."

"This is a lot of gun. Not huge, of course. But if you're not accustomed... It might be better to get something without as much oompfh."

"I'm a woman likes oompfh."

"Uh."

He's blushing.

"This is the one I want."

"Can I get your driver's license? For the application."

"You have to apply to buy a gun?"

"Are you from the ATF? Yes, you have to apply. So I can send your information into the database."

"I thought we had a Constitution."

"Not us. Our grandparents. They decided against."

"Oh, politics. Keep talking. Yummy. Makes my feet sweat."

Donal nodded, fast. Cocked his head. Nodded slow.

He looked at her license. "Same address?"

"Yep."

Donal wrote on a triplet form on a clipboard. She signed. Answered more questions.

"I'll enter your info in the computer and it should just be a minute."

SHIRLEY SAT on a bench out front. Someday she'd buy a watch. At least two hours had passed because the sun moved from beside the post to above it. She tried to fathom the meanness of the man who invented benches made of boards. All the action of the last few days told Shirley to keep her mouth shut and get the gun buy done.

No telling what kind of confrontation would be next, now that she drew problems like a magnet.

She needed lunch. She needed wheels. But she wasn't leaving this joint without a gun. There had to be a problem with her application.

It couldn't have been the time she was arrested in Wichita. There were five girls, all at the same time. They'd earned their way out. What cop would have kept a record of that?

Shirley felt pressure above her eyes. Tension compressing her frontal brain lobe. Compression in her sternum.

...Same thing happened in Seattle as Wichita, except, add breaking and entering.

Shirley got off the bench.

She paced.

The door opened behind her.

"It's approved. We can complete the transaction."

She sighed but the pressure remained in her chest.

That feeling, right there: the fear that 'they' have something on you, because you weren't perfect. You don't need to live like that.

Shirley nodded. "Thanks Viva Shirley."

"What?"

"Let's buy this gun."

Shirley followed Donal inside.

To her right she noticed for the first time a wall rack overflowing with accessories. Almost all were black. Some were flesh colored.

Hmmm.

"You really should take this to the range and familiarize yourself with the firearm's safety features."

"What range?"

"I go to the one on Card Road."

"Never heard of it."

"It's right there. Take the left turn a mile after Burger King."

"How much is this?"

Five hundred fifty nine."

"For a gun?"

His smile flickered. "I want to be delicate here. You shouldn't be buying a forty caliber pistol. You should get some instruction before you take this out of the box. A firearm is a powerful thing. Safe in safe hands. Dangerous, the other way."

"Thanks, I'll take it."

"There's a class here, tomorrow afternoon. No cost to attend."

"I don't think so. I'm kind of a do-it-yourself learner, when it comes to things I don't know about."

He nodded slow. "How will you be paying?"

"Cold hard barrelhead cash."

"You'll be needing ammunition?"

"Lots."

"Five boxes?"

"Sure. How much is that?"

"Twenty six a box."

"Dollars?"

"Uh huh."

"Quite a racket you people got here. I'll still take five."

He turned. Stooped. Stood and placed the ammo next to the plastic case holding her pistol.

"You going to let me see it?"

"Of course." Donal opened the plastic container and withdrew the Ruger SR40c.

"Basic operation. This is your magazine. It holds the cartridges. You place the loaded magazine inside the handle like this. Listen for the click—there—the magazine is in place. Next, grab the slide by placing your fingers on the grooved area on each side, here, and here, and pull back. Release. Don't ease the slide forward. Just release."

The slide slammed forward.

"If we had placed ammunition inside the magazine, the slide mechanism moving forward would have pushed the top cartridge from the magazine into the chamber. The firearm would have been loaded. This mechanism on the side is your safety. When the red is showing, it's ready to shoot. When you see white, it's on safe."

He placed the Ruger in her waiting hand. "One more thing. On this model, if there's a cartridge in the chamber, this little mechanism on top sits up a little higher. See how it's red on the side? So with a glance you can see, red on top, red on the side, means it's ready to fire."

She pointed at the wall.

"Place both hands on the grip." He demonstrated. Spread his feet. Bent his knees and stretched his arms, leaving a slight bend at the elbows. His right hand was a fist with index finger extended, signifying the gun barrel. He cupped his left hand around the fingers of the right. "Do it like this, you'll be steady on your feet and limber enough to aim."

Shirley mimicked his pose. "P-kow!"

"That reminds me. Here. A free set of ear plugs."

"This feels real good in the hands."

"It's a fine weapon."

Shirley placed it in the case.

135

. . .

SHIRLEY SAT on the bench in front of GUNS AND GLORY, getting situated before walking three blocks and buying a Dodge V8 something or other. There was a Toyota dealer closer, but she was a red-blooded American, and felt good after her walk last night.

After a second studying the magazine, and how it fit inside the pistol grip, she determined the direction the bullets should point. Some of this stuff was intuitive. No reason to be afraid of the unknown.

Shirley filled the magazine, the spare, then stood, holding the SR40c at her side.

"What am I going to do with this?"

She tried to tuck it into her pants. No room. Too tight. The barrel pinched. Plus she had five boxes of ammunition.

She turned. Gun arm swung wide.

A woman approaching the hair salon a few doors down pivoted.

That's right. You're a badass.

"I'm a dumbass. I shouldn't have a gun. I'm going to kill somebody."

Damn right. A bunch!

"I should take it inside and get my money back."

No, you should learn how to use it, so no one ever uses your face for a punching bag again.

Shirley swung open the door.

Donal pointed. "The sign, Shirley."

NO LOADED FIREARMS ALLOWED

"How do I unload it?"

Donal frowned. No sadness or anger. Pity. "Let me show you." He held out his hand. She gave him the Ruger.

He turned it so she could see. "Press this button."

She did.

The magazine clicked and popped a quarter inch.

"Two steps. First, remove the magazine."

She pulled it out.

"Second step—and you always do this step, no matter what. Even if you think you don't have to. Pull the slide back and observe the chamber. If there's a bullet in there, it'll eject. Otherwise, you'll see the chamber is empty."

"Most important step," Shirley said. "You should be a teacher. At a gun range or something. I need a way to carry this."

"Our holsters are on the wall. I could show you a couple that would work with the SR40c. Here." He grabbed one from a bin. "This'll fit." He accepted the Ruger from her hand and slid it in the holster. Held the assembly at his hip, slightly back. "It sits right here, out of the way. When you need it, grab and shoot."

"Everyone will see. I need it hidden. So the people in Walmart don't freak out. I like that one." Shirley pointed to a flesh colored bra-holster.

"That's a Flash Bang holster. It has a solid design. The firearm fits in the slot here. You gain access by lifting the shirt. Then pull and shoot. Slick concept."

"Flash him, then bang. I want."

"Might be a problem with the uh, they don't make a plus size."

"Story of my life. What about this one over here? What they call this, the Side Boob Holster? Not in my size either, I bet. Which is ridiculous. They make bra holsters for the iddie biddie titties, but not these." She swung herself to face him. "Check it out. Rack like this? I'm the one that needs protection. But the Side Boob Holster Company has no interest."

Donal opened his mouth. No sound. Then: "Sounds like you found an unserved market. You could start a company. Sew up one of your own, uh, garments. To start. Can you stitch?"

"Yes I can stitch. That isn't the point. I'm bitching and moaning for the pleasure of it. Not because I want to do needle work."

"Still. The niche could work. That's all business is. Find something people want and sell it to them. Meantime, if you don't want to modify one of your garments, just use a regular hip holster."

"I don't want my gun out in the open."

He's looking at you funny.

"I get it. My wife... she was plus. I made her something simple, so she could carry concealed. I could do the same for you. Nothing fancy, but it gets the gun out of sight."

"In my bra?"

He patted his waist, in front, to the side. He shrugged. "Or, I guess if the brassiere was solid."

"Men carry guns there? Up front? Where it could shoot their garbage off?"

"You're not a man."

"Well I got garbage just the same. Where do men hide guns?"

"Some in the front, on the side—but it gets in the way, sitting down. Most conceal in the small of their back, or they wear loose clothes and conceal at the front hip."

"You concealing right now?"

"Of course."

"Where?"

"Then it wouldn't be concealed."

"I like you Donald McGlaughlin."

"Donal."

"Donal."

"O'Laughlin."

"You're pretty damn particular. I'll take the one for the hip. And you'll make me another?"

"I will. Come to the training tomorrow and I'll have it for you. Shirley."

CHAPTER 21

No one at the Pink Panther—or any club—had ever seen Roddy Memmelsdorf's red and white F-150. He slouched behind the wheel.

He'd parked at the back of the lot, facing away from the strip club entrance, and adjusted the right sideview mirror to monitor the parking lot entrance. The rearview kept the main door in sight, and the left sideview displayed the side exit, where some of the girls came outside to smoke.

In three days, all afternoon and half the evening, no one had come out to roust him. That meant nobody inside paid close attention.

On the seat beside him, his grandfather's Ruger Super Red Hawk, a revolver with a Leupold scope. He'd hurt his wrists the only time he'd fired the beastly .44 magnum.

It felt good on the seat, though.

Roddy wore his jacket collar high and a ball cap low on his brow—he'd had to unfasten the tiny buckle on the back to allow the cap to accommodate his swollen head.

He lifted a paper cup from the console and spat blood.

The five men who beat him hadn't returned. Roddy always remembered a face.

But he did see Ulyana arrive each day. She waltzed inside like she owned Flagstaff, nothing on her mind but her perfection. He imagined what she looked like inside the club, all day. How she waved her naked flesh around, gyrating, grinding, spreading, rubbing. He'd seen her up close. With his perfect memory, his extra-spatial reasoning, and the juggernaut of libido coursing through him since his ass whooping, sitting in the truck and staring off into the woods was almost as bad as having her grind those magnificent orbs in his face.

He watched her arrive and leave.

Shop for groceries.

Run laps at the trailer court where she lived, in that tight, may-as-well-be-naked outfit.

And what was up with her and the fat girl? Her mother? Why was she staying at Ulyana's? Had to be her mother—but the genes didn't make sense. If that was her mother, Ulyana was adopted.

They couldn't be best friends. The age difference. The everything difference.

Maybe it had something to do with the trailer that burned. Helping out a neighbor.

The side door opened. Roddy glanced at his watch.

Ten after eight.

Ulyana emerged, holding a gym bag. Without so much as a glance around, she strutted to her car.

He waited.

Her taillights flashed. Exhaust from the pipe. Reverse lights.

Ulyana backed out, swung to the right. Departed.

He twisted the F-150 ignition. Backed. Stopped. Adjusted his rearview and driver sideview. Backed out and followed Ulyana.

Roddy sensed he'd never do anything to Ulyana. But he had fun imagining, sometimes.

All grown men have fantasies.

If he ever snatched a girl, hypothetically, such as, say, for instance, Ulyana the bitch from Philly, he'd have to keep his actions from his wife. Ruth wouldn't be able to handle the violence. Women didn't understand the world the same way. That pain was all in the head. Especially in his case. All in his head, and all mental. Women didn't grasp that sometimes, only force could compel a solution. They didn't get war. Politics. Sales.

Sex.

Ruth would interfere. She was always trying to be gentle. Take a bug outside, instead of crush it. That kind of thing.

On the other hand, she'd been asserting herself since Roddy choked Mister Shonky. Ruth had been finding little ways to grate on him. If he left an ice cream bowl in the sink for her to wash and return to the cupboard, she ignored it. The grocery bill crept higher. He'd asked. Turned out, she switched brands for all her female products. The old, inexpensive ones tested on animals. She simply had to make the change. For her conscience.

Roddy shut his eyes to a stab of pain. Returned his thoughts to fantasy.

Nab a girl, you can't just haul her out in the woods. People find bodies in the woods every day. You think they're buried, but some wild animal that can smell a hot dog from a hundred miles comes along and paws her out.

You don't leave evidence out.

Nor do you take a girl when a bunch of witnesses can point their fingers. "He's the one she had the altercation with."

No, if he ever brought the dream to life, he'd have to find a girl with no connections to him.

But leaving that aside, boy did he have a place.

He'd inherited his grandfather's house and land three years ago. After taking ownership, he inspected the house for maintenance issues, thinking of a quick sale and cash bump to his investment account. Then he thought about the cash-on-cash return of renting it out, instead. Undecided, he mowed the lawn and set off a bug bomb twice a year, beginning and end of summer.

In three years, he never listed the house for sale. Never advertised it for rent. Instead, he removed the mailbox to eliminate junk mail.

The way the house hid back in the woods, accessible only by a single driveway no one knew existed...

Ruth asked what he planned to do with it. Just since Shonky died. He ignored her, but she queried a second and third time. Someday, the house might be a hideaway from work. A place to disappear from the noise.

A not-so-remote hunting camp. Only a half mile from his house, accessible from the same driveway. Until twenty years ago, the whole area was Memmelsdorf land. Over a hundred acres. But his father had sold parcels until only his grandfather's original house and barn remained.

Roddy imagined Ulyana standing in the 1950's kitchen, baking muffins for him. Naked, except he let her wear slippers to protect her feet from the cold linoleum.

He closed his eyes. She smiled at him, all horny from kitchen work... Like women get.

Grandpa's house was old as Flagstaff. Constructed of stone and log. Basement had a dirt floor until the eighties. Roddy remembered being with his father and grandfather when they laid cement, and became modern.

He remembered the small garden, the dill weed growing everywhere. A plum tree.

He'd never take a girl. Regardless of right and wrong, his pride wouldn't allow him to pay for a woman. Or take one against her will.

Roddy would never take a girl. No matter what.

But if he did, that farm house would be the place to take her.

CHAPTER 22

S hirley sat inside her new-used Dodge Durango in the Walmart parking lot. She'd purchased a few items.

Yes mother, the cash was *burning a hole in my pocket.*

Before Walmart, she'd bought a Durango from the dealer a mile down the road. The salesman—a man of prodigious circumference—said it was the lowest, easiest-to enter sport utility vehicle, with tons of room about the hip and legs.

"What colors you got?"

"There's only one Durango on the lot. This one."

"Black. I like."

"What would stop you from driving it home today?"

"Not much. I got my ducks in a basket and I'm knocking them out one by one." She patted the Ruger on her hip.

"In a row?"

"What?"

"Nevermind. Would you like to take it for a drive?"

"Why bother? You only have one."

"Oh. I see."

"We have to fill out forms? An application?"

"For what?"

"You want to sell this damn thing or not?"

"Oh! Will you require financing?"

"I got the financing. Cold hard cash on the barrelhead."

"Very few forms. We'll have you out the door in a half hour."

Three hours later she drove to Walmart, so excited she didn't notice how uncomfortable she was. But now, with her purchasing spree near over, and her holster pressed against the console, it was time to do something about it. If she needed to draw the Ruger and shoot somebody while she was driving, she'd have to pull over, open the door, shift her left ass, then her right, and then make her quick-draw.

Better to have the gun on the seat, so she could grab it without thinking.

Shirley opened the door. Shifted. Slid. Yanked her Ruger and admired it, sideways, a moment. Red on top means a bullet in the chamber. Red on the side means pull the trigger and make a bad guy go sploof.

Both showed red.

Blood tingled in her face.

Her hand time-warp-shifted in her focus.

The gun could literally blow up. Right now. She flattened her hand, to touch less of it.

The safety is on the side. Switch it.

Shirley pushed upward with her thumb until the latch clicked, revealing a white dot.

Test it.

Shirley pointed the Ruger toward the passenger footwell. She grimaced. Squinted. Turtled her head into her shoulders...

She squeez—stopped!

Shirley pressed the button and the window lowered.

She aimed again and increased pressure to her trigger finger. Slow. Easy. Her hand shook. It wouldn't go any farther. She'd depressed the trigger all the way.

There, it's on safe. That was easy.

"There's got to be a better way, Viva Shirley."

She started the Durango and adjusted her rearview: Walmart.

SOMETHING HAPPENED IN WALMART. A man grabbed his daughter by the arm. Hopefully, his daughter. She was in her teens. Developed enough no man could touch her without knowing she was an innie, not an outie. Girls are the same as boys until suddenly they're not. This girl was ten years past. So the man knew what he was and knew what she was, and wrenched her arm so her shoulder blade jutted out her back. He did it to move her, because he didn't like her location. The girl shrank. No fight in her, like it was his place to push and hers to move.

The thought occurred to Shirley that Ruth Memmelsdorf, from the support group, might not even know she shouldn't get the sense punched out of her every time her husband had a bad day. She might have grown up seeing her grandmother, mother, aunts, every woman she knew, showing up at family shindigs with bruises nobody asked about.

Shirley found only one Memmelsdorf in the white pages hanging from a pay phone. It'd be no harm to swing her new Durango and Ruger over to visit.

She drove. The vehicle took some getting used to. One problem: when she pressed the gas pedal, the giant V8 engine roared forward. She was used to a car that needed foreplay. This Durango drove like a man who hadn't seen a woman in three years. Britches down and banging. Every time she turned, the tires squealed.

She drove. Thought about Ruth Memmelsdorf. About VIVA the REVO-LUTION. The house was coming up. She pulled to the side of the road. Puzzled. How on earth could she do surveillance in a vehicle this amazing? Who could possibly not look at it?

It's black. Like invisible.

"Black is not invisible, Viva Shirley."

Have you ever seen a ninja?

"Good point."

There could be one in the back seat. How would you know?

She turned off the engine and twisted until she could worm her right arm into a bag behind the passenger seat. Pulled binoculars from plastic packaging. Tossed the garbage to the back, with the ninja. Held the binoculars to her eyes and spun the adjustment dial.

She yawned. Looked at the clock. Late afternoon. She had to pee. She'd had crotchless panties—before her trailer burned. She needed crotchless pants, for surveillance work. Just hunker down and get relief. She could start a plus-size bra company and add a line of crotchless denim jeans. Or maybe have the zipper go all the way to the back.

In fact—that was another form of discrimination. Zipper discrimination. Men could just yank out their root and go. Why couldn't a woman unzip to her tailbone and squat? Same difference.

She definitely needed to start a company.

Shirley squirmed. That almost felt like a leak. No way she was going to risk tainting her new Durango seats.

She studied the Memmelsdorf house. No action. Just an F-150 with rust visible at a hundred yards. Red, with a white stripe down the side. It looked old. Sat up high on giant mudder tires. Behind it, a boring white sedan, like a salesman might drive.

The Memmelsdorf house was out a ways from town, in the country, but with neighbors. It was a small box, birdcrap white, with three trash cans on the side. A few cords of stacked firewood, and a tiny lodge, where the wood burner was located, for safety. The house sat on an upslope. The driveway was mud. Windows dirty. Smoke came from the wood burner, floating close to the ground, and for Shirley, that somehow summarized a man who would beat his wife.

There were other houses nearby. And plenty of woods. A trail went from the Memmelsdorf house to the forest behind it.

That was a leak. Pee outside!

Shirley opened the door. Exited, crossed behind the vehicle and opened the passenger door. Standing with her legs in last year's clumps of yellow grass, amazed her tire missed a Budweiser bottle, Shirley wriggled her drawers to her knees. She sat on the Durango door jamb and felt the splash about her ankles.

"Gross."

This is not gross. In tactical situations, all heroes pee on their ankles.

She wiggled since she couldn't wipe. Looked into the woods for any staring faces. None. She stood and raised her pants. Turned to close the door and heard the slap of a screen in the distance.

She hunkered.

A man—had to be Roddy Memmelsdorf—stood on his front porch. Faced the Durango.

Shirley shrank.

He trotted down the steps and strode toward her.

She adjusted her blouse. Stood full height. Stepped from behind the Durango, this time around the front. She slipped. Grabbed the grill.

Memmelsdorf walked with flapping arms and a long stride. He didn't appear to be armed. His face was a bruised and pulpy-looking catastrophe. "What you want?" he called. "Who are you? Who you with?"

Her balance regained, Shirley leaned on the hood.

"I'm nobody."

You left your gun on the front seat.

"Nobody." He stopped half way across the road.

You should mother hen his ass.

"Oh dear! Oh my God! What happened to you!" Shirley stepped onto the road. "Are you okay? Have you seen a doctor? You poor dear!"

"What? Who are you?"

"What happened to you? Were you in a car accident?"

"What? No. Stop—"

"Are those stitches?"

"Woman!"

"Huh?"

"Who the hell are you?" Hands on his hips. Chest out.

He needs thumped in the face. Again.

"Oh I'm nobody. I just bought my Durango. I was out driving around. You know. The sheer joy of it. And I had to pee so bad I just pulled over right there. I thought with the Durango being black, you know?"

"What? I know what?"

"You wouldn't see it. You ever see a ninja?"

He stared, jaw set. Up close, she noticed his left eye was pure red, like every vessel was broken.

"Get your Durango out of here. This is private property."

This is the man who beat Ruth.

Shirley beheld. Skinny man. Bony arms. Elbows like wings. Jutting Adam's apple.

He stared.

She connected, held his look. Smiled wide.

You think you're big stuff but I'm going to show you big. I'm going to stomp you like an ant. You and your scrawny elbows.

"I'll just be on my way. I hope you heal up good. That looks nasty."

"Yeah, well it took ten of them to do it."

She opened the driver-side door and glanced at the Ruger, comforted to know she could grab it before he could reach her.

147

He watched her every move. When she left, he'd probably go look at the pee mark to see if she lied.

You see? How can a wimp like that think he's superior to anything?

"Because decent people turn away."

Right.

She closed the door. Started the engine and rolled down the window. She placed the Ruger on her lap. Thought a moment. Left the safety on.

You need to go to that class. And see Donal.

Shirley gassed the engine. Spat gravel. The Durango jumped. She met Roddy's glare with a rakish grin as she drove by.

"Well, Viva Shirley, you better hope Ruth doesn't tell him about the fat girl at the meeting who told her she shouldn't be taking his beatings anymore."

You think she tells him about the meetings?

Shirley adjusted her rearview.

Roddy walked to where she peed.

CHAPTER 23

Another night on Ulyana's couch. Another breakfast without pork.
Viva Shirley insisted on ground beets, greens, and cocoa powder. It felt like insanity, after what the concoction did to her bowels yesterday. But Shirley had to admit to a certain energized, lighter feeling throughout the day. Maybe vegetables made it easier to stay tuned to Viva Shirley's voice. If that was the case, yes, let's have another. Because Viva Shirley was profoundly more uplifting than Old go-ahead-and-beat-me-while-I-pleasure-you Shirley.

After two glasses of vegetables ground into sludge, Shirley negotiated Ulyana's shower and dressed in a couple new items from Walmart.

Today's big thrill: learning how to handle her Ruger. How to quick-draw, rapid fire, and basically, look like a movie star. Or... simply how to avoid killing herself.

She and Ulyana would get together in the evening, after Ulyana's shift ended at the club. They'd visit justice upon Roddy Memmelsdorf.

Via the Internet, Shirley confirmed there was another women's group meeting tonight. If Ruth did not attend, and stayed home, they'd have to configure plan B. As yet to be discovered.

But with luck, Ruth would go to the meeting, and when she came home, a radically different husband would greet her at the door.

The plan?

The outline remained the same. Naked woman, doorstep, handcuffs, physical abuse. But this time Ulyana had to step up. The way little Roddy had glowered at Shirley, her arrival naked on his doorstep would not lead to an invitation inside. He'd be too afraid to enjoy her. Roddy needed a little woman who didn't intimidate him.

The anticipation was killing her. The thought of Roddy crying, promising to be a better husband, upon risk of Shirley coming back and cutting off his little peeper...

You don't have to save the world. Just convert bad men into dead men or eunuchs, one at a time.

After Ulyana returned from the club, they'd swing by and see which option Roddy preferred.

Ulyana left for work.

Shirley gathered leftover cash from yesterday's clothes, counted roughly one thousand, nine hundred fifty three dollars, and put fifteen hundred back into the black duffel.

She admired her shiny black Durango while walking to it. Boarded, and ignited the engine. Admired its throaty grumble.

"I want everything in my life to have the same sass."

You and me forever.

"That's right Viva Shirley. You and me."

She drove to Guns and Glory.

"You're a little early," Donal said.

"I wanted to give you a couple minutes to show off your handiwork."

He frown-smiled. Not attractive on a skinny face comprised entirely of creases.

As if his face has anything to do with what's inside.

"You got it, Viva Shirley."

"What?"

"I'm just mumbling. Can't wait to see what you made. You know, funniest thing, your business idea. I had another."

"Oh?"

Donal walked the length of the glass counter top and stooped at the end. He lifted a paper grocery bag, returned, handed it to her. "Don't be disappointed. This is a down and dirty combat holster. The first rule for tactical gear is that it works, not that it looks good."

"Sounds terrible. But I get it."

"So what's your business idea?"

"Well, you know. It's a liberation thing. Boys can just whip it out and whiz when they want. That's freedom. And I'm not saying men peeing all over the place is subjugating women. That's not where I'm going with this. But you can just stand next to a tree and let's face it, most men, you have to be right up on them to see anything. So nobody knows you're taking a leak."

Donal nodded in slow motion.

"Women, on the other hand, have to drop their drawers. So everybody would see everything—and you know girls are always taught to be prudes. Good girls don't show boys their thingy. So we grow up afraid to just pee where we want. I saw a man whizzing on a brick wall just two weeks ago."

"You want to micturate on a brick wall?"

"Mick who?"

"Urinate. You want to go on a wall?"

"No. Not me. What I'm saying is women don't have the same urinating privileges as men. Well, what if we made pants?"

"I don't follow."

"Yes you do. We'll make jeans. But the zipper starts in front and goes all the way to the top of your backside. Follows the crack all the way around. Get it? Now a gal doesn't have to drop her britches. She just unzips, squats, shifts the panties—if she's wearing any—and cuts loose."

"Maybe if I was a woman it would have more appeal?"

"In fact, she'd have an advantage. She could knock out a number two while she's hunkered down. That'll shift the balance of power."

The door opened. Two women entered. A man approached the door behind them.

"Class is in back," Donal said. "Come through here. I'll be right with you."

The people passed.

Shirley opened the paper bag.

"Something I wanted to ask you last time," Donal said.

She lifted her gaze from the bag. "Yeah?"

"Would you like—I mean—I was thinking. And, uh?"

He's trying to ask you out. Don't do it! Super heroes are unattached. Romance doesn't work because you're always out saving—

"Uh-huh? Would I like?"

"To have dinner me. With me. You know?"

"I'd love to. But I have this little nagging voice inside warning me off. I'm what you might call a complicated woman."

"I thought I'd ask."

"You married?"

"Not anymore."

"What happened?"

"I was on the force. Homicide cop in Phoenix. She just—you know. The big C."

"You shouldn't call her that."

"What?"

"That's the one thing you never call a woman. You don't even pretend to call her a—"

"Cancer?"

"Oh. *Cancer?*"

Heat spread across her face.

Donal swallowed. Blinked. Stepped backward. "Yeah. Well. Hmmm. She was a beautiful woman. But it's time to keep going. Not moving on. Keeping going. She was, uh. Plus size, you know. You're different though. A lot of ways. More spirited than her. Not that I compare. Of course I compare. But not in a bad way. I just wanted to ask you to dinner. Let's get the class started."

"Let's do dinner, Donal. A little food never hurt nobody."

"Tomorrow at six?"

"Magnifique. Vunderbar."

"What time should I pick you up?"

"I'm a modern woman. I got wheels—I'll meet you."

"The Oceanic has great surf and turf."

"Fine."

"Settled. Let's get inside the classroom. One thing you'll learn. I'm punctual."

She followed.

You can't go to dinner with him.

"Yes I can."

It isn't wise to get encumbered. You don't need a man getting in the way, slavering all over you.

"You apparently never had a man slaver your nethers, Viva Shirley."

She entered the back room—a large closet someone had converted to a classroom by installing a white board. Donal stood beside a mop bucket. Shirley maneuvered between the two folding tables and hesitated next to the folding metal chair with a dented leg. Thankfully, the others sat at the front table. She pushed the chair back. Looked at the metal.

Don't do it.

Shirley eased onto the seat. Brutally uncomfortable, but why make a fuss? Just get through the class, go on your date, kill bad guys.

Metal groaned.

The seat shifted a little to the weak leg side.

Something popped. The bands tethering the back legs to the seat broke. Each spindle bent straight out. The seat crashed into the linoleum but her flesh suppressed the sound. Her tail bone screamed in pain. Her face scorched with instant shame. Donal's eyeballs fell from his head and the others, with their backs to Shirley, ducked as if she'd exploded.

Shirley stared. Nothing was broken. Her hands were free. Nothing landed under the chair. Her legs were straight out. Aside from the pain where her tail bone landed on metal, and where the metal holding the backrest gouged into the sides of her back, the eighteen inch drop didn't cause discernable damage.

Donal's mouth opened in slow motion.

Shirley listened as the echoes of her humiliation evaporated into silence. The man at the front table twisted sideways. The girls remained looking forward, shoulders high, rigid.

Donal stepped toward her.

She had to get up! Before Donal could help. Before the skinny girls turned around. Before the other man smirked. Or feigned concern.

Before she burst into tears and went total berserk crybaby.

Shirley reached up to the table for support.

Don't!

She grabbed the edge and pulled—

The table tipped to its side and the edge crashed to her legs. One of the girls shrieked. Donal leaped. The other man jumped from his seat and with Donal, lifted the table from her. Shirley rolled to her right. Pushed off but couldn't lift herself. Her thighs knotted where the table edge had tried to sever them from her body. Tears splashed down her face. Her chin bandage bumped her shirt and reminded her she was even more stupid than she thought. Shirley couldn't see for the salt water. Her lungs pushed air in bursts, heaves. She heard her voice like through a television, a bad actress wailing and sobbing. The table off her, Donal and the man approached like she was a wounded animal needing put down.

"Easy, Shirley, we'll help you. You'll be fine."

They hate you.

"It's okay. Hey, we'll help you. You're going to be fine."

They think you're disgusting.

"We can each take an arm, okay?"

"LEAVE ME ALONE!"

Donal froze. The other man stepped back.

Shirley leaned to her side, pulled her right leg into a crawling position, then her left. Braced with both arms, she knelt. She grabbed Donal's hand and lifted her right leg, placing her foot square on the tile floor. She shoved away the shattered chair. Braced against Donal, she lifted to her feet. Tears rolled. Her lower back ached. Donal again opened his mouth without words. The other man looked away. The two girls still didn't turn around. Shirley didn't even want to see their fake horror. She could already hear how they'd chatter and giggle the moment she left.

Shirley set her jaw. She pointed to her purse on the floor, next to the bag Donal had given her.

"Gimme those."

The man stooped. Handed her both.

Shirley closed to Donal, in her path. More open-mouth don't-know-what-to-say horror.

"Move."

He stepped aside.

Shirley strode from the closet classroom. Marched out to the parking lot, opened her Durango, threw her purse and Donal's bag inside.

She entered.

I told you not to do any of this. I told you everyone thinks you're ridiculous. You're just a loser.

"Stop, Old Shirley."

A loser who doesn't listen to anyone.

"That's not true."

What? You want Viva Shirley, right? Because she tells you what you want to hear. That you're special and wonderful. The truth is you're terrible. No self-esteem because you're not worth any. Ever since you were a fat kid. You'd do anything to please anyone. You knew something was wrong with you. And you always put yourself in situations so bad things happen. You never learn. You're not a super hero. You're super fat. You're not helping anyone. They don't want help. They want you to stop meddling. And now that you've robbed Lester Toungate, and beaten up—"

"Lester's dead."

You think? That bastard won't ever die. And you robbed him and killed his son. And then you beat on a man who knows where you live, and already proved he's willing to knock you senseless. So what does Viva Shirley do? Antagonize him. You should have just played nice. Did what he wanted and held your pride.

"I don't have any pride."

You shouldn't, because you're almost worthless. But you do. That's where your VIVA the NONSENSE came from. Just fat Shirley being proud and stubborn. When the truth is you're nobody. Just like every other nobody.

"Stop it, Old Shirley."

Where's Viva Shirley now that you've humiliated yourself?

"I don't know."

Just like all the people who talk tough. They leave you holding the bag. Say it, Shirley.

"Say what?"

Say it.

"You're being mean."

I'm telling the truth, and you know it. Say it!

"You were right all along, Old Shirley."

CHAPTER 24

F BI Special Agent—special because he had arrest authority—Joe Smith parked his black sedan on the gravel before a giant log cabin, set with Flagstaff's San Francisco Peaks jutting above the green metal roof. Must be a darned heck of a nice view from the back. A house like this probably had a two-thousand square foot deck. With gazebos and benches built right into the perimeter. Joe imagined standing on that deck, a non-alcoholic beer in his hand, looking up at the snowcapped mountains. Maybe with his tie loosened a little, or if he was feeling reckless, loosened a lot.

Joe stepped from his car and with a crisp turn, swung the door closed and launched toward the house. He walked with the stride of a man who'd put something behind him. A man whose demons rotted in an air-tight vault, locked, barred, bolted, nothing left but bones and rotted succubus-flesh.

Special Agent Joe Smith's demon was named Shirley Lyle, and in truth, she roamed free, ready to destroy his career.

He blinked her out of his consciousness. Extracted his ID wallet, containing FBI badge and FBI identification, while he tramped to the front door.

An old man opened before he knocked.

"Mister Toungate?"

The man's nod didn't seem to reveal his identity.

"I am Special Agent Joe Smith with the FBI. I have reason to believe your son has been murdered."

"Which?"

"Lester Junior."

The old man was steady. "How?"

"Unknown. Right now all we have is charred remains found in a burned vehicle registered in his name."

"What's the make? The vehicle."

"Impala."

"I see."

"Do you have time for me to ask a few questions?"

"Go ahead."

"May we step indoors?"

"No."

"Okay. No problem. For starters. Did your son have any enemies? Anyone who would like to see him dead?"

"Of course. Everyone."

"Why do you say that?"

"People don't like him. Don't trust him. He has a mean streak."

"Does the name Shirley Lyle mean anything to you?"

Lester Toungate remained level. Cool. It was his tell.

"No, can't say that name means anything to me. Why?"

"Her name came up elsewhere in our investigation."

"You think he was murdered, I take it?"

"That appears to be the situation. However, it remains for the coroner to make the call."

"But he's in a burned vehicle?"

"That's right."

"So what does the FBI want with the murder of the CEO of a small-town construction company? I thought you boys hunted big game."

"Thank you for your time Mister Toungate."

"Wait. Where was my son found?"

"Inside his car, on the back seat."

The old man frowned. "Where was the car?"

"At the abandoned grocery warehouse on Jackson Street."

"Thank you."

CHAPTER 25

Shirley sat in her Durango. The vehicle was a joke. She was ridiculous sitting in it. Badass SUV with a big fat zero inside. Who keeps getting her ass beat. Cheese grater chin. Bruises at the eye. Ache in the tail bone. Thighs with purple-yellow across the front, like a tree fell on her. What kind of woman—

A stupid woman. A worthless woman. A woman with no future except her past. Every day waking up to the same yesterday. Nothing new under the sun.

"Viva Shirley? Where are you?"

She's hiding. From the truth..

Shirley turned the key to accessory and pushed the radio knob.

Hip hop.

I don't feel like hip hop.

"I don't give a rat's stinkeye, Old Shirley. You're horrible. Leave me alone."

Shirley turned the volume higher.

Where was Ulyana? She was normally home by eight o'clock. She worked the afternoon and early evening shift, flirting with daytime businessmen and gray-collar bosses. Working stiffs were never off during the day. So the pay was better, she said.

The same metrics had always applied to Shirley's business. Charge full boat all day long. He'll pay, because he can. Discounts at night, when most of his money's spent, but you're still short for the electric bill.

Now that she had money, she needed a cell phone. Find out where Ulyana was.

Shirley turned off the radio. Rolled down the window. Noticed a mosquito take immediate advantage. First of the season.

She smeared blood and wings against the glass. Prick already got her. Or someone else.

Whole world made up of parasites. Every animal. Every human being. You either cooperate or you're a victim. Both ways, a cog in somebody else's scheme.

Silence.

"I hate silence."

Because you think about what you are.

"No, because you won't shut up."

Shirley glanced at the clock. "I'll give her another half an hour."

SHIRLEY LOOKED AT THE CLOCK. Forty five minutes had passed. No Ulyana.

She twisted the key in the ignition. The Durango roared. She moved the shifter to reverse.

What are you doing? You can't—

"I'm going to find Ulyana."

Like you can do anything for her. Let's say Lester got her, what are you going to do? Give him a blowjob?

"Lester Toungate is dead. I took his pulse. He didn't have one."

He's evil, and evil doesn't die.

Shirley pressed the gas, reversed. Moved the selector to drive. She turned right out of the Mountain View Mobile Home and RV Resort. Passed Burger King. The cops were finally gone. Must have found their vigilante from North Carolina and his dog.

"I should get a dog."

No dog deserves you.

Ulyana's strip club, the Pink Panther, was only a couple miles away.

Shirley drove slow.

You're going to get into more trouble. Besides, you don't even know where Ulyana is. She might be turning a trick. She doesn't answer to you. Look! A hotel. Twenty nine dollars a night! Let's stay there!

Internet. Continental breakfast.

She pulled into the parking area.

SHIRLEY AWOKE. All night long, she tossed and turned, wondering what had happened to Ulyana. Did Lester Toungate kill her? Did Maddox Heregger kill her too?

After showering, Shirley dressed in yesterday's clothes. She thought about her humiliation at Guns & Glory, and how the snotty girls never bothered to turn around to learn if she was okay. Probably because they knew they wouldn't be able to contain their laughter.

For some people, another person's pain was funny.

Shirley studied her white smile in the hotel mirror. Her Listerine and apples burned in the trailer fire, and she'd forgotten to get more at Walmart.

She remembered pretending to brush her teeth with her finger in second grade. Her teacher said if you don't have a toothbrush, eat an apple —that's just as good. One day she read the label on her toothpaste: *harmful or fatal if swallowed.*

Eat an apple, gargle with Listerine. Live.

She turned in the plastic key card, checked out, and sat inside the Durango. The paper bag Donal gave her was on the passenger side floor.

Shirley keyed the engine, turned on the air-conditioning, and looked straight ahead.

Where was Ulyana?

That's not for you to worry about.

Shirley remembered when they killed Lester's son, El Jay. After a moment of mutual distrust between Shirley and Ulyana, one meth-zombie clubbed Shirley and another was closing in. Ulyana could have fled to save herself. Instead, she'd killed two men, and rescued Shirley.

Plus she'd been instrumental in luring El Jay into handcuffs.

Shirley put the Durango in Drive.

She's probably dead already.

Shirley drove. She turned left from the hotel parking lot and resumed yesterday's route. She'd stopped at the hotel not too far from the Pink Panther strip club. She saw its unlit neon sign a hundred yards away.

The strip club was in an industrial area, with little around it but yellow grass, scrub trees, and farther down the road, an old warehouse.

Between the club and the warehouse, Ulyana's car was parked on the side of the road.

I told you—

"Go die, Old Shirley."

She turned left into the empty Pink Panther lot. Braked and shifted to park, with the Durango pointed toward Ulyana's car.

"If I had come last night I could have helped her."

Shirley wiped her eyes. Bowed her head. She saw the bag Donal gave her. Picked it up, unrolled the paper and withdrew an object made of coat hanger wire and duct tape, bent like an S.

"How is that a gun holster?"

The wire at the top was bent into a tight curve, almost like a clip. The bottom was more open, had space between the curves, and was much narrower than that above.

Shirley held it up. Rotated. Maybe this was the right way. She took her Ruger from the seat and situated it next to the holster. She shifted each like pieces of a puzzle, seeking a fit-pattern.

The skinny end was wrapped in duct tape and inserted snug into the pistol barrel.

Shirley understood. The top part of the S was a hook that would fit over her pants waist. The heavy cloth would hold the Ruger against her underwear, and the lower curve locked the barrel, and prevented the gun from falling down her leg.

Shirley got out of the Durango. She pulled her waist band, inserted the holster and Ruger at the same time.

Everyone can see. It looks stupid.

Ulyana's car was parked fifty yards away on the other side of the road. Shirley thought of grabbing her binoculars, but she didn't need them to see the shattered driver side-window. She climbed back inside the Durango. The Ruger pinched. Adjusting her seat gave no relief.

"I'll deal with it for fifty yards."

You shouldn't even have a—

"Shut up. Until you have something nice to say."

She parked twenty feet behind Ulyana's car, so she wouldn't interfere with the CSI people's investigation, and approached on foot.

The driver's side window was smashed. The door was partly ajar. The back seat was empty. Shirley placed her belly close to the door and with her shirt between finger and metal, opened it.

Blood streaked the armrest.

Time to go… before someone thinks you killed her.

Shirley returned Ulyana's door to how she found it, and walked to the Durango.

A car pulled into Pink Panther lot. Shirley watched as a bald man unlocked the door and entered.

She parked beside his vehicle and went to the same door. Locked. She knuckle rapped.

Nothing.

She side-fisted.

Nothing.

She drove the flat of her foot against the door, hard enough on the fourth kick that she lurched forward. The door opened. The bald man scowled.

"Ve are not hiring."

"I'm not applying. What's your name?"

"What do you vant?"

"A little courtesy. And your name."

"Mykhaltso. Look, I vorking. What you vant?"

"Ulyana works here. Have you seen her? She didn't come home last night. She's missing."

"Not problem of me."

"No, listen. She strips here. Her car is outside with blood on it. What happened to her?"

The bald man closed the door. From inside she heard a metallic click.

Shirley kicked the door.

Placed her hand on the cloth concealing her Ruger SR40c.

Now is not the time.

"Viva Shirley? Is that you?"

Miss me? We need more information before we get ugly with people.

"What information?"

Exactly. We don't even know what we don't know. How sad is that? Let's go back and think about it.

CHAPTER 26

S hirley sat in the Durango. Viva Shirley rode shotgun.

This is where Ulyana disappeared. This is where we start.

"Tell me what to do, Viva. And if Old Shirley pipes up, knock her out. I'm sick of her head trash."

That's what VIVA the REVOLUTION is all about. You can't stop other people's crap until you quit taking your own. But I can't shut her up.

"Well, then I'm screwed."

No—I can't get rid of her—but you can. When she comes back, all you have to do is think of the things you're grateful for. Say no to pessimism! Remind yourself of what you have, and all the good stuff about you. Instead of the bad stuff.

"Yeah, but I'm a lot of things. Mostly not pleasant."

"So what? Who you are, and what you are, all come from your decisions. Make different choices and you'll create a new Shirley.

"Sounds like waving a magic wand."

Over time. That's how it works.

"How do you know all this?"

When Oprah's on, you laugh. Or sometimes you cry. I take notes. We'll talk about it later. For now, we have to find Ulyana.

"Old Shirley said she's dead. The blood on the armrest proves it."

Old Shirley's scared out of her mind—but I don't judge. That blood proves there's blood on the door. Nothing more.

"So what do we do?"

Think for a minute.

"Well, this is where Ulyana disappeared, and where she worked. Seems like we need to investigate what goes on around here."

Shirley leaned closer to the dashboard. The land was mostly flat for a few hundred yards. Shrubs. Yellow grass. On the other side of the terrain, a car drove. It disappeared behind roadside trees, then reemerged.

"I'm going to park by that cover over there and survey this whole place with the binoculars."

Surveil.

"Right. Exactly."

Shirley turned. At the main road, she cut the wheel again, and waited for the left that would take her to where she'd seen the car by the trees. But the turn never came. She drove a half mile and looped through a gas station, back toward the Pink Panther.

Viva Shirley was silent.

"I'm going to figure this out."

Back at the strip club, she studied where the car had been. Waited. Another car came along, from the other direction, facing Shirley. It turned and eventually disappeared behind the trees.

"I didn't go far enough."

Truth. Always go farther. Break the rules! Shake the badge!

Shirley swung out of the Pink Panther lot and this time, passed the gas station where she'd turned. A quarter mile later, she found the road—and then another quick left. She braked. Drove straight but wanted to turn.

She spun the wheel.

This two-lane was lower than the one she'd been on—explaining why she never saw it. She passed metal industrial buildings with big parking lots. The pavement was better here. A thriving world of people making things. Trucks. Forklifts. Pallets stacked beside a chain link fence.

You never made anything. You don't know how to do anything but lay on your back.

"That isn't true. I give a mean foot job. Go back in your slimy hole, Old Shirley."

She kept driving around a curve to the right.

There! She was on the correct road. Across a couple bare acres, the Pink Panther. Shirley slowed and alternated her gaze between the ditch, the field, the strip club, and the approaching clump of roadside trees. Arriving, she drifted to three miles an hour—but found no place to pull over.

She kept driving, seeking a vantage providing both parking and a view of the club. She arrived at another manufacturing area, comprised of multi-acre two story steel buildings painted battleship colors. Giant parking lots that were mostly empty. Chain link fences. She turned, realizing that from this location, the Pink Panther was impossibly distant.

"Well look at that."

She pulled over. Grabbed her binoculars.

Across a grassy distance, at the small brick warehouse down the road from the Pink Panther, the bald Mykhaltso stepped out of a truck and walked to the side door. He knocked and turned around. The door opened and he entered.

"What are you doing, Mikey-Mike?"

A scenario unfolded before her imagination. Ulyana leaves the Pink Panther. Maybe fleeing, running. She leaps into her car and tires squealing, swerves onto the road. Mikey-Mike stands loose, head tilted. He snaps up his right hand and fires a pistol through her window, and Ulyana stops. The bullet grazes her. Blood squirts to the door arm rest. He drags her out, chains her in the warehouse, and ships her to Mother Russia to work in the sex trade.

Shirley nodded. Fast, then slower.

"Why would he let her get in her car when he could have drugged her inside the club? Or grabbed her? Or told her, hey, climb inside this crate, or I'll kill you."

Yeah. And not all Russians sell girls.

Still, Mykhaltso had been suspiciously disinterested in Ulyana's whereabouts. He didn't care—which seemed strange. Ulyana was lovely and if he worked at the Pink Panther, he'd seen the exact contours of her loveliness.

Maybe he cared, but didn't want you to see. You know. A tough guy. Forbidden love.

Either way, this was valuable intel. The man who ran the show—who Ulyana said would never trust a bank with his money—was probably inside the brick warehouse down the road from the strip club.

That was information worth knowing.

CHAPTER 27

L ester followed Shirley.
　　The big girl was loco, and Lester was good at math. After his go-bag of money disappeared, Shirley boasted a new wardrobe, a new Dodge Durango, and was spending time at the gun dealer.

Now, with Ulyana not at her place, Shirley seemed hell bent on finding her. Maybe they wanted to do more shopping—with Lester's money.

Ah, whatever. The heist gnawed his gnuts but what do you expect from trailer trash but theft and other nonsense? Watching the woman was comical—and came at a good time. The Almighty had scored a couple points on Lester in the last few days. The way a human being scores points thumping an ant into the next room.

The last weeks had been among the most interesting in his life. A neutral observer might believe the deity Lester had spent an entire lifetime scoffing and mocking had at last risen to take the bait.

But not Lester. The best proof that God didn't exist was the fact that Lester still did. No moral divinity would tolerate him.

But what if that was just grandiose thinking? Lester's big ego?

Now that we're being candid, Lester... What if you're a nobody on the coldblooded scale?

"I'm the only evil man I know."

But how many does God? Quite a number. And give the Creator some credit. If He exists, and made you, is He surprised? You're the disease He designed you to be. In His mercy, He blinded you to it.

Lester sat, blinking.

He shook his head. Slight pain. Not much.

Shirley.

Well, if she wanted to go private detective or movie hero, track down Ulyana, spend some more of his money, she'd have a day. Bottom line for Shirley was the same as Ulyana, and Paul, and El Jay.

But the picture was growing. Cosmic nonsense aside, the situation kept unfolding, exposing players that were invisible before.

When Clyde Munsinger came looking to extort him a week ago, Lester thought the boy-genius had connived a plan on his own. Lester believed his son Paul, and other son, El Jay, were in cahoots against him, and the whole thing wrapped up clean when he offed Clyde, then Paul. El Jay's sudden disappearance confirmed his treason. The explosive part of the situation was contained.

But the plot was bigger than he'd thought. By a number of players.

Shirley idled her SUV at the strip club. Drove to Ulyana's abandoned car. Walked around it. Motored away from the club, turned left, and not a mile down the road swerved at a gas station and turned around.

Lester did too—other side of the road.

But... not a half mile back the way she came, she three-pointed again.

Stark raving stupid, the only word for it.

Lester looked to the right and hoped she didn't recognize his truck passing her for the second time.

He took a residential street, turned in a driveway, and emerged in time to see her swerve left, well beyond her initial turnaround. Evidence said she didn't have a path to where she wanted to go.

Lester paused for a moment of self-congratulation... the lubrication that kept him sane.

Most folks would assume Shirley didn't know where she wanted to go. Not Lester.

Everybody wanted something. No one did squat without a motive. Asinine, most of the time, poorly considered, flawed in execution. But no matter what a person did—and the weaker sex was no different—nobody did nothing without wanting something first.

A corollary insight: every person who pursued something did so only after justifying the right to want and pursue. No one eats ice cream without feeling at some level he deserves a treat. Ice cream, or human leg meat, like that Dahmer fellow. Everybody, it turns out, is a stand-up guy.

Worked the other way, too. Most people avoid taking what they're convinced they don't have a right to take.

Shirley Lyle: A week ago, standing in her trailer as El Jay dumped her belongings and broke her glasses, Shirley was weak sauce. Sputtering useless. Barely mustered a pot of coffee. But something changed in her the other night; she hurled a chair and charged like a one-woman buffalo stampede.

An idea, disbelieved, is nothing at all. But when a thought is perceived like knowledge, when the opinion stands on legs as strong as two plus two is four—in short—when a gal believes she has a right to something, you have to consider new possibilities.

A convinced woman was dangerous.

Soon, Lester would put her down. And Ulyana—once he'd enjoyed her company.

But that rule... Lester was the exception.

He alone, of all the people he'd ever met, was willing to take something without the requisite lie that he deserved it, was right to have it, or was somehow improving society by expropriating it.

When he first consolidated his position in Flagstaff as the man who brought in the pills, the ganja, the man he replaced begged for his life on his knees. Why the hell any man would ever willingly fall to his knees was another mystery. But David Wygoner looked up and said, "We can help each other. We can go into business together."

He said to Lester—not the first time he heard it—"You get what you want by helping other people get what they want."

"David, I feel poetic tonight, and I'm going to give you a chance to save your life. All I want is the truth. Rock bottom, heart-of-heart. A cold look in the mirror kind of truth. You're on an island. There's one coconut. Your buddy wants the coconut. You want it. How do you get what you want by giving it to him?"

"Well, see, you cooperate. You share. In all advanced societies—"

Lester shot him.

Afterward Lester thought, if David had said, you're right, I was just making a pitch to save my life, Lester might have let him live. Because he said he would.

While Lester mused, Shirley drove the road to the industrial park. She slowed at a clump of trees, then raced ahead. Stopped roadside near the cluster of manufacturers at the T.

With nowhere to wait her out, Lester drove by a third time, and swung right, staying out of her view.

The woman was oblivious.

Lester glanced over the area. Chain fences surrounded the parking lots. Entrances with guard booths. No choice. He pulled to the third gate and stopped. Rolled down his window.

"I am indeed lost."

"What you looking for?"

"Wasn't there a Ford dealership down here somewhere?"

"You must be thinking of the one on the boulevard."

Lester rolled his eyes. "Don't grow old."

He backed out and again passed Shirley. Her head still pointed the other direction.

"Girl can focus. I'll give her that."

He looked across the hood of the Durango. She watched an old warehouse across the field.

A bald man walked to the side door.

Vanko Demyan owned the joint. Plus the strip club, and thirty other businesses Lester had discovered over the years. The bald man was Mykhaltso Babyak, a lieutenant who worked mostly on the clean side.

Lester's detente with the Russian was almost as old a Reagan's with Gorbachev. The Russians arrived in 1990. Vanko was the youngest son of Old Man Demyan. No one knew his name. He fought a war to establish a foothold in Phoenix, and sent Vanko to conquer the North. Vanko worked with Columbians, moving cocaine. Lester started with the simple stuff: weed, pills. The nod-and-wink drugs the sheriff would confess he experimented with in college. Nobody got too riled about weed and speed. Later, once he owned the right people, Lester added methamphetamine to the menu.

He'd only met Vanko once. They sat in a coffee house while Lester's people and Vanko's people stared past each other up by the window. The meeting lasted ten minutes. They shook hands, and Lester always figured they had a deal as long as they both found it convenient. Demko didn't want to mess with the lesser drugs, but he did want to ensure no one used them to move into his territory. Upon learning Lester had no interest in high profile drugs, and real profit, they fashioned a common-sense accord. Each had exclusivity, and a promise from the other not to infringe.

But Lester had always doubted. Now, seventeen odd years later (if the meeting was 1991. Who the hell could remember that far?) Lester's distrust was confirmed. His premonition was correct. Shirley... Ulyana... Paul... El Jay...

All revolving around Vanko Demyan.

The only way Vanko could know Paul and El Jay were gone from the picture was if he was working with them. Meaning the whole setup was Vanko's work. Clyde Munsinger, Shirley Lyle, Paul, El Jay, and that pretty blonde he'd soon tap one last time, Ulyana—all working at Vanko's behest to oust Lester.

Why not just kill Lester?

That was the devilish part. By leaving him alive, Lester would have no choice but to trade his business for his freedom from prison.

Vanko, Vanko, Vanko.

Lester could be a wily son of a bitch too.

In time.

If it was just about the money the girls stole, they would both already be dead. He would kill Shirley here and Ulyana later. But from experience, Lester waited. When you think you're looking at a tree, but suddenly see a forest, you don't grab an axe because it's handy.

Nor a chain saw.

You wait for a book of matches.

CHAPTER 28

S hirley sat in her Durango, parked at the Pink Panther.

You should report Ulyana missing. To the police. They can help look for her.

"I've already wasted a day. And all you want is to fritter away more time answering questions—while every minute Ulyana could be in a pit with a madman telling her to put on the lotion. Besides, everyone knows Ulyana is the Russian stripper. She doesn't have family around. No senator for a mother, or anyone else who can pull some strings and put the law on her side. She takes off her clothes for a living—"

One step up from you.

"Shut up Old Shirley. You know damn well how they think. A woman who flaunts the goods gets what she deserves. I can just hear the police... 'You know, she probably went home with somebody.' Or, 'You're putting us in a quandary. We don't got the resources to hunt for your missing ho *and* pass out speeding tickets.'"

Shirley thumped the steering wheel.

If the police actually believed Ulyana missing, they'd ask Shirley a bunch of questions that could tangle her up. They might think she had something to do with Ulyana's disappearance, and she'd maybe feel she had to prove her bonafides. She and Ulyana were running mates. Her tongue might slip—and explain how they killed El Jay. The way they did it

—alternating thirty electric stim pads with a blowjob—hard not to tell a story like that.

Her gaze drifted to where Ulyana's car was, yesterday, on the side of the road. She'd returned to make a more thorough study of the evidence, only to find the location empty.

Ulyana?

"No. She hasn't been back to the trailer. Where else would she go?"

She's not even missing.

"Double shut up, Old Shirley. Viva, knock her ass out. We're on a mission."

You should still report her missing.

"With what proof? Glass on the side of the road?"

Shirley lowered her window for the fresh air.

The bottom line: Some crimes were only crimes because the hoity-toities got their panties in a wad. To the police, the people who ran afoul of these hocus-pocus crimes—they were the real problem. Cops imagined a perfect society where no one farted, spat, smoked weed, drove too fast, took money for sex, or committed an occasional well-intentioned homicide. And like Confucius say, if your enemy goes missing and might be dead, let sleeping dogs keep sleeping.

Shirley squirmed in her seat. Looked at her Ruger.

Now what?

Who took Ulyana? She could only think of three candidates.

Maddix Heregger. He'd seen Ulyana before she clocked him, and was likely one of the guys who frequented the Pink Panther. A lot of crossover between their client bases.

Lester Toungate. Viva Shirley kept insisting Lester wasn't dead. That was a horrifying thought. Lester already knew the pleasures of Ulyana. Easy to imagine he took her, bound her wrists and ankles, and locked her in his closet.

Plus, Shirley and Ulyana killed his son and stole a million in cash. Bottom line, Lester was dead. But if he wasn't, he took Ulyana.

So, two people likely wanted Ulyana dead: Maddix Heregger, and the corpse of Lester Toungate.

But a third candidate could easily want her alive. Shirley didn't know his name, but he owned the Russian strip club. Sold drugs. Ran women. And other shenanigans.

A girl like Ulyana would be hard to control, but bad actors always had their methods. They'd grab her, inject her with dope, and ship her in a freight container to the other side of the world, where women still did what men said.

Like you did?

"I'm getting plenty tired of your nonsense."

Just keeping it real.

"Oh go to hell."

In total, three candidates: Maddix, Lester, and the Russian.

Of the three, one was dead, and one had a fresh-broken arm and maybe a couple fractured skull bones.

That left the Russian.

Shirley had seen Mykhaltso enter the warehouse farther down the road. It wouldn't be easy, but she needed to—

A stakeout!

"That's right Viva! Where you been? Binoculars. Potato chips and a pee cup."

She fired up the Durango, repositioned from the back of the lot to the side, windshield pointed toward the warehouse, another few hundred yards down the road. Nothing but a flatland of yellow grass and occasional shrubs between. She had a perfect line of sight to the door on the left side of the warehouse, beside all the garage-doors of the loading bays, where bald Mykhaltso went in to see his boss.

Shirley lifted her binoculars and placed the eye cups against her sockets. Twisted the adjustment and the warehouse resolved. Nothing there. No vehicles. No guard walking around with a cigarette and an Uzi.

Fine. One less man to sneak up behind and slit his throat with a razor.

Bwah!

"Old Shirley! I swear to—

Rapping at the window!

Shirley jumped. Swung her face around with the binoculars still at her eyes. Gouged her right socket.

"WHA!"

Rapping again.

She lowered the field glasses.

Bald Mykhaltso. He made the rolling down the window signal. Shirley shrugged. Mouthed "WHA?" again.

Mykhaltso tried her door handle. It opened.

"You are koming vith me."

"Hell I am, you bald weenie."

He reached to his back and his hand emerged with a pistol. He let it hang at his side.

"Where did you say we're going?"

He looked at her, top to bottom, spending too much time admiring her hips.

"Stay."

Mykhaltso stepped around the back of the vehicle.

Now's your chance!

Shirley slammed her door. Revved the engine. Reached to the shifter.

The passenger door opened.

Mykhaltso entered. "Don't be stupid. Back out. Slow. Turn left at road."

The only thing down there was an empty field... and the warehouse.

"Don't you dare think for a minute—"

He glanced at her. "Drive."

Shirley thought fast... No reason to avoid capture. He'd kidnap her too, and lead her right to Ulyana. She was a human horse. A trojan human. A human trojan horse.

"You know I hooked for a living, right? That's why you're taking me to be with the rest of them."

Mykhaltso frowned. "Don't talk."

"What's this? You're taking me to the audition? I don't do drugs. I insist on that. But the rest? You've heard of women that can make a golf ball blow up a garden hose, right? Well let me say, you don't carry around four hundred pounds of guilty sinful pleasure without a serious set of lungs."

Mykhaltso shook his head.

"Thirty years, I been in the game. You think about that."

"Quiet."

"What's that sound? I can hear your balls rolling from here."

Mykhaltso turned on the radio. Hip hop.

Shirley felt the motion in her hips. The wiggle in her spine that set the rest of her body undulating.

"Just drive." Mykhaltso slammed his palm to the knob.

"Easy, Love."

He pointed at the warehouse.

She pulled into the lot and parked near the door he entered the day before.

"Keys." He held his hand open.

She placed them on his palm. "I get the Durango back at the end of the tour, right? You gonna park it inside? My baby gets garaged. That has to be part of the deal."

Mykhaltso exited. Waited by her door.

Facing him through her window, Shirley glanced downward and to the left. "This thing won't open itself."

Mykhaltso glared. He opened the drivers' side door. Shirley unloaded herself.

"Lift your arms."

"My ass."

He lifted her arms, patted her sides. Then up under her boobs. Then her hips.

"Uhn."

He patted her Ruger. Mykhaltso pulled it out. Studied it. "Red and red. Here and here. This gun could fire, right now."

"It isn't the gun. It's the person holding it."

He placed the safety on. Tossed the Ruger into the Durango and closed the door. He strode to the warehouse. Knocked four times, a different pause between each.

That's from the bear song Ulyana sang in the shower—for El Jay...

The door opened, swung inside. No one stood there.

Weird.

"Inside," Mykhaltso said.

Shirley stepped into the darkness. Her eyes adjusted. The air was cool.

A man sat at an oak rolltop at the corner, with his back to the entrance. He didn't watch television, or he'd know better. The desk rested on an oval carpet, and had a lamp on top. Two more by the chairs behind him. He swiveled.

You're dynamic! Charismatic!

Shirley sashayed toward him, snapping her fingers at the conclusion of each second step.

The man leaned back into his chair. Jaw open just enough to denote happy astonishment. He lifted his hand, and his mouth broke into a smile.

"You are Shirley Lyle, of whom I have heard so much."

"It's only true if it's naughty."

"Please, sit. We have things to discuss."

"I don't need to sit. Who are you? Because I'm only here to talk to the big head. The honcho man. What's you're name?"

"Vanko."

"That's not American. What is that? Alaskan or something?"

"Close. Russian."

"First name or last?"

"First."

"And your last?"

"Demyan. I am Vanko Demyan."

"I thought so. You look like Lester might have, if he was ever young."

"You know Lester? Toungate?"

Shirley smacked her lips.

"And you think he looks like me. Interesting."

"I know some things about him that could be useful to a man such as yourself."

"By such as yourself, you mean, his competitor?"

"That's right, Love."

"Two things. One, we are not competitors. We long ago decided to coexist. Two, I am afraid my friend Lester is in poor health. Whatever information you have, it will not be as useful as you think."

"Well, that isn't what I wanted to talk to you about anyway. I'm a woman. I got tricks up my sleeve they stopped teaching in Chicago in 1932, when the great Madame Longwood retired. You wouldn't have heard of her, you being a communist, and her being American. Anyway I got three holes, two hands, and two feet just as dexterous. I got thirty years popping corks and Love, I never told a man a story without a happy ending. I'm not coming on as some teenager, doesn't know dick from a doorknob. I'm rocked and socked, ready for bidness on day one. I'm here to negotiate my requirements."

He cocked his head. "You misunderstand much."

"I'm not a regular shipping crate kind of girl, for starters. And I got a pretty new Dodge Durango. I'll need that garaged, for the duration. Mikey already said that was all right."

Mykhaltso grabbed Shirley's arm and steered her toward a chair. She shoved him off. Planted her right leg forward and her left hand on her hip. Thrust her chest forward.

"Sit, Shirley Lyle. I misspoke. We do not have things to discuss. I have a single question. Why are you spying on me?"

Don't lie. He must have seen you yesterday.

"I, uh."

"That's a lie. Stop thinking about being clever. I know why you are here. Say it."

"You took Ulyana. I'm going to knock heads together until I find her."

"I thought so. But I did not take Ulyana. I value her very much, in my organization. Let me just say, you and I are on the same side of this problem."

"Why should I trust you?"

"You should not. However, if I was the man you believe, and did to Ulyana what you suspect, I would do the same to you. If you think I killed her, then I would kill you. Does that make sense?"

"You're not going to kill me, so you didn't kill her."

"Approximately. Okay. I'll accept that."

Shirley head-tilted and shrugged. "I'll think about it. If you didn't take her, who did?"

"I do not know. You might ask the people she works with."

"I did. They blew me off." She nodded at Mykhaltso. "That one did."

"His English is not so good. You might try others. Regardless. Ulyana is very important for my plans. That is all you must know. Mykhaltso, take Miss Lyle back to her transportation."

That's code for 'kill her.'

"Wait, I'm not ready to leave yet. If you didn't take Ulyana, why is her car missing? You nabbed her outside the strip club and when I caught on you moved her car to get rid of the evidence. Now you have her in a shipping crate so you can send her to Pennsylvania or something."

"If I wanted her in Pennsylvania, I would tell her to go. And she would go."

"If you didn't kidnap her, then take me to her car so I can gather evidence."

Vanko turned to Mykhaltso. Shrugged. "Take her."

Shirley studied Vanko.

Mykhaltso waved his arm toward the door.

Don't do it! He's just going to kill you!

"Viva, what say you?"

Rock and load.

Shirley followed Mykhaltso. At the door, she turned to Demko. "If I don't find my girl, I'm coming back."

His eye twitched. "Hope you find her."

The door closed behind Shirley. Mykhaltso already sat in the passenger seat of the Durango. Shirley opened the door. He waved her Ruger by the barrel. "I vill keep this."

Shirley climbed inside and started the engine.

Mykhaltso directed her to the Pink Panther lot, where he exited the Durango. After he got in his truck, she followed him away from town. Shirley recognized his next turn and the one after that.

He was taking her to where she and Ulyana burned El Jay's corpse.

He's taking you there to kill you.

"I think you're right."

Then why are you following him?

"He has my gun. I want two, not zero. I need one for reserve. Never knew they were so hard to hang onto."

How will you buy another gun when you're dead?

"Viva Shirley? You in there somewhere?"

Mykhaltso's truck slowed at the entrance. Shirley got up on his bumper. She saw the ramp and bay door on the right corner of the warehouse.

She guessed the distance was thirty yards. The building was easily two hundred yards long. If she gunned the engine, she could crash Mykhaltso into the cement block wall. While he sat there stunned like a thumped rabbit, she'd run up and punch him in the throat. Grab her Ruger, and whatever gun he was carrying.

Then she'd have two.

Mykhaltso's truck surged forward and angled left, not rightward as she expected. Shirley stomped the gas. Drew close. Mykhaltso raced along the front bays and squealed tires around the corner. No brake lights.

Shirley's guts rolled as she anticipated crashing into whatever was parked around the corner. She tapped the brake, turned the wheel, stomped the pedal to the floor and rounded the corner with rubber squealing. Mykhaltso extended his lead. The Durango roared. Mykhaltso swung wide and disappeared behind the back of the warehouse.

Shirley followed.

Red lights!

Shirley stomped her brake pedal with both feet. The Durango slid sideways, around Mykhaltso's truck, and screeched to a halt with the nose pointing at Ulyana's car.

Mykhaltso lowered his window and dangled Shirley's Ruger. He pitched it with the barrel pointed at her.

Shirley flinched.

The gun bounced.

Mykhaltso sped away.

CHAPTER 29

"I'm going to tell you straight up," Shirley said.

Donal stood beside her. He'd risen from the table upon seeing her enter the restaurant, and now held the back of her chair.

"Aside from being a laughingstock, I'm trouble. You don't want anything to do with me—"

A bearded man at an adjacent table glanced at her. She couldn't read his hidden mouth, but his shriveled, bloodshot eyes were piqued.

"Mind your own bee's knees."

Shirley turned to Donal.

Donal motioned her to sit. She sat.

"I'm a woman with an appetite for mischief. When I have a bad day, I'm a slobbering wretch. And lately when I have a good day, people die. I don't have baggage. I have a caravan."

Donal returned to his seat.

"I'm north of overweight. Doctor says I'll die young. I hate myself and love myself. I don't take garbage from nobody. Well, being honest, I take lots, but you won't ever know from one minute to the next whether I will or won't. If you guess wrong, I'll hold it against you. Or not. My choice."

"Whoa. What are we doing here? Let's have dinner. You don't need to account for anything."

"I'm trying to say I'm unpredictable—and here's the straight dope on why you don't want nothing to do with me."

He leaned.

She leaned.

A pretty waitress with a button nose and button boobs arrived. She smiled.

"Go away," Shirley said.

Server smiled bigger. Turned.

Donal raised his eyebrows. Leaned even closer. "You were saying something about straight dope?"

Shirley glanced left and right. "I've been with more men than Tiger Woods."

Donal sat up. "Isn't he straight? I mean—"

"You didn't let me finish. More than he's been with women. By ten thousand. I made a career of sleeping with men. And other assorted sundries."

The bearded man dropped his fork on his plate. Looked away.

"Yeah, look away, you. Hey, I know you. I did you a couple times— Mitch? Frank? What was your name? You've got a birthmark on your ass and a pecker so skinny I wanted to pick my teeth."

The man tossed his napkin and stood. Huffed. The man left.

Donal said, "Sundries?"

"I keep a mental folder for my pretentious words. *Ergo.* That's my favorite. *Per se.* I don't get to use sundries as often. I drop them in sometimes when I'm nervous. SO.... this is nice, you asking me to dinner, but I'm bad news. And I only came because I need a favor."

Donal's corrugated face gave away nothing. He hadn't gotten up and left, so that said something. Maybe one out of a hundred thousand men would see a woman behind the front.

"Okay," Donal said. "I'm hooked. I want to know how the story comes out."

"What story? There's no story."

"Sure there is. You didn't lay all that out because you want to play me. You're being honest. You might have a favor to ask, but you're interested. I can see it. You're laying a foundation."

"Yeah, that's all I'm laying. Like I said. We're not building anything. I spent thirty years servicing men for money. I've had enough wood—

pardon my French—to stock a shipyard."

"I've been with one woman in my life."

Shirley closed her open mouth. Blinked. "Yeah, see. I don't even know how that works. You're probably all up tight. Scoot your eyeballs to the wall when people kiss on television."

"No. Just loyal."

"Earlier, you said you was married. She died of cancer."

"High school sweetheart."

"Then what? Kids?"

"Never happened. We didn't try to force it."

"Then what?"

"Well, we were married from age eighteen to forty nine. I'm fifty eight. We already discussed how she died."

Shirley grimaced. "I don't know what to say."

"No need to say anything. I had the best years of my life with her. I won't replace her. But I want to keep living. She'd want me to."

Shirley studied the weave of the table cloth. "Do you miss her?"

"Yes. But that's the funny thing. After a long enough time, you start to feel like things are the way they are. I miss her, but I miss the time with her. The moment. I miss who we were and what we did together. I'm not angry any more. I accept she's gone."

Button boobs returned. "Still thinking about your order? Would you like to hear today's specials? Can I get you anything to drink, to start?"

Shirley said, "Donal, what do you say? Want to order?"

"Sure. On the positive side, we won't talk as much. Go ahead, if you know what you want."

"I haven't looked at the menu. But I'm feeling adventurous. Bring me today's special—so long as it isn't fish."

"And to drink?"

"Water."

"And for you?"

Donal nodded. "I'll have what she's having."

The server left.

Donal cleared his throat. "So what's the favor?"

"Thank you. I'm not the touchy-feely type. I don't know how to—you know—show compassion very well."

"Sometimes silence is compassionate. The favor?"

"My friend. She's disappeared. She helped me with a couple things. You used to be a homicide cop?"

"In Phoenix. Retired with thirty."

"Were you any good at it?"

"I cleared my share."

"Do you do any work on the side. Like, you know. Magnum P.I.?"

"No."

"Well my friend is a stripper. She disappeared. She knows some dangerous people and I don't know exactly where to start. Like, can you run fingerprints?"

"No. Do you have fingerprints?"

"How do I get them? See, there's a whole world out there I need help with."

"Let's go back to the beginning. How do you know she's missing?"

"She didn't show up when we were supposed to go do something together."

"Okay. So here's a plan. We can't find her right now. Let's enjoy our dinner, and when we're done, we go someplace we can talk. Outside, or something. I'll see if I know anything that can help you find your friend."

THEY SAT ON A SIDEWALK BENCH. Donal crossed his arms at his belly. "She surprised me, you know. Bringing out the deep fried catfish."

"People don't listen."

"It was good."

"Yeah. Except I didn't want fish."

"So, back to Ulyana. It could be the Russians. They told you where they moved the car. That doesn't really mean anything, one way or the other. Second, it could be the dead drug lord. Or third, the fellow who beat you up. And you beat him up."

"Right."

"Anyone else you can think of?"

"No."

"Okay. So what help did you want from me? What do you need?"

"The Russians told me where they dumped her car. I thought you could take prints and do, you know, what cops do at a car."

"I'm retired. Cops don't like retired cops getting in their way."

"What way? They aren't involved at all. And don't you wish you were still on the job? Making a difference?"

"Sometimes. But I have the gun store now. That makes a difference. You need to report Ulyana missing, before anything else. The real police can do a whole lot more than a retired cop and a wannabe."

"They're not going to do anything to find a stripper working for a drug lord."

Donal closed his eyes. She watched his face. His mouth remained flat. His chest filled with air. He released the breath. Opened his eyes. "Okay. Let's find Ulyana. But you need to know one thing."

"What?"

"She's probably dead."

"I know. But if she isn't, we need to get her back."

"Can you take me to the vehicle tomorrow morning?"

"Yes."

I have a couple errands first thing. But if you pick me up around ten we can check out Ulyana's car."

CHAPTER 30

With her eyes on the road and her hands upon the Durango steering wheel, Shirley shot a quick look to Donal. "This thing's supposed to go where?"

"Between your bosoms."

"I love that word."

"Rightly so. Don't get me wrong, the holster works just fine on your hip. But I made it for your, uhm, bountiful, bodacious—"

"That's so sweet, thank you."

"Just tuck it right—"

"I get it. Thank you."

Donal studied the scene out the side window. Adjusted how the seatbelt crossed his sport coat. "I checked out Heregger. He's not your guy. He was in the hospital until yesterday morning."

"Damn. After Ulyana disappeared."

"Right. Lucky for you, he declined to press charges. He didn't take Ulyana, but he'll be a problem for you, later."

"How did you find that out? About the charges?"

"Some of the guys on the force up here used to be on the force in Phoenix. I'm a retired cop. We're friendly, you know. If we see something, we pass it along. Makes it easy to shake hands and ask questions."

"Oh."

"I also reported Ulyana missing."

Shirley flinched. Thumped the steering wheel. "I can't believe you did that! I told you I didn't want to be mixed up in this, as far as the law is concerned."

Donal kept his eyes forward.

She looked at him. "You aren't going to say anything?"

"I guess duty comes first."

"Before loyalty. And keeping your word? I can't believe this." Shirley shook her head. Drove a mile. "Well, I bet they didn't care anyhow."

"Not true. She's a missing person like any other. She'll be treated the same way. A detail has already been assigned."

"What did you tell them?"

"Everything you told me."

"Just ducky."

Shirley turned at the open warehouse gate. "So I guess when I round this corner I'll see a bunch of Flagstaff's finest, investigating the scene."

Shirley braked and turned. She stopped beside Ulyana's car.

"Wow, just swimming with cops. CSI. FBI. Even your wonderful Alcohol, Tobacco, and Guns. All you super-concerned law people."

"Wonder if I gave the wrong address."

"They know this warehouse. Everybody does. They don't care, because Ulyana's a stripper."

She parked the Durango and turned off the engine. Donal opened the door.

"Don't touch anything," he said. "All we can do is observe what's in plain sight."

He exited. Shirley climbed out and pointed. "The window is shot out, and there's blood on the arm rest."

"You said the Russians told you they moved this, right?"

Shirley nodded.

The door was ajar. Donal yanked out his shirt tail. Placed it between finger and metal and pulled open the door.

That's what you did, girl! You got skills!

"That's interesting."

"What?"

"No glass."

"I saw that too. That means whoever fired was inside. But Ulyana didn't have a gun. Unless she found one, somewhere."

"Lots of variables. It's just as likely the gun was fired while the door was open. Maybe during a struggle."

Shirley slumped against the Durango. "Ulyana could be dead."

His face softened. "That was always a possibility."

"What else do you see? What about the blood?"

"There's not much of it. That's from a scratch."

"Then she could be alive?"

"Right now, she could be dead or alive. She could have just wandered off somewhere. We don't know. But if someone took her, no. I don't want to sound callous, but if some guy grabbed her and she's still alive, she won't be for long. Bad guys tie things off."

Shirley wiped the corner of her eye.

"But this is helpful information. This is helpful," Donal said. "I'm going to make a phone call, make sure the PD knows the location of the vehicle."

Donal fished a cell phone from his pocket and walked away. His voice started out low, but grew more insistent. He gestured with his free hand. After a moment he returned his phone to his pocket but continued staring into the distance.

He turned.

"Can't do anything more here. Can't risk contaminating the scene. Let's go to where you found the car, before it was moved."

SHIRLEY PARKED at the Pink Panther. She walked with Donal across the lot and road. Her legs ached from the hundred miler she put in around the trailer park, a couple days back. But through the discomfort, she noticed an improvement. Not more energy. More desire.

"Here's where Ulyana's car was. See the glass, and over here, there was a bullet. Somewhere."

"A shell casing?"

"There. In the weeds. See it?"

Donal removed his cell phone. Snapped photos of the glass and brass.

"Could we get a sammich bag from the club?"

Donal reached into his jacket pocket. "I happen to have brought an evidence bag."

"A second ago you were smiling. Now you quit. Why?"

"Nothing."

He lifted the shell casing with a pen and dropped it in the bag.

"You're not telling the truth. What's up?"

He frowned. "The location of the brass, compared to everything else. The glass is over here, so this is where Ulyana's driver's side door was. The shell casing is here. Behind the back of the car."

"So?"

"Pistols eject from the right."

Donal withdrew a firearm so fast she didn't see where he'd had it hidden.

"See? If I'm standing here, and fire the gun, it ejects the brass out this port, and lands over here." He pointed to the grass where he'd bagged the shell casing. "Who ever fired the gun was standing back here, not up there."

"She could have taken his gun and shot from there."

"Then she never would have been missing to begin with."

"I don't understand why this matters. There still isn't any blood except on the car. So what if he shot through the window from back there?"

"I agree."

"So why make a big deal?"   ·

"I didn't. I just quit smiling for a second." His brows locked tight around his eyes, bunched at the middle. "You're taking everything I say like some grand pronouncement. Ease up."

Ease up. Just go be a woman somewhere. Let the men handle it. Go knit a sweater.

"I'm gonna find who did this. I'm not going to stop. If she's dead or alive I'm not going to stop. This is what the REVOLUTION is all about. Not quitting. Adversity can go to hell. If someone doesn't stand up and say the little people are people too, then everybody just thinks... I don't know. Whatever nonsense they already got in their heads. Don't look at me like that! This world's insane, and the only way to change it is to change me. And for you to change you. Can't you see that?"

"Now I'm the problem? Try to help a—"

"Woman? You don't even hear me. I've got to stop being a person who does nothing when a good person would do something. I can't call other people the problem unless I call myself the problem first. That's why I have to find Ulyana."

Donal's mouth was flat. "You need to let the police deal with this."

"That's how we do it, all the time. Not my problem. We got other people for that. The police. The army. The doctors. The parents. Always somebody else we can point at. If they just did their jobs. I'm saying no! It's all our jobs. A woman goes missing, the whole damn world ought to stop rotating. But look at this. Crime scene, right here. Where's the police? The doctors? The politicians?"

"The police will come."

"When it damn well suits them—and long after they could have done anything that changes the outcome."

"Well, they're equipped for this, and you're not. Shirley—what have you done—"

"Gotta have a pedigree to give a damn, nowadays? World gone to hell in a basket and you want a college diploma to say I'm not going to be the problem anymore?"

"You aren't equipped to solve—"

"I'm not trying to solve! I'm trying to prevent. If Ulyana's alive, I want her to stay that way!"

"That's not—"

"I've had it with bullies. Look at me? What? I'm fat? Stupid? A woman? Forty—ish? Only qualified citizens get to care about how degenerate their society's become? So they can pass the buck of doing something to the official office of doing something, which never does nothing?"

"You're taking everything I say and—"

"Finishing it with the truth before you can spin it to a lie. Donal, it was nice of you to help. But I'm so pissed. I'm going to figure this out on my own. You take your baggie back to the police. I'll even drive you. But this thing in me—I'm fighting to keep it alive and you're trying to smother it. It shouldn't take a rebel to give a damn."

Donal's mouth remained part open. He closed it. Snapped several photos of the road, the Pink Panther, and a couple more of the broken glass.

He turned. "Well, I guess that's it."

CHAPTER 31

D usk.

Lester sat in his Dodge Ram with the headlights off but the engine running. He looked at the concrete ramp leading inside the warehouse. Sunlight lit the first few yards, but beyond, blackness. The other bay doors—set four feet high on the dock, to meet backed-in tractor trailers—were closed.

Long ago, workers used the concrete ramp to drive forklifts and other vehicles in and out of the warehouse.

Nostalgia.

The company that owned the warehouse went bankrupt in 1990. Receivership trustees in New York, to save the greater business, attempted to amputate the western operation. They sought to sell the building and property to other grocers with stores in the area. Those other grocers already had warehouses. So the receivers tried selling the albatross to regional grocers interested in expanding into Northern Arizona. But by late 1990, businesses sniffed the next recession.

Lester had cash in the basement, in boxes, waiting to be used as payment for fake services through one of his front businesses. The money from those businesses flowed into various checking accounts. He bought things and sold things. Mixed the cash around the economy until no government accountant could ever discern the origin.

One of Lester's earliest insights about money came to him when he was looking for new ways to launder drug cash.

Contrary to what his high school teachers said, money didn't retain value. Folks defined money as a store of value—but when the feds control the printing press, and nothing backs the currency but the integrity of the charlatans in Washington, currency leaks value like a sieve.

Hard assets were much better at storing value. Houses. Cars. Antiques. Lester bought them all, not even guessing they'd appreciate. So long as they didn't lose value, they'd be three percent per year ahead. And if a market existed that would facilitate the sale of the asset in a reasonably short time, such as a month, why bother holding cash?

Day to day spending. His go-bag. No other reason.

Lester always kept an eye out for property that promised to retain value.

The warehouse failed that test. Internal rate of return was negative. But the external return, hard to calculate the benefit. A great ecosystem lived inside. Cops stayed away. Corpses piled up in the back room. A population of users and pushers flourished. All great for business.

By the time Lester considered buying, homeless had occupied the building at least eighteen months. Spray paint everywhere. Excrement. Waste. Ramshackle apartments made of pallet wood and outdoor debris, treehouses in the pallet racks. In Lester's estimation, no new company would be interested. Cleaning would be a multi-million dollar project.

The warehouse never sold. Lester stopped keeping track, but eventually curiosity bit. He dug through some newspapers. The receiver eventually thrust the warehouse on another business that held debt of the bankrupt grocer. As if a warehouse filled with bodies and drug addicts was fungible.

Lester imagined some arm twisting went into that deal.

The warehouse became a community, filled with bands of homeless, drug addicts and runaways. Lester enjoyed the lawlessness. Police didn't venture inside, in the beginning. Once they did, they didn't care. City government, slipped a little cash, questioned the wisdom of removing the homeless from the shelter they preferred, only to send them to another, on the city dime, that they didn't.

Homeless folks built dwellings in the product racks, thirty feet high and a three hundred feet long. Bleeding hearts tried, from time to time, to provide assistance. One group tried to raise money to install sun lights, of all things. The effort died. Others attempted to teach the warehouse dwellers about hygiene, and gave pep talks about how to write resumes and find jobs.

Eventually the area developed a reputation; indigents in Phoenix and Tucson heard about the warehouse in Flag, if they ever passed through.

It was the kind of thing Lester Toungate could spend a great deal of time thinking about.

Lester exited his truck. Checked the handle—locked. He entered via the ramp with his .357 in his right hand and a flashlight in his left.

In his pocket, a Ziploc baggie.

He entered the darkness. The hair on the back of his neck stood. Always stood, entering the human wild.

The only sound came from grit underfoot. Lester directed his flashlight toward the pallet racks, and dragged the expanded beam of light across them, from left to right. Domiciles everywhere, but no faces.

"I got Barbs. Phennies," Lester said. "Tooies. Hell, I got Christmas Trees. All yours, for some information."

He listened.

Lester directed his flashlight to the far corners of the warehouse, slowly scanning the reach of light into the darkness. The old-style twelve volt lantern illuminated the first thirty yards, but beyond, shadows.

Warehouse dwellers never came out, at first. Took a little encouragement. Lester holstered his .357.

"Ahhh."

He caught a trace of the scent of rotting flesh.

Any society that survives very long finds a way to deal with its dead. Especially communities made up of societies unwanted, the homeless, and especially the drug addicts.

The original warehouse had been constructed as a rectangle. Business was good. The firm bought additional grocery stores, which created the need for additional warehouse space, to hold the goods to stock them. They knocked down part of the wall in the back and added floor space equal to half of the original. Business continued to be good, they acquired still more stores, and needed more space. For the second expansion, however, instead of knocking down walls, the designers left them in place. The new addition was closed off, except for two giant bay doors, tall enough to allow forklifts to enter, and wide enough for two to pass side by side.

Twenty-five percent of the entire warehouse could be closed off.

Lester thought when he brought Paul there to dispose of their first corpse together, the warehouse dwellers would quickly learn from his example, and utilize the back quarter for their bone fields. But when he drove his truck inside to dump the body, and pulled the chain to roll up the door, his headlights shined on a dozen dead indigents in varying decay.

The quarter of the warehouse containing the bodies was perpendicular to the opening Lester entered through. Although the doors remained closed, warehouse dwellers preferred to live opposite that part of the building.

Lester turned to his right and walked beside the cement block wall. He wondered at how much grit accumulated underfoot, when the people living there had to cross a quarter-mile of blacktop to reach the entrance.

A shadow moved.

Lester halted. Aimed the light.

If one of them was in front of him, Lester knew from experience another would be approaching from the side, and another from the rear. That is why it took a little while to engage them. They had to set up their ambush.

"I got the drugs. I also got bullets, and a few questions. Come on up boys, let's work something out."

Lester stopped walking, turned his back to the block wall. He stepped 5 feet forward and placed the lantern on the floor. He returned to the wall, and waited.

No one came from the source of original motion. That person was a decoy. Two forms approached from Lester's hard left, following him. As they neared he discerned instruments in their hands. The warehouse boys liked torque wrenches, from the maintenance section.

They neared.

"I'm the one who comes around, time to time." Lester tossed the baggie of drugs so it landed close to the lantern. "I want you both to stand on the other side of that lamp. Stand together. If I see movement on the sides, I know you're up to no good and I start shooting."

The two figures became men. Their beards and hair were tangled; their clothes ripped and filthy, stinking of old sweat and rot. They moved like predators. These men were strong. The enforcers always ate better.

They walked to where Lester directed, and stopped. The one on the left turned and glanced around them, then faced Lester and smiled. The gleeful madman. He placed his hands at his groin, and holding the wrench, swung it back and forth.

The other man held his wrench at his side, and stared.

"There was a car found here, a few days ago. See it?"

The man on the left cleared his throat. Grinned.

"What can you tell me?"

"There was..." He coughed. "There was two cars. Which you mean?"

"Both."

The man placed his wrench on his shoulder and scratched his head. "First was a week ago. Same as comes here every month."

"You see what happened?"

A nod.

"How were they killed?"

"Shot."

Lester nodded. "You see who? Was it the same people they met every time?"

The man shook his head sideways. "New people."

Interesting. He spoke of a drug meet El Jay had told Lester about, their men getting hit. Even if the mules weren't killed by the same men they met every time, they were killed by someone who knew the meet was taking place. Someone on the inside was connected.

"Okay. You get a look? What they look like?"

The man shrugged. "One was dark hair. Other kind of gray."

It would have been nice to have been able to show them photographs of Lester and Paul, but Lester was not sentimental. He had no images of his sons.

"White pants. The man with dark hair had white pants."

El Jay.

Lester absorbed the information. Confirmation that at least one of his sons had mutinied. He already had good information that Paul had also been making a move. This last bit of information confirmed they were working together to unseat their father. Each probably had a plan to dispose of his brother, following. Lester nodded, smiled. At least he taught them something.

The man answering the questions stepped toward the bag of pills.

"Not yet. Tell me about the second car."

Another shrug. "Two girls."

Lester nodded.

"They came in two cars and left one parked beside the one from before."

"Just leave it?"

"Nah. Burned. Smoke cleared us out."

"Then what?"

"Police came."

"Yeah? How long?"

"Next day."

Lester drifted in thought. How would the police know to come, unless they were tipped? Or involved.

Ahh—several pieces of the puzzle clicked.

FBI agent Smith was setting up Lester. He didn't have to tell him about his son. Didn't have to drop Shirley Lyle's name. The FBI wouldn't even be involved in a homicide case unless it was connected to something big enough to grab a couple headlines, if they got arrests.

Lester had assumed it was a RICO case—but this made more sense. Besides, with RICO, he'd have seen them tailing him. Snapping pictures and the like.

If Joe Smith was off the reservation with this investigation, it was because he was involved—or he had a beef with Shirley Lyle.

"What did the girls look like?"

"Fat. Skinny."

Lester nodded. "Skinny girl have blonde hair? Nice rack?"

The man held Lester's stare. His teeth glowed white.

"Thank you for your candor. Go ahead." Lester nodded toward the Ziploc baggie. "Take it, and move back a ways."

Remaining close to the wall, Lester exited the warehouse.

CHAPTER 32

S hirley stood on Ulyana's front patio with a key in her hand. The board under her left foot bowed. She shifted to her right foot and dragged her left backward. The gray paint had long ago flaked, leaving the exposed wood to rot.

Shirley reached forward with the key and froze.

The metal door's paint was marred. The dented edge gapped at the jamb. Someone had pried it open.

A chill shot down Shirley's back. She reached for her hip and realized she'd holstered the Ruger farther north, in the mountains. She yanked her shirt from the collar, snatched her Ruger from under her bra, where it rode her left breast, and allowed her pistol hand to hang free at her side.

Shirley sniffed. Gazed. Twisted to the left. She observed the stillness. Her vision tunneled and all her focus shifted forward in her mind. She became aware of herself in this precise, tingling location of space-time.

Hair stood on her neck.

She rotated a full circle, observing minutia. Madge Wilson unloaded groceries. A boy rode an old banana-seat bicycle that squeaked each time the warped part of the wheel rotated past the fender. One of the newer neighbors had a Porsche. It sat there, red. Sexy.

Confident no one would rush her from behind, Shirley pushed the nose of the Ruger into the door. The latch clicked open.

They killed Ulyana and now they're here to kill you.

"I know that."

Why are we going inside?

"We're sick of being killed. Get Viva Shirley. I need her."

Shirley blinked three times and kicked out with her right foot. The door slammed open. She lowered her pistol hand and followed through with the weight of the kick, sliding sideways into the trailer. Snapped her Ruger arm level with the hallway, held at a forty-five degree gangsta tilt.

"What do I do, Viva?"

Listen.

Nothing.

If someone's here to kill you, he'll be down the hallway, in Ulyana's room. Or in the rooms behind you.

"Gee, the whole trailer. Thanks."

Ruger SR40c aimed at the opposite hallway, Shirley twisted her head to the right. Wrinkled her brow.

In case you haven't figured it out yet, I'm not your secret superhero power. I can't sense things you don't sense. I don't have x-ray vision.

"Yeah, but you're smarter than me."

Well... Yeah.

"So what do I do now?"

Clear the house. Room by room. You've seen television. Get to work!

Shirley stepped toward the hallway.

No! Closest rooms first!

She. Nimble as possible, she approached the first bedroom door. She grabbed the knob with her left hand and pointed the Ruger. Glanced to her right. A bathroom, door closed. And at a right angle, a short wall and the door to the second bedroom.

She played a scenario in her mind. If she opened the door of the first bedroom and went inside to clear it, anyone in the bathroom or second bedroom could trap her inside. Grease her with a machine gun. Starve her out. Burn the trailer down around her.

She pushed open the door, and keeping her body in the hallway, peeked inside.

Ulyana's junk. Lamp seemed in the right place. A desk with a journal. Books—always the same. Philosophy, religion, physics, apologetics. Shirley didn't know what Ulyana thought she needed to apologize for. A chair with part of the cushion worn away, exposing dirty-yellow foam. A stain on the carpet where someone spilled a red-hued soft drink. Wine? Maybe in Russia they didn't have good stain cleaners. Or Philadelphia. Another reason to stick with ice and clear-colored spirits—

Focus!

Shirley closed the door, stepped to her right, and opened the bathroom door.

Empty—but someone had recently left skid marks inside the toilet bowl.

Break in, leave a nasty mess in someone else's toilet. The mark of a real asshole.

"Focus, Viva." Shirley smiled.

She closed the door. Pivoted and opened the second bedroom.

Empty...

Shirley looked at the closet. She glanced back, into the living room. So far, no one had charged out of the master bedroom on the other side of the kitchen. She had a moment.

Shirley rushed the closet—flung open the door—stood to the side with her Ruger pointed—

Nothing.

She clamped her teeth. Nostrils flared. Her assassin had to be across the trailer, other side. Master bedroom. Or master bath.

You're about to break this wide open! Whoever took Ulyana is here for you. Go kill his ass, and we'll save Ulyana.

"How will I know where Ulyana is?"

Ask him, then kill him.

"Okay."

Shirley looked at her Ruger. White on top. White on the side.

She flipped off the safety. Racked it.

Red and red.

She stepped into the living room, around the dining room divider, and through the kitchen.

"Keeping things on the up and up, whoever you are, as soon as you tell me where you put Ulyana, I'm going to kill your sorry ass."

Nice. Maybe you should kill him, and then tell him.

Shirley stood motionless. Would she kill him? Saying you're going to do something nasty, and actually doing it, were two different things. She remembered once telling her son Brass, when he was nine, if he used foul language in the house again she'd beat his ass raw. She was in a mood. He stuck his tongue out, which was the same as cussing, in her mind. She swatted, caught his arm and lifted him off the ground.

She stayed her hand. Couldn't do it.

Brass cavorted. Wriggled—his arm hurt, hanging by it—and she knew she had to follow through on what she'd said, or her son would know she'd never validate a threat.

Yeah, kill the assassin. Then he'll trust you.

"This is the bastard who took Ulyana."

Shirley twisted the knob and shoved wide the door.

There! Inside...

Nothing.

Shirley became aware of a giant gulp of air trapped in her lungs. She burped it out. Lowered her gun arm. Planted hands on hips.

"I would have *so* killed him."

She shook her head.

The closet! Under the bed! Behind the bed! Check it out!

Shirley eased into the room. She lifted her gun hand again and rotated from left to right, stopping with the pistol trained on the closet door. She stepped forward and reached with her left hand, and stopped, her finger-tips a quarter inch from the knob.

She listened.

Nothing.

She flung open the door!

"Aaaagggghhhh!"

She aimed, back and forth, up and down.

Nothing.

She shook her head. Sat on the edge of Ulyana's bed and her gaze drifted to a cordless phone on the night table. Shirley grabbed it. Pressed nine numbers. Hesitated. Pressed the tenth.

The phone buzzed.

"Hello?"

"Brass, this is your mother."

SHE REMINDED him about the thumb drive, and all that happened after-ward. How she'd found her spirit and started to soar. Or at least imagined what a little wind whipping about her clothes and hair might feel like. How she'd taken action! Beat the man who raped her—broke his face and arm. Put him in the hospital. And that was just the start.

"There was another guy I was spying on. He beat his wife. I met her at the women's self hate group, on Wednesday. She doesn't even know there's a different world possible. That's what VIVA the REVOLUTION is all about. Doing everything possible to make every single woman know—

"ARE YOU NUTS? You put a man in the hospital? How'd you know he wasn't going to kill you? Or won't, when he gets out?"

"I don't. I'll be ready and kill him first."

"You are nuts. What happened to you? You can't do this. You can't just be somebody else if you don't like who you are. You have to be who you are. And be happy with that. Or content with that."

"You know what I always did, right? You know how I made a living all those years. With men."

"Of course."

"And you want me to just be what I am and always have been. Relax in it."

"Ma. Ma! All this danger. Stress. Worrying about this guy killing you— because you're trying to be something you're not. You can't wink an eye and be a hero. It doesn't work that way. You've been acting so weird lately, like—"

"I want to matter? Even if only to me? A little damn bit."

"No, not *matter*. Of course you matter. But you're trying to be… you should stop trying to change… And let yourself… no! *Give yourself permission to* have lower expectations. It's not as bad as it sounds. Not that you don't try. But you let yourself fail. Because it doesn't hurt as much as getting killed. That's all. I love you."

Shirley lowered the receiver from her ear. She pressed the OFF button and tossed the cordless to the other side of the mattress.

She sat on the bed, with Ulyana's beat up dresser in front of her, the mirror on top reflecting her full, red-faced puffy ugliness.

Her chin trembled. Tears filled her eyes. She let them wash up from inside, and flow over with sorrow and ache. She had so much potential, when she was a kid. She blinked fast. Couldn't see for all the salt water. As a little kid. She was smart and could really see people. She was pretty, back then. Not fat pretty, and not "beautiful inside," but regular pretty. So many different things could have happened, except she messed them all up. A colossal failure. A wasted human. Nothing but one disaster after another. A prostitute. Unwed mother. Couldn't raise a supportive son. Couldn't save her best and only friend.

She cleared her throat. Succumbed to a moment of utter hopelessness —and spat phlegm to the carpet.

Looked at the gooey slimy mess and wept more, that she did it.

"I can't even get murdered!"

A new torrent of tears flooded her cheeks.

"I don't know how my life could get any worse."

Shirley, Shirley. Never say that...

Shirley blinked. Again. "Wait a minute." She wiped her eyes with her sleeve. "Wait a damn minute." She stared at Ulyana's dresser.

"If no one was waiting inside to kill me—why break open the front door?

Her eyes sprung wide. Her heart bounced into her throat and stopped there, trapped. Her brain slipped into the air and floated.

"Oh no. No. Not this. All my life I got nothing. Now I finally got something. Not this."

She looked in the closet at Ulyana's pink backpack, where she'd crammed her share of Lester Toungate's drug money.

Drug money? My dimpled derriere! Drug money. That's freedom money! VIVA the REVOLUTION money—for Ulyana. Money that says she never needs to shave another inch if she doesn't want.

The bag looked unmolested. Shirley nudged it with her foot. Sort of heavy—like a half million dollars.

Unless they swapped it out with newspapers.

Shirley tucked her pistol back into her bra. Realized it could fire.

Relax. Your boob doesn't have a trigger finger.

She worked to her knees and unzipped Ulyana's bag. Saw green. She studied the wrinkled bills, how some were dark with the oily dirt of ten thousand hands, and marveled at how they still had the same worth as a clean bill, straight from the bank.

"Well, Ulyana has her money."

Shirley zipped the backpack and positioned it behind a few long dresses that swooped to the carpet. Closed the closet.

What about your five hundred large?

In the living room she stood before the sofa, her head drifting back and forth. "Nobody took my money."

Sweat stood on her brow. She dragged her sleeve across. Closed her eyes.

"Nobody took my money."

She bent her right knee and with the sofa armrest for support, eased her left to the carpet. She followed with her right. Kneeling, she bent forward and rested her arms and head on the sofa cushion. She adjusted to a more comfortable position. Less weight on the kneecaps.

"Dear God, I don't talk to You enough. I don't know any hymns—but only because I don't know any. I'm a jerk. A broken, brazen Jezebel like the woman you wanted her bones eaten by the dogs. I was flipping through and saw that. I'm like her. Just horrible. But if you could overlook all my sins and transgressions... and let me keep the money we stole... I'll give away half to the poor. Or that pastor on TV—Benny. No? If that don't please, I'll find a homeless guy or something. Some orphans."

Shirley closed her mouth. Ground her head back and forth, pressing into the cushion. Squeezed out stress-tears. Imagined herself dead broke, no home, no friend, no skills but making men's eyes roll back in their heads.

She lifted from the sofa. Pushed upright. Sniffled.

"No, I won't give away half. You know it, and I won't lie. I want that money. Why not me? That's what I want to know. Why the hell not me for a change?"

Shirley shifted to the side of the sofa, bent, grabbed the base, heaved it forward. She braced on the armrest and leaned over the back.

She studied the empty space a long time.

CHAPTER 33

Head crushed against the pillow, Lester struggled for air. He pushed —but his arms were weak against her flesh. Like being in a dream, running in slow motion. What flesh he shifted away was replaced by more.

His empty lungs burned. His diaphragm was unable to move. Lester tried to kick but her flesh pinned his legs. Without being able to breathe, he smelled baby powder.

Delicious, divine irony, he realized, that he would die under a whale. Not inside one, like Jonah. In Lester's grasping, flailing awareness, he sensed the weakness of the irony. Jonah didn't die *inside* the whale. He escaped, bleached white, after three days.

Another divine let down.

Lester allowed his panic to ebb. This was it. Nothing grand or special. No weeping grandchildren. No pomp. In one sudden moment everything changed and he knew the clock had ticked down to his very last moments. He would die with all the ceremony of a cat fart.

Held motionless, powerless, his lungs collapsing and his greatest realizations as yet inchoate, Lester knew he was powerless against the cosmic injustice. The darkness overwhelmed.

Lester submitted.

A sound—like a shutter croaking in the wind.

Was he on the other side, already? No dreamy film; no river Styx. No warriors. No virgins. Would he wake up reincarnated as a worm?

The sound, again.

Wait a minute! Why could he breathe? Enough!

Lester opened his eyes. Inhaled, hard.

Shirley turned black and slipped into mental shadows.

There! Again! So faint he almost imagined it... the sound—

Automatic, he rolled, ejected his leg from under the covers and slid his body after. He stood and without a sound lifted his .357 magnum from the lamp table. Lester crept to his bedroom door. His hand drifted to his chest, where a moment ago, he dreamed it crushed under the weight of Shirley Lyle.

He paused, grateful to be alive. No one to thank.

The sound... like something created by the wind except Lester believed more in men. It came from inside the house. Lester rotated the door knob. He felt the silent twitch of the latch spring.

Lester stepped aside. He raised his pistol arm level with his belly, with the nose pointed at the aperture.

The hallway opened to a great room, lit by moonlight that entered through the upper windows. The lower were curtained. Lester glanced backward. His bedroom was black. He was invisible.

Had Shirley Lyle returned to finish a job she'd started at the burning trailer?

If so, was it time to kill her?

Lester considered. He had one exceedingly good reason to do so: she and Ulyana had stolen a million dollars from him. Had to be them.

But while he hated to lose the cash, the loss didn't create an existential threat.

What Shirley Lyle knew about his money laundering, and could prove with the thumb drive, did.

Killing her now was not the smart play. Unless things just worked out that way. It would be nice to move on to other problems.

Lester stepped forward, easing the ball of his bare foot to the hardwood floor. Fully in the hallway, he paused. No further sound issued before him.

Did he actually hear something? Or was it part of the dream?

Lester lowered his pistol.

He stepped forward again.

Click!

A flashlight beam splashed him in yellow. He shoved off with his right leg and hit the wall at the same moment orange sparked in front of him—another shot, and another—

Lester's arm jerked—grazed by another bullet. The other two penetrated his door with a soft splat sound. His assassin must have intended to cap Lester in his sleep, and only brought a .22. Lester grinned. He shook his right arm loose. Wondered why only three shots... Pistol jammed?

Or just another amateur?

With his left-arm pressed to the wall, he lifted his bullet-creased right arm and fired the .357, aiming one foot right of the tiny flash he'd seen. The pistol erupted in his hand and the flash lit the hallway.

Lester saw no one. Big girl could move.

She'd likely hidden behind the pine hutch. He could blast through it and be done, but he liked the heirloom.

Instead, Lester ducked into his bedroom. Turned on the light and in the massive closet, swung open an unlocked gun safe. It stood five feet tall, five wide, and six deep. The original guts of the safe had racks for dozens of rifles. Lester had long ago removed them. He spun the dial, ducked, entered, and pulled the door closed by a finger hole drilled into the interior metal wall. He groped in the darkness along the floor. Heard footsteps hurrying in the hallway.

Lester found a slot and pulled. The floor lifted up and away from him, revealing the dim glow of the basement, illuminated in scant moonlight from the twelve inch windows above the ground. He stepped to the stairs leading to the basement floor.

He'd gotten the idea from a documentary about Mexican cartels.

After five steps Lester's head was below the two by eight supports. He scanned the dim basement, then glanced to the twelve-inch windows above ground level. Necessary risks weren't worth pondering. He continued down.

Above him, heavy footsteps pounded across his bedroom, back and forth. In a moment his attacker would discover the air holes drilled into the safe, clues designed to lead to a conclusion, but not oversell it.

Pistol fire above. One after another. From the sound, his attacker shot at the air holes.

His feet found concrete.

Lester preferred an empty basement, and only located the water heater and oil furnace there. Kept navigation in the dark easy. He cocked his .357 and walked to the staircase leading to the kitchen. Glad for the 2 x 4 reinforcements that made the steps silent, Lester ascended to the kitchen door. He listened.

Nothing.

He pulled the door toward him, tight in the frame, and twisted the knob. Soundless. He pushed. Left it open. Walked left of the table, preserving him from the line of sight from his bedroom. Lester held his pistol in front and entered the hallway.

From his bedroom he heard footsteps, loud. Like a big woman.

Lester floated closer. He stopped shy of the door.

Gunfire! Sounded like a cap gun. Each pistol shot zinged with a secondary percussion. His adversary was firing into the gun safe. Six shots. A magazine release clicked.

Lester stepped into his bedroom.

A man spun. Threw up his hands.

Mykhaltso.

Lester fired, placing a red dot in Mykhaltso's chest. The Russian stood. Stared. Dropped forward.

Anything other than an instant execution risked a frenzied attempt at survival.

Lester watched blood expand on his floor.

As far as puzzle pieces went, this one placed pretty damn easy.

CHAPTER 34

Lester left the body of the dead Russian at the warehouse. Not because he'd been thinking about the warehouse, but because Vanko Demyan also sold drugs to the pallet dwellers. Mykhaltso's body showing up where the Russians did business would point suspicion more toward Vanko, and his enterprise, than Lester.

The sun rose as he returned home. Lester made coffee. Sat and pressed his eyes.

Though Shirley's latest attempt to kill him was a dream, and the bald Russian turned out to be real, Lester found himself pondering Shirley. One thing at a time. Of course he would have to revisit the big picture with Vanko. Their working relationship no longer existed. Vanko was likely behind El Jay's and Paul's treason. He was certainly behind Mykhaltso's attempt to kill him. While Lester spent endless time on the disaster called Shirley Lyle, Vanko waged war.

Well, fine. But first things first. He'd deal with Shirley Lyle, and Vanko Demyan next.

Shirley Lyle.

What he knew of her history didn't mesh with her success at stymieing him. In his eighty-three years, Lester had been familiar with several women of the night. Enjoyed a couple; offed a couple. From the sample, he felt confident extrapolating a few general insights.

Hookers were like dogs.

Not junkyard or working dogs.

They were like froufrou dogs, shampooed hair, pink toenails, bells on their necks just as annoying as their ear-dagger barks. Get one riled, it'll yip and nip until it gets its way or you pitch it through a window. No in-betweens.

But Shirley Lyle wasn't an ordinary hooker. She didn't yip and nip. She threw chairs and charged. You don't chuck Shirley Lyle through a window. And if you do get her down, she's Rocky Balboa. She gets up swinging.

While Vanko moved chess pieces, Shirley Lyle clasped her hands together and smashed through board and table.

Time to end Shirley Lyle.

Best thing would be to drive a vehicle not registered in his name and not associated with him in any way. That meant stealing one. Grand theft had never been Lester's style; he had no skills.

Instead: the next best thing. A car no one would recognize as his.

He pressed the garage door button, waited, and when the door cleared four feet, slid the shifter into reverse. The Toyota Prius hummed as he tapped the pedal and squirted onto the driveway. He stopped, looked over the vehicle's dashboard to refamiliarize himself.

The Prius was not his vehicle of choice for day to day duty. It was tiny. No horsepower, or at least nothing close to the torque his Ram boasted. It was robin's egg blue, gay as a jaybird—but a perfect cloak for a whiskered old drug man whose greatest affection in life was for a dog.

The plan?

Since her trailer burned, Shirley stayed with Ulyana. Lester paused at the thought of her. With all the action over the last couple of weeks, he'd had no satisfaction. He'd have to remedy that.

Shirley?

There was a thought. She made a living at sex, so there might be something in it for him. But tying her up and poking her would hardly shatter her psyche and make her confess the location of the thumb drive. And in that case, why bother?

Lester wasn't like other men. He only counted the women he killed.

Ulyana would be much better. First deal with Shirley. Then the prize. Lester wriggled his butt into the seat. Widened his legs and adjusted his mess.

He'd pick up Shirley at Ulyana's trailer and follow. Eventually, she'd lead him to his money, the thumb drive, or most likely, a place where he could nab her.

Take her to the warehouse?

No. If you want to extract information, you want privacy. And in this case, you want efficiency. You want to break her mind, get the memory stick, and be rid of the body.

You do that in a garage with pneumatic tools and a hydraulic lift.

Lester looked at a bag sitting on the passenger seat. Inside, a Taser, rope and duct tape.

Beside the bag, an Obama *HOPE > FEAR* baseball cap. Glasses with thick plastic rims.

Lester donned the garb and drove.

CHAPTER 35

The metal was warped where the money thief inserted a prybar. The door didn't close all the way and the latch no longer caught. Shirley slept all night on the sofa with Ruger in hand, propped toward the door. When dawn came she rolled her face into the back and put a pillow over her head. At last she rose, thinking she'd pee, mix a drink, and knock herself out.

Her elbow hurt. Her eyes were crusty with salt. Her money was gone.... But the perfect girl, who was missing and didn't even need the money, got to keep hers. And Shirley's son, thinking of the best she would ever be, told her to be happy being a hooker.

Her heart ached.

It's all the stress.

"I know."

Shirley searched Ulyana's cupboards. Had to be liquor somewhere. Ulyana was twenty-something. What twenty-something didn't have alcohol in the house? Shirley flung open the freezer. No ice cream. She opened the refrigerator. Carrots. Lettuce. Tomatoes. Bell peppers. Cucumbers. Kimchi. Organic-no-sweetener-added, plain vomit yogurt.

That's the difference between self love and self hate. Doesn't matter if you strip or screw, you respect yourself or you don't.

She grabbed a bottle of water. After all night crying, friendless, money-less, jobless… she was dehydrated.

Shirley accidentally slammed the refrigerator door.

"I should go out tonight. Blow off some steam. Find a bar and spend some of Ulyana's never-have-to-shave money."

Bad idea.

She took three steps toward Ulyana's bedroom, to see if she was convinced.

Not really.

But no harm in washing the salt off her face. She went to the bathroom and stood in front of the mirror. Studied the splotchy red marks on her forehead. And neck. The puffiness of her cheeks. Swelling around her eyes. White bandage on her chin, yellow at the edge, needing replaced. Probably smelled like Gettysburg under there.

What the hell was that?

Shirley marched to the front door.

It opened.

"Maddix."

He smiled. Winced. A sling held his broken arm. With the other, he pointed a pistol at her.

"Ahhh, shit. I don't have time for this. I'm trying to get drunk for breakfast."

Maddix wrinkled his face.

"I should have smothered you when I had the chance. Hey, dammit. I want my money back."

How many years have you been servicing this asshole?

"Five, at least."

"What?"

"Shut up, Maddix."

So think about all the times he pinched hard enough to leave a bruise. The punches. The insults. Humiliation. Taunts and manipulation. Mental torment. Time spent crying in the bathroom, after he left.

"You know what, Maddix? You shouldn't have come here, your head all bandaged up and arm broke." *You're a weak ass man. Even with the gun.* "You're a weak ass man. Even with that stupid gun."

Shirley eased her hand to her breast. No Ruger.

The couch!

Maddix coughed. "Step away from the door. Back up." He waved his pistol, but when the gesture was done, the barrel still pointed at her chest. "You made a big mistake, woman."

"I'm a big girl. I make them."

She remembered Maddix the last time... every time... how he used words to break her down, before he used his fists.

He brought a gun because you crushed his ribs. Ulyana broke his head. And his arm. Fuck him up! You can do this!

Shirley stepped back and shifted left, hiding her arm behind the open door.

Maddix stepped forward. Shirley caught his look and smiled with clenched teeth. She slammed the door on his foot, catching it on the rebound and slamming it again. Metal thunked. His gun?

"Ahh! You bitch!"

Maddix grabbed her arm with his left hand while his right arm dangled in the cast. His eyes were bloodshot and his forehead glistened with oily sweat. He drove the top of his skull into her, and shifting to the side, his shoulder. Air popped from her lungs. He drove her back. She stutter-stepped and toppled.

Shirley swung her arm toward the Ruger, just beyond reach.

Maddix punched her belly with his good arm.

Two super powers! You can float and take a fist to the gut!

He drove his fist into her belly again.

Shirley heaved with her thighs—lifting her weight and his—and lurched farther onto the couch. She grabbed the Ruger. It felt righteous.

Red on top.

Maddix reared a few inches and drove his forehead to her sternum. He punched her temple.

Shirley blanked.

He punched her head again, shooting fireworks through her mind.

"This next one..." Maddix pressed his face to Shirley's. She breathed in coffee. Cologne. "This one is going to end your misery."

He pulled back his fist.

Shirley twisted her eyeballs.

Red on the side.

Shirley drove the Ruger SR40c to Maddix Heregger's ribs and squeezed the trigger. The pistol barked. Bounced back. Maddix punched again, with all his force. He wrestled with more fury.

She squeezed the trigger again. Again—and wondered if a bullet could bounce from his bones and kill her.

Maddix slacked from her, mouth open, air escaping. His open eyes were already empty. She pushed. He slumped away.

Shirley climbed to her feet, still aiming the Ruger. Her heart jumped and pounded.

Maddix Heregger's blood dripped from his shirt and expanded into Ulyana's carpet. His face seemed to lighten in color, his eyes fixed on a carpet stain.

"Imagine that. The last thing you see as your miserable life evaporates is this nasty carpet."

Shirley kicked him. "You killed Ulyana! Then came back for me! Right?"

Yeah! Kick him! Wait a minute. No! He was in the hospital when Ulyana disappeared.

"Damn! That's right. Couldn't have been him."

So you don't get to give up.

"I didn't give up!"

No, you just punched the refrigerator and cried. Thought about killing yourself because the money you stole got stole back. All because Brass told you to be happy being yourself.

"Being a whore."

You said that. Not him. And Donal got his words tangled up trying to say the same thing. Like either one of them knows you better than you.

"Look at this face!" Shirley pointed. "Does this look like a face that's going to save the world? What kind of future do you see in this beat-up mug?"

Shirley-babe. Don't be silly.

"What?"

Your face doesn't show the future. It shows the past.

Shirley flinched like she'd been slapped. "Holy shit, Viva! What you said!"

So pull yourself together! Ulyana's still out there. If she isn't dead she's alive, and that means something!

Shirley looked at her Ruger. Noticed the red on top and red at the safety—both indicating the gun was ready to fire. She pushed the selector to the white dot and placed the barrel to her nose. Inhaled the acrid stink of burned powder. Wished she'd thought of smelling it right after she pulled the trigger three times.

We go back to the starting point. There was a gunshot outside the Pink Panther.

"Someone heard something."

You need to beat it out of them.

"If I have to kill them."

Okay, but not first. Kill them after.

CHAPTER 36

Vanko Demyan motioned Burian Tkach—Mykhaltso's new temporary roommate—forward.

"You find Mykhaltso?"

"No."

"You check the club. And his room?"

A nod.

Vanko lowered his eyes. Mykhaltso hadn't served in the Russian special forces, Spetsnaz. Still, he toted an infantry rifle and knew how to handle himself. His punctuality never deviated from perfect. The man's life revolved around service to Vanko.

Protocol was, report the job complete. Immediately. If Mykhaltso didn't show by the next morning, he was dead.

Burian halted five feet from Vanko's desk and stood with arms loose at his sides. One leg a little forward. A fighter stance.

Vanko sipped coffee and studied Burian.

Gray hair. Wrinkled face, cut by a scar across his cheek to the edge of his mouth. A medium-sized man who carried himself like more. Burian got off the boat three days ago. From the stories, he would have been a better man for the task than Mykhaltso. Burian's years in the KGB, followed by his years in private security, might have given him an edge.

But Burian was new and Vanko wanted the problem solved with as few unknown risks as possible. Lester Toungate wasn't a good test for a new guy.

Although Lester could have killed Mykhaltso on level ground, it didn't add up. As the attacker, Mykhaltso had the prerogative to choose the time and location of his strike. The ground wasn't supposed to be on level ground. Fire a rifle from two hundred yards and be done.

Vanko struggled to conceive the circumstances that aligned in Lester's favor to allow him to overcome Mykhaltso in the dead of night.

Burian watched.

In the beginning, in the 90s, when Vanko and Lester decided to cool the tension between them, a truce made sense. They sold different products to different markets, and though crossover occurred, it was minimal.

Beyond that, Vanko heard stories. Lester Toungate was hard to kill. He survived car crashes. Bullet wounds. A knifing. When Vanko arrived and did his due diligence, everyone said Lester was a better friend than enemy, so long as you never trust your friends.

A few years into their detente, Vanko considered coordinating their businesses, or taking on joint ventures that would exploit the best of their organizations. Increase profits and keep his enemy closer. He never crossed the bridge. No opportunity presented.

Meanwhile, Lester got old and weak. Sentimental, his sons said.

Vanko said, "So what is he doing now? Lester?"

"Following the girl."

"The girl—what girl?"

"The one looking for the blonde. Ulyana. In here the other day."

Vanko let his mind drift.

Despite himself, he liked Shirley Lyle. She reminded him of his earliest memories of his grandmother. If she'd showed up with a dish of pelmeni, he would have had a heart attack. The illusion would have been perfect.

He'd been kind to Shirley. *Sentimental.*

And he told her Lester would not be around for long.

He placed his hand on his lower lip and pulled. His gaze blurred. Shirley had mentioned Lester to him, not the other way around.

Ulyana was not missing. She was with Lester. Imagine Mykhaltso, prepared for murder, finding Ulyana in Lester's bed. Could surprise cause a moment of confused delay?

Especially when Mykhaltso pursued the stripper with a lover's interest? Always singing the bear song, because she sang it once from stage?

Vanko placed his head in his hands.

Ulyana as a double agent... Vanko had sent her to Toungate's organization. She brought back good information, but that's the way turncoats survived. They gave up truth, their existence a lie.

If Shirley Lyle and Ulyana were working with Lester Toungate all along... was Vanko the stooge while Lester called the shots?

What trap waited to be sprung?

Was Mykhaltso dead? Or on the other side?

Vanko locked eyes with Burian.

"How do you like the states?"

He shrugged. "I go where I told."

"I have a task for you. A daylight job. After, maybe you go home."

CHAPTER 37

S hirley stopped at the patio with the doorknob in her hand, looking at Maddix Heregger's corpse.

Smart thing would be to call the police and give them a heads up. They'd probably want to know she killed a guy. But it was the same old thing. They'd keep her answering questions for hours or days, while Ulyana might be fighting moment by moment to stay alive.

Sometimes the ends justified the means, and that was fine by Shirley. She'd get good and mean. Sort out the bodies later.

But the door didn't lock.

Shirley returned to Ulyana's bedroom closet and grabbed her pink backpack full of money. With one strap over her shoulder, her Ruger firmly ensconced between her mammaries, and a narrow squint at her eyes, Shirley pulled the trailer door as closed as possible and fired up her Durango. She placed Ulyana's backpack behind the driver's seat.

Anyone who wanted that money would have to go through her to get it.

Donal.

"No."

I don't mean that. He's not your type, anyway.

"Then don't go around saying his name all the time. Our affair was brief, but torrid. My heart is still in pieces."

What I meant is that you might call him to find out if the police found finger-prints yet. Maybe they matched them. They could have information from the shell casing, or the blood. They might have suspects you didn't think about.

"No, it's too soon. You've seen every episode of CSI that I have. And if they do know something they won't tell him. And the way I left things; I doubt he wants to chat."

She put the Durango in drive and a moment later passed the trailer court office. Something must be going on with the estate of Clyde Munsinger, the former owner. An old man in a blue Toyota Prius nodded at her.

He looks familiar.

"I wonder why. Let's see. At least one man a day, year in, year out, thirty years. Three hundred and sixty-five times thirty. Let's round it to three hundred times thirty. Nine thousand. Plus all the others from the sixty-fives I dropped. Thirty years of sixty-fives. That's got to be another couple thousand. I've had sex with eleven thousand men."

They all look familiar?

"Bingo."

Shirley eased out of the trailer court and headed for the Pink Panther.

SHE STOOD at the Pink Panther door, attack stance. Shoulders back. Chest high and mighty. Legs and hips set. She shoved open the door and the men inside stared. Hip hop music boomed. She felt it in her chest. Hard to avoid walking in time with the beat, maybe adding pep to her step. A girl strutted on the stage, but it was beyond the bar, in the back. Hard to see anything but skin, from the distance.

A man sat at the far end of the bar looking as flat and desperate as his half-empty draft beer. Needed a shave. Likely a bath. His lower lip was big and his nose too long. He sat with the stool out from the bar but his skinny upper body propped on his elbows and his head slumped to his forearms.

Too exhausted to have seen anything that night.

A woman—presumably also employed by the club—stood bare chested and lethargic beside him.

Shirley looked back to the bar. Another woman—the bartender—did the vertical eyeball dance. Took in Shirley head to toe, three times. Elvis lip.

"You Jazalyn?" Shirley said, above the pulsing noise.

The woman smirked. Wrinkled her nose, as a greeting.

Jazalyn—the manager always giving Ulyana problems because she was coming up too fast. She'd be no help. Shirley looked around, forcing herself to feel at ease despite knowing time was short. There were only a few people at the club. None looked promising.

Shirley leaned. "I need information about Ulyana. She disappeared, and someone here knows something."

"Piss off."

"Vanko said I could talk to people here."

"Whatever."

Shirley fake smiled. Stood upright. Maybe she'd try the man as flat as his beer.

Stop! Think! You've got resources. You're big. They can't push you around. You're smart. They can't out think you or trick you. And you're armed. Worst case, you can shoot everybody here. Society will understand. Ulyana needs you! VIVA the REVOLUTION!

Shirley pushed the stool aside and got her chest and arms over the bar. Leaned as far as she could before her belly hurt. She locked eyes with Jazalyn.

"Any more attitude from you, and I'm a punch you in the face."

Jazalyn stepped back.

"I thought so."

Shirley held her eye until the other looked away, even though it was only to pick up a glass. "You want something? To drink?"

"Save it. Was you here the last night Ulyana worked?"

"No."

"Who was? Who can I talk to?"

Jazalyn shrugged. Busied herself moving bottles.

Shirley backed from the bar. A man shot pool by himself. He was young, wore a tank top that showed a tattoo of a naked girl, bent over so her rear end was the ball of his shoulder. He looked at Shirley. She studied the gap between his teeth and the way his eyeballs seemed too close together, like he was forever contemplating the bridge of his nose. The man chalked his cue stick. Took his shot.

Shirley walked toward the pool table. "So how's that working?"

"What?"

"You got a tattoo that makes men want to screw your shoulder."

"Look, I'm kinda busy. Not interested. Sell it somewhere else."

Shirley held his look. Nodded. He was taking her as a natural part of the scene. That was good.

"Pretty blonde girl takes her clothes off here. She's Russian. Ulyana. You know her?"

The man took another shot. Ignored her.

Shirley leaned on the pool table. "She's a friend. Hasn't been around for days."

He lined up another shot. Drove stick to ball.

Shirley snatched the cue ball from the table.

"I'm looking to make sure she's okay. She's my friend."

The man stepped toward Shirley.

"Easy, little man. I go three-fifty on a light day. I'll pry the gum off the tables with your teeth."

"I'm not a regular here. I don't know her."

"You wasn't here three days ago? You didn't hear the gunshot outside?"

"Like I said, *woman.*"

"Oh no, no, no." Shirley closed her eyes.

Choose your battles. Seriously. It was a true statement.

Shirley opened her eyes. Smiled big. Tossed him the cue ball. "Thanks, little man."

Beyond him, from the back of the club, another man emerged from a closed door. He wore a black leather vest and no shirt. Gray hair in a pony tail.

He didn't stop walking until he was deep in her space. "You need to leave."

"No."

"Go."

"I ain't the subject of your verb, asshole. I'm a gerund. Or participle, or some damn thing. I ain't your subject. You don't boss me around. Besides. Vanko told me to come here and ask some questions, since y'all were so unhelpful the first time."

Shirley looked to her right. The skinny man from the bar, with barely enough ambition to suck his beer, stood next to her. He kept his arms straight down, and his eyes locked on hers. Menacing. He could grab her. Push her. Punch her. Cut her.

Shirley backed a step and bumped into another man. She turned—the pool player trying to get his shoulder laid. He mimicked the other two men. Arms aggressively straight down. Kind of balling the shoulders, rotating them forward. Eye to eye stares. Smirks that said Shirley was outnumbered. They'd do as they pleased.

She smelled cigarette.

She backed again, and ran into a fourth man. Shirley spun. She hadn't seen him before. He stared at her. Cigarette in mouth, smoke drifting over his nose, past his squinty eyes.

Her heart pounded. Blood drained from her face. Sweat broke cold on her brow.

VIVA the REVOLUTION!

"Just so you know... Any of you touches me, like you're trying to move me from where I'm standing... you manhandle me, there's going to be a consequence. You don't disrespect my person without a response ten times as bad as what you gave. It'll probably involve bullets. And definitely teeth. And if I don't get you right now, it'll be after I find out who you are and where you sleep. Hands off! Or I'll haunt your ass."

Facing the older man who addressed her, Shirley stepped forward. Her breast hit him first. Then her belly. He remained planted. She leaned, pushed, drove him aside. All the while expecting to feel the other men grab, pull, punch.

Removed from her path, the man stared. The others stood where they stood.

Five feet away, she turned and studied each face. None of their expressions had changed. The music pounded.

If there was a gunshot outside right now, would you hear it?

"No."

The gray man's eyes flickered.

"If I find one of you assholes took Ulyana, or had anything to do with it. Even just looking the other way. Or not speaking up when you had the chance. If you know something and don't tell me, you're the problem, and I'm going to wipe the earth's ass and get rid of you. I'll find you."

She reached for her holster, and instead of yanking her top down from the neck, just patted there. Nodded. Held their eyeballs with hers, but like a vise.

Shirley spun and exited the club.

She stood in front under the awning, breathing. Cooling her mind. Stilling her heart. She leaned to the cement block wall.

From around the corner, a metal door croaked on rusty hinges.

The four men?

Shirley yanked her top down and pulled her Ruger forty.

Red on top.

Red on the side.

Shirley stalked to the corner. Inhaled deep. Held her breath while the oxygen permeated her cells. Let the air out slow.

You're totally in control. Totally.

She held her pistol arm straight down, ready to swing up and fire in one motion.

Don't shout or scream or anything. Just in case it's not them. That would be embarrassing.

Shirley leaned forward, placed her open hand against the cement block wall, and eased her head around the corner.

Tits.

It was the woman who stood beside the skinny man. Outside, bare chested. Bright sun. Thong. Shirley nodded. "Howdy."

Make her a sister.

Shirley eased back behind the wall and snugged the Ruger back into her bra. She straightened her top. Adjusted her hips. Strode around the corner and kicked a beer can she hadn't seen. It clattered across the gravel. The woman looked up from her cigarette. Drew smoke into her mouth.

"I figured you and me was on the same team. You look like a gal that brooks no nonsense so I'll lay it out. You know Ulyana. She's disappeared."

"Yeah."

"So she's one of us. If it was you that disappeared, you'd want her to tell the investigator everything she knows. Because if we're not in it together, we're in it apart. That means you never get a moment's peace. Because everyone's an enemy. Don't make it like that. Don't make me your enemy. Join the revolution."

"What revolution?"

"VIVA the REVOLUTION. That one. Where we don't take crap no more. From nobody. Got it?"

Uncertain smile.

"Look, sister. There's only two sides. Good and evil. Right and wrong. You can't sit the fence. Not when I'm about to knock your ass off. You better decide which side you want to fall on. Either you want the best for all or the best for yourself."

"Yeah. I got something for you."

"What?"

"I saw him. The one."

"You saw a man take Ulyana? You saw it go down?"

"No. But I saw the man who did, yo. I know it."

"What happened?"

"I come out here and smoke three, four times a day. I don't know how many times I seen him, hiding out there in the parking lot. You don't even know he's in his truck 'less you see the shadow move."

"Who?"

"After Ulyana disappeared, he stopped hanging out in the parking lot. I didn't know it was him at first, then I remembered the ass beating Mykhaltso gave him. He tried grabbing Ulyana and they threw them out."

"Wait a minute. You can smoke inside. Why come outside?"

"Quiet. Just need some quiet every now and then. I'm getting old you know? Can't take it."

Shirley looked at her boobs. Couldn't help it. Yeah. Getting old.

"Happens to the best of us, sister."

"He's a real creep-o. After they threw him out, one time Ulyana found him waiting on her. She went back inside, you know, for security to help her."

"What did he look like? What's his name?"

"Rocky, or something."

"Without his name, how did you guys know not to let him back in?"

"It's just us. We all know everybody—at least to see them."

"Describe him."

"Different sometimes. At first he was just a guy. Short hair. Business-type. Last I saw him, his hair was blonde and kinda long. Mustache. Nose with a crook.

"How can I locate him? Has he been around, at all, lately?"

The woman shook her hair. Exhaled a long burst of smoke toward the sky. "You a cop or something?"

"I'm a retired working girl and Ulyana is my friend. That's all. I need to find this man."

"All I know is he drives an old Ford."

Shirley shook her head. Something clicked. "A truck?"

"F-150."

"Two tone colors, red with a white stripe down the side?"

Saggy nodded.

Shirley strode to the woman. Took her face in both hands and kissed her forehead.

CHAPTER 38

Shirley shouted at her cell phone, sitting on the passenger seat. "I know where Ulyana is!"

She shifted to drive and spat gravel out the back wheels. Fishtailed. Cut right to clear a parked Volvo, accelerated, braked, slid on rocks to the road, squealed right on the pavement.

"Shirley?"

"That's right. I know you and me got some past between us but you need to be here when I get Ulyana. I don't want this getting any crazier than need be, for the sake of the law."

"What?"

"What the hell you mean, what? What I said!"

"Let me get my brain around this. How did you find out who has her? Who is it? Where are you now? What's that sound?"

"Yes!"

"Well?"

"I went back to the strip club and found a girl who would answer some questions."

Shirley glanced at the speedometer. Ninety. She eased off the gas. Looked at the stoplight coming up ahead.

Brake!

She tapped. Stomped.

"What did the girl say?"

"Ulyana was having trouble with a guy there. Repeat trouble. A real stalker-weirdo. I think he's the same one who beat a girl I know from the shelter. I already checked them out once, before Ulyana disappeared."

"Sounds like a great lead. But you never know until—"

"I'm going to 614 Pioneer Road. I'll be raising hell when you get there."

SHIRLEY MISSED THE DRIVEWAY. She stopped. Looked out the window at each house, separated by fifty yards of lawn between them. Memory came to her. She saw the man leave his porch and march toward her. Standing in the middle-of-the-road, aggravated.

Shirley checked the rearview. Put the Durango in reverse and motored to the last house she passed. She swerved and backed into the drive. Hit the brakes and the Durango slid. She grabbed the keys, patted the Ruger in her bra and slammed the door behind her.

Up the steps to the house. Didn't notice climbing them. Pounded, and the door opened with her hand still drumming.

Ruth Memmelsdorf stood there. "You."

"Where's your man?"

"I didn't appreciate you bad mouthing my husband at the support group. You have strong opinions and they aren't welcome here."

"You've got a few bats loose and I don't have time. Where's your husband?"

Shirley peered into the house. Listened for footsteps. She saw part of the kitchen. Part of the living room wall. Photos.

Engine sound.

Shirley turned. A sedan raced up the road. Braked hard and swung in beside the Durango. The door opened and Donal popped out. His motions short and quick, he joined Shirley on the step.

"Where is your husband?" Shirley said. "Where's Roddy?"

"Ma'am, please." Donal smiled. Raised hands, no threat. "Your husband was seen with a person who is now missing. Time is of extreme essence. We need to talk to Rod."

"Where is Roddy?"

"I don't know."

"The missing girl... she might still be alive. We need to know, now."

"Roddy's not here. I don't know where he is."

Sirens.

"What?" Shirley turned.

"What have you done?" Ruth Memmelsdorf said.

"Yeah, Donal! What'd you do?"

Two police cruisers bounced onto the lawn. One made a divot with the front bumper. A uniformed man stepped from each vehicle and they approached together.

Ruth Memmelsdorf slumped against the door. Her eyes glared while her mouth clamped and crow-tracked at the edges. With the door opened farther, Shirley saw inside the living room. A photo on the wall—a house in the woods. A man—Roddy—beside a dead deer on a four wheeler's rack.

Donal touched Shirley's arm. "Let's give the police some room," he said.

"You didn't have the right to call them."

"You wanted police here. I'm not police anymore."

"You didn't have the right to overrule my decision."

"You ended the call."

The two officers turned sideways and split Shirley and Donal.

"Ma'am? May we come inside and talk to you a minute? See if we can find a resolution?"

The two police officers stepped inside the house.

Shirley retreated down the steps. Stood at the front bumper of her Durango. This, where she stood, was where the red and white truck had been parked. To the front right of the Durango, tire tracks led through the yard. The grass was matted over.

Donal spent a moment with his hands in his pockets, closer to the steps. He approached.

"I had to call them. I'm no longer on the force. I don't have any authority, and you sure don't."

Save yourself for the real fight.

"Fine. But you have a habit of doing things that change things for other people without telling them. It's disrespectful, and I vowed I'd never let another person disrespect me without calling bullshit."

"That wasn't my intent." Donal studied his shoes, and then the ground, and then the sidewalk. He walked a few steps. Turned. Walked a few more.

"Would you stop?"

"I thought we had something interesting going, and I don't know what I said..."

"Oh geez. Just stop walking. This isn't Talladega."

The two police officers stepped from the house. Ruth Memmelsdorf glared at Shirley and closed the door.

"What the hell?" Shirley put her hand on her hip.

"Your girl's not even missing. Ulyana. I just talked to her on the phone, at the club."

Shirley's mouth went slack. She raised her left brow. "That doesn't make any sense. I was just there."

"Yeah, well I just talked to her. She said she was away for a little while and now she's back."

Shirley strode from the Durango to the sidewalk, blocking their path to their vehicles. "Where was she?"

"She didn't say."

"You didn't ask? What the hell kind of cop doesn't ask?"

"Don't get all hysterical, or I'll run you in. If you don't believe me about the girl, go to the club and see for yourself."

"So this is hysterical. Wow."

Misogynistic asshole. Hey! Don't repeat that!

"Misogynistic asshole. I'll run your ass in."

Shirley remained standing in the middle of the sidewalk. The two officers traded looks. One sniffed. Shook his head. They walked around her in the grass.

Shirley turned to Donal. "Am I being hysterical?"

"I think he was afraid you might *become* hysterical. Not that you already were behaving that way."

"Oh. Well I think they were being dick-sterical."

One of the officers looked up as he opened his door. He shook his head. Smiled. Climbed inside his patrol car.

"Every barrel has a bad apple," Donal said.

"Yeah. Whatever. This crap happens every minute of every day. Once you see it, you can't stop."

"Yeah. Well, about that. I'm sorry. You're right. I should have tried to call you back before I told the police. This is your show—and just because I have protective feelings for you, doesn't give me the right to interfere when I think you're making a mistake."

Shirley studied Donal.

Wow. Man can romance a girl...

"Thanks. Wow. Cool. But I'm still pissed off at you."

"So you aren't buying that Ulyana's back at the club?"

"I was just there. Before coming here. It doesn't make any sense."

"Let's go to the club."

NEITHER SPOKE ON THE DRIVE. Donal pressed buttons on his cell phone. Standing at the double doors outside the club, Donal said, "Wait a second." He dialed.

"Yeah, this is Donal O'Loughlin, from the Phoenix PD. Retired. One of my colleagues called a moment ago and spoke with Ulyana. We need to get her back on the phone. Forgot to ask her a simple question. Very basic info. Can you get her for me, please?"

Shirley waited.

"Miss Ulyana?" Donal said.

He nodded.

Shirley burst through the door.

Jazalyn stood behind the bar, phone at her ear.

Shirley strode toward her. Pivoted before reaching the stools and marched to the entry at the far end. She swung around the bar and approached Jazalyn.

"You can't be back here!"

Shirley stopped with inches between them. She drove her fist into Jazalyn's face.

Jazalyn staggered backward. Dropped to her knees. Found support on a rack of glasses—and knocked several to the floor. They shattered. She looked up at Shirley with blood flowing from her nose.

"I told you."

Shirley turned. Donal stood close to the door, his hand next to his belt. Must be where he concealed his firearm.

Shirley backed out of the bar space. "Your mother should have beat you more."

241

She swung open the door and Donal followed her to the Durango. He entered the passenger seat without word. Shirley entered. She closed her eyes and saw the double dirt tracks through Ruth Memmelsdorf's yard. Curved behind the house and what? Continued into the woods?

In her mind's eye she saw the photo of the cabin, the four wheeler and the dead deer.

She drove.

Passed that nice looking older gentleman in the Prius—again. He didn't see her this time. Good thing! Stupid coincidence! He'd probably think she was following him!

Stop light. Pulled next to a car with subwoofers hitting it so hard the reflection on the windows pulsed with the beat. Spinnie hubcaps and purple neon under glow. In daylight.

Men.

Donal said, "You want to take another run at Ruth Memmelsdorf?"

"In the Durango?"

"Uh."

"No. I have another plan."

CHAPTER 39

Shirley slowed to thirty miles per hour before arriving at the Memmelsdorf residence. Donal braced. Shirley hit the driveway diagonal, shot into the lawn. Swerved, engine roaring. She followed the matted grass around the house. Spun out, sideways. Braked. Donal grinned. "Four wheel drive?"

"Good idea. How?"

Donal reached across. Pointed at the 4-hi selector switch.

"I got it."

He gave a curt nod. Smiled.

She turned the dial to 4-hi.

"You're still in the doghouse."

The matted grass led through an S curve through the back of the lawn, missing an outdoor wood-burning stove shed before disappearing into shrubs and low hanging tree limbs. The leaves were out but not full. Though the path was wide enough for the Durango, the tracks through the overgrown grass on the trail were narrower.

That's going to scratch the paint.

"VIVA the REVOLUTION!"

"Okay."

Shirley hit the path into the woods at a straight angle. The trail was smooth, as if long ago it had been well maintained.

"Interesting."

Shirley glanced at Donal.

"The path is straight," Donal said. "Whoever made it cut out some trees. Moved some earth."

"That's significant because?"

"You wouldn't take the time and energy to cut a path like this to ride a four Wheeler."

"You saw the photo too?"

He nodded. In the light of the forest, Donal's face looked appropriately rugged. Handsome ma—

"Look out!"

Shirley stomped the brake. A tree was across the road.

Donal leaned close to the windshield, turned his head left and right. "Over there. I think that's how they get around this. See the tracks?"

"Yeah, but how do I miss that trunk? And that tree?"

"Didn't you say Roddy had an F-150 truck? Any place he can go in that truck you can go in this."

"How?"

"If it was me driving, I'd get out of the vehicle and do a walk-through. And if I had a passenger, say, a man with outdoor skills, I'd ask him to be my ground guide."

"Good advice. If only there was a man with outdoor skills around."

"Ha."

"Thank you."

Shirley exited the Durango, not realizing she stopped in a low lying draw. Her feet shifted in the moist dirt. With all the ferns and leaves, it was hard to see exactly what was under foot. Arms poised, step-by-step, she walked around the fallen tree. It came down intact, yanking up a 12 foot circle of roots and dirt, leaving a pool that collected water.

She saw a path forward. Shirley turned. Donal was beside her. "I didn't hear you."

"Skills."

"Would you mind guiding me through?"

Back inside the vehicle, Shirley turned the wheel and crept forward. She followed Donal's instructions, even when he told her to turn farther right, when she was sure she would scrape paint down to the metal on a mean looking tree. A moment later she was back on the path, no harm done.

Donal got back inside.

Shirley gassed it.

A minute passed. "Why would somebody live this far away from civilization?"

"I have a feeling there wasn't much civilization around here, when these folks came."

Shirley slowed. Ahead, in the distance between the leaves, something looked different. The pattern changed.

"I think that's a house up there," she said.

"I don't see it."

"Yeah. That's it."

"You want to come up with a plan before we go charging in? Or just charge in?"

"Well, Ruth is back at the house, and Roddy only saw me once. I don't see a telephone line coming back here. You got cell phone coverage?"

He looked. "No."

"So she can't tell him we're coming. Since he only saw me once, maybe he won't remember. I always wanted to do the lost cat routine."

"Yeah, that's a good one. Top notch."

Shirley crept forward, and rehearsed the words she would say. She speeded up, and then slowed when the road led to a clearing.

"Okay. Do you want to stop here, while we are still out of sight?" Donal pulled his firearm and checked the load. "So what's your plan?"

"I go to the door. Casual. I'll tell him I'm looking for my cat."

Donal nodded. "Good, so far."

"This is just reconnoitering. You scout around the back while I do my thing up front. I'll keep him at the door as long as I can. I want you checking windows and doing cop stuff. See where Ulyana is. See if there's a way into the basement, from the outside. Watch for curtains moving. Listen for Morse code. All that stuff. After that, we meet back here and come up with a plan to get her out."

"Okay. Good. But just one thing."

"What?"

"If I see her, and she's in immediate danger, I'm obligated to act. I won't ask your permission."

"Perfect."

Donal opened the Durango door and slipped outside without a sound. He stepped between the trees with his gun drawn, pointing downward. He walked a few yards, then stopped behind a boulder, and examined the terrain. Stooped low, he darted a few steps and froze behind cover. She caught glimpses of him circling the clearing until he arrived at the back, where he sat low in the weeds with his pistol hand resting on his knee.

Shirley put the Durango in drive and crept up to the house. She parked beside Roddy Memmelsdorf's red and white F-150.

Outside the Durango, Shirley adjusted her rack, felt the comforting presence of steel on her skin.

"BOOTSIE! Here, key-key! Where are you, key-key? Don't you hide from me, you little hairball. I'll make key-key burritos. Yes, key-key burritos. You little hairball."

Shirley arrived at the door and hammered with the ball of her hand.

"Here, little Bootsie. Key-key!"

The door swung.

A pistol emerged, pointed at her.

The door opened all the way. Ruth Memmelsdorf stood in the opening with her knees shoulder width apart, slightly bent, and a pistol grip in both her hands.

Shirley jerked back. "Didn't expect that!"

Over Ruth's shoulder, Shirley saw a window on the other side of the house. Donal appeared at the right side and crept to the left. He disappeared.

Shirley cleared her throat. "Why even go to the women's shelter? If you were in it all along?"

"Because he killed my cat."

"Why—"

"Shut up. Be quiet. Inside." She flicked her pistol upward. Backed a step. "This is an old door. Made before fat people I guess. Turn sideways if you must."

Shirley gritted her teeth.

Motion to her right.

Donal emerged around the corner. Empty hands in the air. He winced.

"Stop," Roddy said, from around the corner.

Donal stopped.

"Real slow. Easy."

Donal stepped forward.

Roddy came into view holding a mammoth-sized pistol on Donal. He looked at Shirley. "Guess we got to bury two more. Wish we had a backhoe."

"You killed her? Ulyana's dead? Why? What'd she ever do to you?" Shirley faced Ruth. "Or you? What are you doing? He's crazy. You don't have to be."

"I told you to come inside the house. Do it. Now!"

Shirley turned sideways.

"Did you pat her down?" Roddy said.

"How would I do that, and still hold a gun on her? Look at her. She ain't armed. And it won't be but a minute anyway."

Shirley side-stepped into the house. Watched Donal and Roddy.

You got this, Babe.

She took it all in—the scowl on Roddy's face, the twinkle in Donal's eye, saying don't worry about me, I got this. You worry about you. Kick some ass, Babe. Kick some ass. She saw the guns—one in Roddy's hand, the other—Donal's—in Roddy's front pocket... The sound of insects in the still air. She was a general looking through field glasses, given the luxury of arriving at the battlefield before the first shots rang, while everything moved in slow motion.

It's all on you, Babe.

"Talk to me, Viva."

Ruth said, "Shut up."

"I talk to myself. Sorry. Do you have a bathroom? I really need to pee. It's a nervous thing."

"Pee your pants. I don't care."

Inside the house, Shirley glanced around. She'd entered the kitchen. Linoleum probably laid in the fifties. Gashes under the kitchen chairs were worn to silver-streaked wood. Cuckoo clock. Those used to be popular. In the other room, partly visible through an arch, gold shag carpet. A wood-framed sofa.

And a black duffel.

Her money?

Roddy stole her money?

With her side perpendicular to the door and her right shoulder pointing to Ruth, Shirley slammed the door with Donal outside. Ruth jumped. Shirley yanked down her top and quick drew her Ruger.

She glared over the top of her barrel and met Ruth's eyes, staring over hers.

"Time for some girl talk."

CHAPTER 40

Lester Toungate kept his distance. If Shirley ever saw him, she didn't let on. Amazing, you think of someone as an idiot, and that's what you see. Then think of her as a genius, and all her silly moves construct a web so intricate it must be by design.

Shirley Lyle, master underworld operator.

Lester shook his head.

Nah. She was too stupid to fake.

Back there—she looked right at him, then looked away, like she was afraid he'd noticed her.

And when she came to bring his gun back? No one's smart enough to do that. Leave the gun, like a message.

Or was she?

Back and forth. To the Pink Panther. Then some guy's run down house. Then to the Pink Panther for three minutes. Then back to the same house, except she didn't park the Durango. She shredded the yard, spun out around the stove shed, righted herself, and took the path into the woods.

Maybe she finally found Ulyana.

He was rooting for her. He'd take them both... Put Shirley in the garage and Ulyana on the saddle.

Lester drove a short distance, turned around and parked facing the house. After a moment a black sedan tooled by, with the driver looking down and away, presumably at his cell phone.

That would be the FBI agent who kindly nudged Lester toward killing Shirley Lyle.

Just because someone else wanted Shirley dead, didn't make it any less valuable for Lester.

He still needed to get his mind around a complication. When Shirley first stopped at this house, a man joined her. He wore plain clothes but had a military bearing. Two police officers arrived, stayed ten minutes, then departed. So Ulyana wasn't here. But the skinny man with short-cropped-hair and square shoulders accompanied Shirley to the Pink Panther—and then back to the same house.

Kill him?

Sometimes extra bodies were necessary—and that was okay. Regardless, Lester's patience was thin. Whether she was a bull in a china shop or underworld mastermind, it was time to chain Shirley Lyle to a hydraulic lift and set her feet in cement.

She'd talk before he filled the first bucket. Nobody held out. That was movie nonsense.

But if she did keep mum, he'd start with a one-inch spade drill.

CHAPTER 41

"Let's both ease up," Shirley said. "Just a little. That make sense?"

"What do you mean?"

"Let's lower the guns. Still keep them in hand. So we can shoot each other, you know. But maybe decentralize the tension."

"De-escalate?"

"Okay, we'll do it your way. We'll de-escalate the tension."

Each lowered her firearm.

From outside, voices. Shirley distinguished Donal's from Roddy's, but not what they were saying.

"Let's be civilized," Shirley said. "Just you and me. We got the brawn outside. Let's let the brains do the work. Sound groovy? We can sort this whole thing out, you and me."

Ruth tilted her head. Sucked in a quick breath. "You think this was his idea."

"What does that mean?"

"You're just as sexist as everybody else. It wasn't his idea. Isn't."

"Isn't? Meaning, Ulyana's still alive?"

"She's downstairs. All these old houses were built with prison cells. Did you know that? They used them for potatoes."

Great! We've isolated the family genius.

"I'm glad she's alive. Very glad. Right? That's a wonderful thing. That means there's no real trouble here. You let her go, and tell the police how it went down. Roddy did everything. I'll tell them about seeing you at the support group, bruised and abused. And they'll dig it. You'll get off. No worries. And you'll be free. No more ass beatings from the old man all the time. Me and Ulyana started a revolution. That's why I came to save her. We girls got to stick together." Shirley winked. "Check this out. You let her go, and we'll make you a member of VIVA the REVOLUTION. Ground floor. We're not even popular yet. But you wait! We'll fight crime together. The three of us. Screw Charley. We'll be our own damn angels, right? You picking up what I'm putting down?"

"You really, *really* don't get it."

"Don't get what?"

"Roddy wanted her. I wasn't enough. How could I be, with her perfect body hanging out? Round and fertile. Prancing around on a stage. He's a man. What did she expect?"

"I don't understand. Roddy beats you. He's keeping a kidnapped woman in the basement. Why haven't you freed her? He isn't home all the time. You've had plenty of chances."

"Yeah, we keep coming back to what you don't understand."

Ruth swung her pistol and pointed at Shirley's head. "Move, and you'll die."

Shirley shook her head. "Okay, now I'm really confused."

"I know who you are. What? You think you can make a scene at our group and no one's going to find out who you are? And by the way, you were wrong. You cut me off when I said I'm powerless over some things, but not what matters. I was about to say—and thank God you cut me off— that I had a plan to bring Roddy under my thumb. You think I went to that women's group for support?"

Shirley's skin tingled. Her face grew hot.

"No. I guess you went so a lot of women would know Roddy had a history of beating you. I just don't understand how you could do that to one of your sisters."

"That slut? Takes her clothes off and wonders why men get horny and say stupid things? If strippers and hookers and sluts weren't all over the place, good men would stay home."

"And you'd have a happy marriage. *Ergo...* that means therefore, in

Greek. *Ergo*, you've been keeping Ulyana. He brought her here, but you've been keeping her."

"I'm going to shoot myself. This is unbelievable. No. Roddy didn't kidnap Ulyana, you daft prat. *I did!*"

"Wha? How?"

"Like this." Ruth twitched her pistol barrel toward the entrance to the basement. "Move. Or you die, right now."

Shirley shook her head. "Nah. Wait a damn minute. I need to understand this. You were going to kill her and then kill Roddy?"

"No! I was going to kill the one woman he wanted, and make it look like he did it, so I could threaten to expose him for the rest of my life. DO YOU FINALLY GET IT?"

Shirley beheld Ruth through wide awake eyes. She saw the whole picture—a flash—Ruth on the stage, presenting herself as weak and broken, perfect camouflage because so many women were. While inside, she was ready to murder—

A shout from the porch!

Scuffle!

Curses and grunts.

The window shattered and a bullet zinged inside. Ruth flinched. Shifted her pistol arm toward the window and the scuffle beyond.

Shirley snapped up her Ruger and squeezed the trigger. The pistol blasted. Ruth's head popped back and blood sprayed the wall.

She collapsed.

Outside—more scuffles. Taut voices and grunts.

"All right!" Roddy shouted. "Ruth! You in there? Come on out! Both of you. Right now, or he dies!"

Shirley dropped to her knees. Shoved away Ruth's gun. With her .40 pointed at the door, she placed her left hand on Ruth's neck. No pulse.

"Ruth? Baby? You in there?"

Shirley glanced.

Red on top.

Red on the side.

She dragged a chair and sat. Elevated her head. Roddy was only ten feet away, at most. Though he used Donal as a shield, his head emerged to the right of Donal's, with enough sticking out to see his eyeball.

Shirley placed the gun barrel in a V of broken glass, allowing her to pivot up and down.

"Don't be stupid, bitch!" Roddy said. "Throw the gun out the window or your man dies. Right now. I ain't kidding!"

Shirley lined up the three white dots on the top of the barrel.

Even if the beads were wrong, the tube pointed straight at Roddy's head.

Worked pretty good last time.

Shirley fired.

CHAPTER 42

Agent Joe Smith sat at the Wal Mart parking lot, hand on the center console, tapping thumb, pointer, index, ring and pinky finger in a perfect nonstop beat.

Whole setup run amok. Heart a-patter.

Never should have hooked up with a hooker. He recognized right from the beginning: mess with darkness, it pulls you in.

Joe slipped lower in his seat, in case anyone happened to be looking.

He couldn't suspend the situation any longer. The FBI sent him from Phoenix to Flagstaff based on Shirley Lyle's tip. She was supposed to provide information for him about a drug dealer.

Instead, she created a murder victim, and made him an accessory.

Joe couldn't allow the FBI to become aware of the case, whether the victim was a bigtime drug dealer or not. Nobody investigated deeper than the FBI. As soon as someone interviewed Shirley, she'd say "Your agent paid me for sex. He was with me when it all went down."

The truth wouldn't help her, but it would destroy him.

Now the FBI wanted him home. Joe told his boss back in Phoenix, there was no drug dealer. A woman with an axe to grind against her old love interest. Now they wanted him home.

If Lester didn't kill Shirley Lyle—

"Oh no!"

The whole time he hadn't even realized it. The blonde girl.

"Oh, no-no-no."

She could put him at the scene, too.

There was no other way.

If he didn't take action—today, while he had opportunity—he would eventually go down as an accessory to the murder of Lester Toungate's son El Jay.

He had no choice.

Joe Smith had to ensure the two women who might destroy him were dead.

He stepped out of his car. Slammed the door. Turned back to watch the lights flash as he hit the fob. He strode to Walmart and grabbed two 5-hour energy shots.

The poop was about to get real.

CHAPTER 43

Both Donal and Roddy fell. The red exploded out of Roddy's head, though, not Donal's.

Donal didn't have to fall down. He's faking.

"Old Shirley. Not welcome. Go home."

Shirley picked up the gun beside Ruth. Opened the door.

Donal sat on his butt, knees bent, one hand braced behind him, the other rubbing the side of his head. Roddy sprawled on his back, very much a corpse.

"I felt that bullet, you know? Wow. I thought I was dead. But I don't guess I am. Did you know you'd hit me with hot powder?"

"Ulyana's in the basement!"

"You closed the door. He had the gun—"

"I was trying to talk to Ruth—Ulyana's in—"

"Did you kill her?"

Shirley turned from Donal and hurried to the basement door Ruth had urged her toward at gunpoint. It opened, revealing downstairs darkness. Shirley groped for a light switch.

Still outside, on his butt, Donal said, "Don't worry. It was a clean shoot. Ulyana's downstairs?"

Shirley glanced about the kitchen. No flashlight handy. The light situation in the basement must be self-evident. Turning sideways because the house was built by skeletons, she placed her left foot on the first step. It gave a little, and the edge was round from a hundred years of wear.

Her stomach butterflies fluttered. The board held. She eased her foot to the next. Two more steps. The guard rail wobbled. She braced against the stone wall.

"Why would they make a basement without a light switch?"

A shadow crossed the doorway above her.

"Because the house was built a long time before electricity," Donal said.

"So they did a half-ass job when—"

"SHIRLEY!"

"ULYANA! That you, Babe?"

"SHIRLEY!"

"Where are you?"

"Here!"

"Where's here?"

"With the roots and fruits!"

"That doesn't help. I can't see in the dark. You behind a wall or something?"

"I'm in a root cellar."

The stairs shook. Donal rumbled down behind her. Shirley stepped. Stepped. Stepped.

"Don't hurry me, dammit. I'll trip and break my neck."

Donal waited.

"The light bulb should be over this way."

"Grab your phone."

A moment later, Donal's hand glowed white.

"See—there."

"I got it."

"Over here!" Ulyana said.

Donal stepped across the cement. Pulled a string and a yellow light bulb lit.

"Ohh." Shirley took in the root cellar door. Three feet up the stone wall, a large square door, she guessed two feet by two feet. Held closed by a series of wood latches, like on a medieval castle door, but small. She lifted all three from their cradles and chucked them. Pulled the door open and inside, in more yellow light, looking serene, Ulyana sat on folded blankets.

The root cellar floor was waist-high. Ulyana and Shirley were at eye level.

"Is she inside that?" Donal said. "I mean, Miss, uh Ulyana, uh. You in there? What is your condition?"

"Alive. Happy. Who are you?"

"Donal O'Loughlin. And you're, uh, happy. After four days in a root cellar?"

"Can you move? You aren't tied or anything?"

Ulyana rocked forward to her hands and knees. "No, she never tied me. I'm kind of sick of the spiders. That's the only thing that made it bad."

"Oh dear. They broke your mind."

Ulyana laughed. "No. I'm the happiest I've ever been. It was really amazing. What a blessing. Uh—could you move over a little?"

Shirley backed from the entry. Ulyana swung her legs and wriggled over the sill to her feet.

"I almost killed twenty people to find you, and you're not even crying. Why aren't you freaking out? If I was in there I'd be covered in tears and turds. You aren't right in the head. Donal, she ain't right in the head."

"No, I am. Really I am. I learned so much. I saw—"

"What? Learned what?"

"Everything."

Shirley grabbed Ulyana's shoulders. Patted her. Grasped her head and kissed her brow. Shook her.

"I'm fine. Really. Uh... I need a shower. I want out of here. I'm fine."

"They didn't hurt you? I mean, *hurt you.*"

"No. Hey, uhm. Can we all move toward the stairs?"

"What do you mean, you learned everything? About the Memmelsdorfs?"

"They're dead, aren't they?"

"Yes," Shirley said. "Had to. They had guns on us."

"That's too bad. Their choices."

"So it was Ruth? Really? She stopped you with a gun?"

"No, she stopped me with a wave. To talk. Then she pulled a gun."

Donal said, "Let's get you out of the basement, okay?"

"No," Shirley said. "Hold on. Ruth brought you here? And Roddy fell in line?"

"Roddy was a wimp. Ruth called his bluff, I guess. Any time he questioned her, she said something about Mister Shonky. I don't know. If you don't mind, I promised myself that if I lived, I'd spend the rest of my life in the light. I'm ready to go upstairs."

"Oh, yeah. Should have said something. I'm sorry. Let's go."

Donal led, then Ulyana. When they were both completely off the stairs, Shirley followed.

You saved her.

"Did I? She seems in pretty good shape, for a girl kidnapped by two psychos."

Yes. And you need to learn what she learned. Trust me. You need to know.

"Okay, Viva. If the stairs hold, someday I'll ask."

CHAPTER 44

Burian Tkach sat on a black BMW R1200GS, a motorcycle equally at home on roads or trails. One of his targets—the old man Lester—lived in a log cabin set back from a suburb defined by perfect lawns and massive front windows. Wearing a helmet and riding a motorcycle, Burian felt comfortable scouting the environment without giving himself away. A quick tour in and out.

The road dead-ended a quarter mile beyond Lester's home. When Lester left, it would be through the community.

Burian drove into a copse of trees, and waited.

Finally, a Prius departed Lester Toungate's garage. Burian thumbed the start button. The driver wore a blue and white baseball cap and giant sunglasses. Burian clicked the shifter. He detected motion to his right—a black sedan about to pull out. Burian kept the clutch handle tight and his foot on the brake.

The sedan had been sitting there when Burian arrived. It looked like the kind of vehicle preferred by government people. No one got into the car while Burian watched. Whoever pulled out after the Prius was waiting the whole time. Burian let the car pass and after a moment, eased the BMW through the foliage, over the bank, and onto the road.

The black sedan held back from the Prius, but turn after turn, followed.

An order for a daylight hit was sacrosanct. Nothing gets in the way.

Part of the job is the killing, but another part is the audacity of it. The daylight job carries more risks, and with it comes a concession from the bosses who ordered them. A sweetener.

The assignment was absolute. No amount of risk was reason to stand down. If the target was suddenly surrounded by an infantry platoon, you attack—and die.

But... due to the increase risk... Collateral damage was fine. Spectacle was okay, even desired. Nightly news, hostages, anything needed to escape the greater danger was acceptable.

The target dies. You go home.

In this instance, three targets. Two females. Shirley and Ulyana. One male, Lester, probably there with his own designs on the girls. And a fourth target, the government man, if he interfered.

The targets die, Burian, and you go home.

The End...

NEXT?

For two free kindle novel downloads, a behind the scenes peek at the next book in the series (no spoilers), along with all the funky one-of-a-kind items at the Baer Creighton Shop...

Enter the following in your browser:

https://baercreighton.com/product/8-shirley-fn-lyle-one-at-a-time-boys/

ABOUT THE AUTHOR

Howdy. I appreciate you reading my books—more than you can know. If you've read this far, (not only the third book in the series, but the stuff at the back of the book as well), you and I are fellow travelers. I suspect you sense something is not quite right with the world. It's not as good as it's supposed to be. We human beings aren't as good as our ideals. Yet, we prize and want to fight for them.

I do my absolute best to write stories that portray the human situation with brutal transparency, but also I strive to tell stories that are not as bleak as the human condition sometimes seems. There's no limit to the darkness. Light is rare. But it exists, and I hope when you complete one of my novels, you find your values validated. I hope I encourage you to fight the good fight, just as you encourage me when you buy my books, review them, and join my Facebook group, the Red Meat Lit Street Team. Y'all are an awesome community. It's good that we're in this fight together, and I'm grateful you're out there. Thank you.

Remember, light wins in the end.

Made in the USA
Las Vegas, NV
13 January 2021